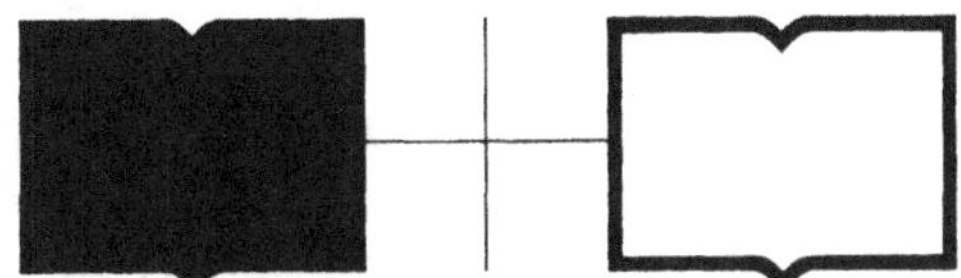

Toronto Reprint Library of Canadian Prose and Poetry

Douglas Lochhead, General Editor

This series is intended to provide for libraries a varied selection of titles of Canadian prose and poetry which have been long out-of-print. Each work is a reprint of a reliable edition, is in a contemporary library binding, and is appropriate for public circulation. The Toronto Reprint Library makes available lesser known works of popular writers and, in some cases, the only works of little known poets and prose writers. All form part of Canada's literary history; all help to provide a better knowledge of our cultural and social past.

The Toronto Reprint Library is produced in short-run editions made possible by special techniques, some of which have been developed for the series by the University of Toronto Press.

This series should not be confused with Literature of Canada: Poetry and Prose in Reprint, also under the general editorship of Douglas Lochhead.

UNIVERSITY OF TORONTO PRESS

Toronto Reprint Library of Canadian Prose and Poetry
© University of Toronto Press 1973
Toronto and Buffalo
Reprinted in paperback 2014
ISBN 978-0-8020-7503-1 (cloth)
ISBN 978-1-4426-5189-0 (paper)

No other edition known.

"GUILTY"

FORGIVEN = RECLAIMED

*"TRUTH IS STRANGER
THAN FICTION"*

A CANADIAN STORY FROM REAL LIFE

BY

LANCE BILTON

Entered according to Act of the Parliament of Canada, in the year 1906,
by The Rolla L. Crain Co., Limited, at the Department of Agriculture.

THE ROLLA L. CRAIN CO., LIMITED,
Printers and Publishers,
OTTAWA, CANADA

CONTENTS

AUTHOR'S NOTE

Because of the very enthusiastic welcome given Stuart Taggart's already famous painting "Guilty;" because of the privilege to use the central figure of his picture as a frontispiece for this book, and also because the conception of "Guilty" was evolved by the artist from facts depicted in this story which bears the same title, the author has mustered sufficient courage to consent to its publication.

Although certain names are fictitious, the characters are all sketched from life, and no doubt will be recognized by at least a few. If such be the case, will the reader please deal as leniently with the author as possible, and endeavour to study the various characters from his view point.

Should the history of Chris Cainsford's follies, failures, successes, defeats, debauchery, degradation, despair, and final victory over fierce appetite and mad passion, stand as a warning, and breath encouragement and hope to a few unfortunates, causing them to follow his example and go to the same source for help to renounce evil, then the author will have achieved his object in writing this story.

Should the history of Nora's love, devotion, courage, self-sacrifice, steadfast hope, forgiveness and care, prove an incentive to other sorrowing ones of her sex to continue hoping, trusting, praying for the dawn of a brighter day, then the author will have been doubly repaid.

Should George Littlejohn's example act as a slight spur to other generous sympathetic gentlemen to help the fallen and encourage the despairing, then "Guilty" will not have been published in vain, and Pilot will have made true friends.

This story is dedicated to the memory of one of God's noblemen—my father.

Sincerely,

LANCE BILTON.

PART I.

GOOD AND EVIL

CHAPTER I.

GEORGE LITTLEJOHN'S DISCOVERY

Rap! Rap! Rap! "Come in."

Rap! Rap! Rap! "COME IN."

Rap! Rap! Rap! Rap! Bang! "COME IN."

The last attack on the office door made it shake on its hinges. The last imperative "Come in" was shouted so loudly that things fairly trembled; then silence.

"What does it mean? Who can it be? Some of the boys I'll be bound." As these thoughts flashed through his mind, Chris Cainsford sprang to the door; yanked it open, and found, no one! Quickly glancing down the passage leading to the stair, he got a glimpse of a man's back covered by a black coat.

As the man turned to descend the stair, he evidently saw Cainsford, for immediately he retraced his steps, and, as he drew near, fixed on him a pair of keen bright eyes, while he nervously thrust his hand into the pocket of his rich lambskin overcoat. He came closer and closer, still fumbling in his pocket.

Now, Chris Cainsford was no coward, but the singular actions of the stranger and the recent loud rapping, together with the fact that just a few days previously he had read of a prominent judge who was treacherously shot to death while answering his door-bell, formed a combination of circumstances that caused Cainsford a nervous twinge, and as the stranger came very close he involuntarily stepped back through the office door, followed by his visitor, who now succeeded in drawing from his pocket a long oddly formed weapon. Instead, however, of using it on Cainsford, he placed the small end in his ear, gave the big end a little shake, as he said, in a rich mellow voice, "Don't be afraid, it is not loaded. Are you the lawyer?" And he fixed a searching gaze on the young man's face.

By this time Cainsford had recovered from his momentary embarrassment, and understood the cause of the loud rapping, and why the stranger had not entered when bidden. He must be deaf as a post and no mistake, thought he, or he certainly would have heard that last "Come in." The remembrance of the awful howl, intended for one of his chums, made Cainsford feel a little ashamed, as he looked into the honest rugged face of the old gentleman before him; and besides he noticed how well dressed he was. This may have had something to do with the answer he spoke into the trumpet very respectfully, but not very distinctly, "I am exceedingly sorry I kept you waiting at the door." Evidently he was misunderstood, for the visitor shook his trumpet, shoved it into his pocket and said, with a merry twinkle in his eye, "Don't matter much, if he went out by the door he'll perhaps come in by the window. Good-day," and he was out in the hall before Cainsford seized his arm, and shouted in his ear: "I'm the man; I'm the lawyer; What do you want?" Out came the trumpet; it was satisfactorily adjusted; then the rich mellow voice innocently enquired: "Did you wish to speak to me?" Cainsford this time frantically shouted into the trumpet. "What do you want? I'm the man, I'm the lawyer. What do you want?"

"I don't want you to break my machine, nor burst my ear. I know I am a little hard of hearing, but you don't have to bellow enough to break glass, and it appears to be a little hard on you,—judging by the redness of your face. You had better let me do the talking, it don't hurt me, though hearing does, at times."

The last two words were added in a low sweet tone, accompanied by a little smile, just a glimmer, that appeared to exactly suit the rugged, honest, rosy face with its grey side whiskers, and bushy eyebrows. That smile was like oil on troubled waters.

Cainsford was naturally impulsive, and inclined to be quick tempered. He was just about ready to show the old man to the door. (It might have been better for all concerned if he had). He could not resist that smile, however, and at once became good natured; placed a chair for his visitor, and with a hearty laugh motioned for him to talk. The trumpet was again placed in position, and its owner proceeded to ask the following questions:

"Is there much business going on in this town?"

"Yes." With a nod.

"Much building being done?"

"Yes."

"New railway has caused a sort of boom hasn't it?"

"Yes."

"Is it healthy, and will it continue, do you think?"

"Yes."

"If a man had a little money to invest would it be wise to invest in this town, at this time?"

"Yes." Very emphatically.

"Could six per cent. and good security be got?"

"Yes."

"Would you be willing to invest it for me?"

The questions were asked in a business-like tone, without a pause. The answers were as promptly given.

Then Cainsford leaning over, spoke distinctly into the tube. "I could have placed two thousand dollars this very day, at seven per cent, and good security."

"What kind of security?"

"First mortgage. Man owns valuable corner lot; is building, and wants money to complete it."

"That sounds pretty good, sure. Well, I'll consult my wife and let you know about it later. How much do I owe you?"

Cainsford shook his head.

"Oh! yes, you cannot spend time hollering at a deaf man for nothing."

He produced a well-filled purse and laid a two dollar bill on the table. Then picked up his cap, shook hands, bowed, walked briskly to the door, paused, and as he recrossed the floor placed the trumpet in position and asked:

"What is this your name is? I saw it somewhere, but did not pay much attention."

"Cainsford" was the answer, spoken distinctly into the tube.

The old gentleman gave a perceptible start.

"Say, did you ever know a preacher by that name?"

"Yes, firstrate. I lived with one till I went to college."

"What was his first name?"

"Jeremiah."

"You don't mean that you are a son of Reverend Jerry Cainsford?"

"The same at your service."

The long, steady, piercing gaze from those level grey eyes almost made Cainsford uncomfortable, then the eyes fell, the lids trembled, and two big tears stole down the rugged face, while the mellow voice, now with a quiver in it, softly said:

"You do look some like him, but darker. Why bless me, if you are a son of Jeremiah Cainsford, the preacher, you go right on and invest that two thousand dollars, and here it is."

The old gentleman eagerly drew forth a pocket book from inside his vest, and while the strong fingers of the sinewy hand shook slightly, handed the surprised young lawyer a certified check for two thousand dollars.

"Why, man, you should be proud of your name and prouder of your father. I'm delighted to meet you for his sake. He taught me everything I know, just about, that is any good. He taught me how to read, how to write, how to add, how to spell, how to live, and best of all, how to be ready to die."

The rugged, rosy face twitched while the trembling lips whispered with a sob in the voice:

"God bless him! God bless him."

"It's fifty years since I went to school to him, but I haven't forgot, no, I haven't forgot."

And these two, the strong young man, and the strong old man, clasp hands with a fervent lingering pressure, as they silently gaze at each other.

While they are thus engaged we will try and describe young lawyer Cainsford as he appeared that day.

He is of noble physique, full six feet in height.   His broad, square shoulders give the impression of plenty of muscular force; his arms are long and strong.   His full breast denotes endurance, but before one can take in all the details of the well knit, graceful figure he is unconsciously compelled to note the noble head, thickly covered with coal black, wavy hair, the broad well developed intellectual forehead, the not too handsome nose, the well kept black moustache which scarcely covers the full upper lip, but adds to the rounded beauty of the dimpled chin.   If there is a weak point it is the chin.   However, what strikes and rivets one's attention in this peculiarly powerful face is the full dark eyes, with their jet black, heavy, arching brows.   They possess a fascination all their own. At present they are as mild as the eyes of a gazelle, and the expression of kindliness and sympathy is intensified by the moisture of the dark lashes, for strong Chris Cainsford has been moved to tears by the earnest words of the deaf man, whose hand he holds. Nothing is more sacred to him than the memory of his dear, dead father; nothing has the same power to call forth the best that is in him, as reference to that father's earnest, useful, godly life and example.

These same eyes, however, were mostly responsible

for the name "Crazy Chris," which he bore at school and college. When angry, or excited, or when performing one of his many daring feats, they would glow like live coals, and seem illumined by a sort of mad light, gleaming under the jet black brows and shooting forth what appeared like sparks of scorching fire. In many a school fight, Chris Cainsford's opponent, or opponents, had been beaten and cowed as much by the crazy burning eyes as by his sturdy blows. Now he is a man, and not often called "Crazy Chris"; however, it is rumored that he is a bit wild. His more intimate well-wishers whisper: "What a pity Cainsford gambles and drinks." "All in a lifetime, only wild oats," is the usual reply.

He has been in practice but a short time, has already made a name, and is considered a clever lawyer. His business prospects are first class. Socially, he is a great favorite, is brilliant company, an accomplished violinist, a skilled horseman, and has a singularly strong control over animals. He can hold his own in any game where muscle, courage, quickness and endurance is required, is generous to a fault, besides being considered the handsomest man in town. Truly he is a fine specimen of young Canadian manhood.

CHAPTER II.

The Deaf Man's Story

While still holding the elder man's hand, Cainsford gently forced him to a seat, at the same time speaking distinctly into the trumpet:

"The school; tell me about it.   When did you meet my father last?   How did you happen to call to-day?"

As the old gentleman fixed himself comfortably in the arm-chair he said, the merry twinkle again appearing in his eye: "I'm a better talker than hearer.   If you have time to listen, I have time to talk, and I tell you I like the subject—could not have a better than Jeremiah Cainsford.   If you get tired just holler into this old machine," and he gave the trumpet a shake.

"My name is George Littlejohn.   I'm sixty year's old; am a Presbyterian and a Grit.   Like Eben Holden, "I never lied in a horse trade, and never caught a fish "bigger" than t'was.""

"About fifty years ago a new teacher came to our neighborhood and opened school in the old log school house on the hill.   I was just a barefoot youngster then, but I remember it as well as if it was yesterday. Our former teacher was quite an old man and I think liked his drop.   Sometimes he was over-exacting; sometimes over-careless; sometimes he would come late, with red eyes and lowering brow, and then woe betide the small fry.   The older scholars generally did as they liked, and took advantage of the teacher's varied humors. Of course, we made no advancement. When Jeremiah Cainsford came things were different. He was a believer, to a certain extent, in the old adage, "Spare the rod and spoil the child." He did not let us spoil anyhow. He had some pretty hard tussles with the large boys, and big Joe Delaney, the bully of the school, gave him lots of trouble."

"One day, however, the climax was reached when Joe and his followers decided they'd run the school, and if it came to the pinch put the teacher out. Joe started the row by chewing up a big wad of paper and throwing it across, with pretty good aim, at one of the girls. The teacher saw him do it, and there came a light into his eye that made me tremble; then he spoke quietly, in a creepy sort of voice that seemed to make you cold, and just suited the light in his eye. "Delaney! get that filthy paper and put it in the stove then apologize to Nellie Gibson.'"

"Delaney did not move."

"'Delaney did you hear?'"

"Delaney rose slowly from his seat, squared his big shoulders, clinched his dirty fists, and growled 'I'll be d—— if I do.' At this the bully's friends left their seats in a dogged sort of way and edged toward him. The teacher looked at each of the five burly forms with that awful light coming and going in his eyes; then he quietly drew out the big strap and sprang down the aisle. Delaney, who had reached for the poker was not quite quick enough, and got a left hander that knocked him into the middle of about a fortnight, judging from the way he stayed sprawled there, with his head under a bench.

"I was just about scart to death, but saw that teacher, your father, jump over three seats to the door, just in time to stop the biggist of Joe's friends from getting out. He yanked him back, locked the door, put the key into his pocket, and seized Will Weese, (that was the fellow's name), and shook him till his back teeth rattled, then off came his coat; and using the big strap flogged the four fighting chaps to a standstill. How, they did howl and beg for mercy, but your father that day made a job of it, and never let up till they apologized—first to him, then to the school.

"As they sat rubbing the sore spots, and wondering what had happened, he seized big Joe and shook him as easily as a terrier shakes a rat. It appeared to bring him to himself a little; for as his blinking eyes were caught by those two burning ones of the teacher, and he saw the shaking finger point to the wad of paper, he staggered over, picked it up and in a dazed sort of way put it in the stove. Those two burning eyes never left Delaney's face for a second, and the iron voice said, "apologize," and the strong arm pointed to Nellie Gibson. Joe blinked a time or two, then slouched over and said brokenly, "Nellie, I'm— I'm —sorry," and great sobs burst from him, and he cried like a child; although he never was as near being a man before."

"Say! if you're anything like your pa you're a wonderful powerful man. Why! that left hander knocked more ignorance out of, and that shake shook more sense into Joe Delaney, than all his previous schooling. He never got back the one nor lost the other; and do you believe me, inside of three month's Joe and Jerry were thicker than thieves. I mind one day I was

down to the pond having a skate, and they came along.
"Will you let me put on your skates for you, Mr.
Cainsford?" said Joe kind and soft like.   "Thank you,
Joe, if it is not too much trouble."   They were the old
fashioned skates with a screw for the heel, and straps
to fasten them on.   Joe fixed them in good style; your
pa helped Joe with his, and away they went across the
pond, holding on to the same "shinney stick."

"How had they made it up?   Oh! I don't know
exactly; but after that flogging was over, and school
had recovered from their scare, your father kind of
broke down and begged our pardon if he had mani-
fested too much anger, said that he was paid to teach
us and could not honestly earn the money unless
he had order and obedience.   If he could not secure
it by kindness, it was his duty to adopt other methods;
if he had been too severe in this case he was sorry.   As
he said this his voice shook, and a tear or two ran
down his face.   I think the tears, the shaky voice, and
the next morning's prayer, did most to make us love
him, for from the day of the big lickin' to the day he
left, the strap was seldom needed, and scarce ever seen.

"The day he left was a great day, but a sorrowful
one.   Joe Delaney got up a subscription, coaxed his
father to give more than any one else; worked more
than any three at fixing up and decorating the old
school house.   He read the farewell address, too, in a
manly way, but with a quiver in the voice, and with a
trembling hand presented our beloved teacher with a
gold watch and chain.   What your father said in
reply I could not repeat if I wanted to.   When he
finished and wished us "God Speed" there was no dry
eye in the old school house, and it was packed to the
door.

"The last time I saw him was about twenty-two years ago, and he wore that watch, and said it kept good time. He had come to visit us, and to baptize my second boy. Your father had married Nellie Gibson and me. We were sweethearts when he left the school to enter the ministry, we stayed sweethearts till we grew up, and when grandfather gave me a farm, we got married, and have been sweethearts ever since. We put off our wedding day three months so that we could have your father say the words for us —we both loved him so. At that time he lived away up west, and could not very well leave his charge, so we waited. I tell you it was a happy day, the day he came and gave me Nellie Gibson for my very own. Who do you suppose was best man? Why Joe Delaney. He'd got to be a fine looking big fellow, and did his part as proud as a prince.

Two years afterward your father baptized my oldest boy. We couldn't seem to have anybody else perform "sacred things" for us, and the last time I saw him he baptized my youngest boy. We just had the two."

Here the mellow voice faltered, the bright eyes dimmed. There was a moment's pause before the narrator continued brokenly:

"Oh! he was a noble boy. We named him after your father, and as he christened him when he said, "Jeremiah Cainsford Littlejohn, I baptize thee in the name of the Father, and of the Son, and of the Holy Ghost," we all felt the solemnity of it all, and as he added, "The Lord bless the child," tear drops as well as water drops fell on the curly head."

Another pause. Then the mellow voice continued more strongly:

"The Lord did bless him; a better boy never lived. I think the name he bore helped to make him good. He got a sudden call, but was ready for it; he died as he lived, nobly."

For a moment the grey head was bowed, then the voice continued:

"You read, no doubt, about the great railway accident near Morrisburg last October, and about the young man who went back into the upset burning car to save the little girl whose mother had been killed? He succeeded in clambering back with her to a broken window, and having reached her out, was trying to get through himself, when something that held the car gave way at the end where the fire was fiercest. The car gave a lurch, toppled over, and went crashing down the steep embankment, a seething, fiery furnace, nothing could live in it a second. The papers called that young man a "hero," and that young man was my boy, Jerry.

"I went to the scene of the accident the next day, but all I could find to bring home and bury was a few charred bones."

The voice faltered, one great convulsive sob shook the sturdy frame as the trembling lips whispered, "Yes, the papers called him a hero—but—they—did'nt —know—how—good—and true a one my Jerry was."

For some time after the story was finished the two men sat in silence, Mr. Littlejohn then got up, crossed the room, turned, put on his glasses and said in his brisk business tone:

"If you'll give me a pen I'll endorse that check. I've talked more than I intended, but I think it's done me good and I hope you'll be none the worse."

Cainsford dipped the pen into the ink and handed it and the check to Mr. Littlejohn, who slowly wrote his name across its back, as he said:

"This check represents part of Jerry's insurance, the other two thousand he left to his mother. I'm anxious that this half should be well invested for it belongs to a splendid girl. Her name is Nora Dean; she is the orphan daughter of Mrs. Littlejohn's only sister. We're about all the living relations she has. Her father and mother died when she was quite young, then she came to live with us, and helped make our home bright and happy, till she went to study for a nurse. Last year she graduated, and is now head nurse in the new hospital. She doesn't know Jerry left her the money, her name was not mentioned in the policy, but Jerry told his mother and me that if anything happened him, he would like Nora to have half of his insurance.

"If you can place the money satisfactorily, please make out the papers in her name; I'll tell her about it when she can 'stand it better.' Jerry and she were great chums, and loved each other as brother and sister. His sudden death nearly broke her heart. People call her beautiful, and they have a right to; she has the prettiest hair you ever saw, why its just like sunshine, and her heart's as good as gold, but you'll think me an awful talker, and I guess I am, but you see I can't listen very well, (here the grey eyes brightened, and the little smile glimmered). If you meet her you'll think as I do, that she is a girl in a thousand."

As George Littlejohn uttered the word thousand the office door opened, and two young men stepped in.

"Hope we're not intruding?" said one.

"No, boys, take a seat a minute, am about through,' said Cainsford.

Mr. Littlejohn got up, shook hands with Cainsford, who motioned for the trumpet, and spoke into it.

"Wait till I write you an acknowledgement for the money."

"No, never mind, think I wouldn't trust Jeremiah Cainsford's son. Good-bye for now, good luck for ever;" and nodding to the new comers, George Littlejohn was gone.

CHAPTER III.

BIRDS OF EVIL OMEN

"Well I'll be ———, Cain, but your a lucky dog!" said the taller and broader of the two young men who had just entered the office.

"Who's the old geezer with the hearin' horn? He thinks he's struck an honest lawyer does he? Haw! Haw! He must be blind as well as deaf. Did he leave you a thousand? I heard him mention that little amount as we came in, and he wouldn't take even an acknowledgment. By gad, he must come from away back, or he'd know better than trust a struggling lawyer. Haw! Haw! Hoo-pee! ain't that so, Cain."

"I say, hold on Gregg; don't you see the danger signal in Cain's eye?" said the speaker's companion, as he coolly swung a slim walking stick. "You may be very much mistaken, the old coon was more likely talking about sheepskins than toad skins. He! He! He!"

"Didn't you notice he wore a lamb overcoat? He looked as if it belonged to him, too; but you can't judge by appearances. Like enough he's an old wolf in a young lamb's clothing." Again the speaker gave a discordant, mirthless he, he, he, and continued:

"If he is not, and if he did leave a thousand with our honest Chris, without a receipt, whose business is it? Do you not think our learned friend capable of taking advantage of a trifling circumstance like that, without any hint from a poor customs officer, or a half paid church organist? Oh, you may leave it to him; oh, yes, you may certainly leave it to him." Again he laughed his mirthless laugh, and gave the companion he called Gregg an insinuating wink from a watery eye.

"That is all right, Teary," said the first speaker, "but I maintain that if he knew as much about young Chris, as he thinks he knows about old Jerry, he'd have accepted the acknowledgment with many thanks. Ha! Ha! What do you think, Cain; what do you think, eh?"

"I think you a low insulting coward, and Stancy a miserable meddling sneak," Cainsford fairly hissed, and his dark eyes glared upon the two, while his muscular fingers grasped the thumbs of each hand as if to hold himself in check, as he continued:

"If you were not both half drunk I'd throw you out." The voice, though not loud, was so charged with vemon; the powerful, trembling form so filled with menace; the flashing dark eye so fierce, that the two young men for a moment stood in speechless, awe-stricken silence, while Cainsford went on:

"If I hear another word in disparagement of that grand old man, or the slightest slur cast upon the name of my dead father, you'll wish you had never entered this office. It makes me wild to think that two drunken rowdies have the audacity to come here, and to my very face belittle my dead father's best friend, and make a by-word of that father's name."

Here Greggson assayed to speak, but was made dumb by a commanding gesture, as Cainsford continued bitterly:

"Truly, I must have fallen pretty low or you would never have dared to do it, drunk or sober."

Then with a mirthless laugh, he continued: "If George Littlejohn knew the sort of company I sometimes keep, he would never have entrusted me with his money, no never."

At this point the one called Stancy, cringingly offered a weak apology, saying that no offence was intended, just a little banter, would not hurt his feelings for the world; that they had had a horn or two, or it never would have occurred.

While he continues to reiterate their heartfelt sorrow, speaking for his companion as well as himself, we will endeavor to describe the worthy pair—beginning with the speaker. His figure is rather spare, of medium height, with drooping shoulders, long arms, white hands, and thoroughly well kept nails. He is well dressed in dark blue coat and vest, shepherd plaid trousers, patent leather shoes, and immaculate

linen. In a light blue silk tie he wears what looks like
a valuable pin. Coal black hair, worn rather long,
is combed well back from his narrow forehead. His
eyes are of an undecided light blue color; his brows
straight and dark, in strong contrast to the colorless
eyes, giving them a notable peculiarity, which is added
to by a persistent tear, or tears, which seem determined to make a dwelling place in the corner of his
right eye. If one is hastily brushed away it is immediately replaced by another. This peculiarity has
given Mark P. Stancy, the nickname of Teary. The
affliction developed shortly after he had the eye
straightened by a specialist. From Stancy's birth it
had been decidedly crossed. The operation was
entirely successful, but the eye was never afterwards
entirely free from a tear, as if in reproach for the pain
it had suffered.

One could never be sure whether Stancy was glad
or sorry, merry or downhearted. His complexion was
ever the same. The sun had never succeeded in
tanning his cool pale face. The most direct insult
was not capable of producing a flush on the marble
cheek; or of causing a tone of indignation in his
metallic voice. He gave lessons in voice culture to
others, but entirely failed to cultivate his own. When
Stancy became angry, it was in a sort of underhand
way, only made manifest by a larger tear than usual
in the watery eye. If he attempted retaliation for
insult or injury, he did it in a roundabout manner, and
always struck in the dark. Cainsford had given him
the most appropriate name, when he called him a
miserable sneak. Mark P. Stancy was employed by
one of the leading churches of L—— as organist.

Those who liked him least, however, were obliged to admit that he could play.

His companion Greggson is very unlike him; he is taller, and of a much heavier build. His large close cropped head is set on a short thick neck, between heavy, broad, rounded shoulders, denoting great strength. He is carelessly dressed in grey tweed, his clothes do not appear to fit well. He has a round red face, clean shaven. His eyes are small, of a dark grey color, and somewhat shifty in expression. He is square-jawed, and thick-lipped; his lips when parted reveal a set of beautiful, even, strong, white teeth. They are so perfect that they attract attention, and have a tendency to redeem, somewhat, a very homely face. These teeth have been Ance Greggson's pride from his youth. He is want to say that he can bite a nail in two. Some of his old schoolmates could show marks of these same strong teeth, which they had received years ago during some slight misunderstanding with their owner. Now, their perfect symmetry is marred by a gold crowned one, occupying a prominent position in the upper row. When angry, Greggson has a habit of curling his upper lip to one side, exposing his teeth in such a manner that it gives him a truly ferocious expression.

During Cainsford's passionate threats, and Stancy's reiterated apologies, he stood with bowed head, his face wearing a sullen, hang-dog expression. When Cainsford turned to pace up and down, his little eyes followed every move, every lineament of his face showing intense hate; even emotionless Stancy shivered as he caught sight of it. It changed instantly, and a forced smile appeared as Cainsford again looked his way, and he said gruffly:

"Look-a-here, Cain, what is the use of being so short and cranky with old friends. You know me long enough surely, to overlook a little slip of the tongue, not meant to raise your dander. As Teary says, I don't think it would have happened if the brandy hadn't got to our heads a little. You've been there yourself, and know how it goes. Haw! Haw!"

"Why, Cain, I'm no ways near ready to quarrel with you, no sir, not by a ——— sight. It just about tickled me to death when the old man got me the appointment for this town, and why do you suppose? Just because I knew my old schoolmate was livin' here, and I knew I'd be near him once more. You have no idea, Cain, how glad I was when you took me up and introduced me round, never seeming to remember the fights we used to have, never seeming to bear ill-will. Why, old man, you made it a darn sight easier for me in more ways than one, you can easy see. I don't want anything to come between us. Instead of coming here to quarrel with you, I came on purpose to ask you to drive out to the rifle range for a shoot. The other lads will be there. I'll furnish the rig and it won't cost you a cent; and say, Chris, I want you to shake hands and forget this little misunderstanding. You may be sure I'll be on my guard in the future."

Greggson emphasized the last words, and held out his hand, Cainsford willingly grasped it, but as he looked searchingly into the other's face, he received a peculiar shock, akin to positive aversion. The forced smile was more like a satisfied sneer. The impression was only momentary, however, and he gave Greggson's hand a hearty friendly shake. Chris Cainsford was as forgiving as he was passionate, and as generous as he was forgiving. He thought that possibly he had been too hasty in his resentment, and decided to tell Stancy and Greggson of the noble character of the deaf man, and of the warm friendship which had existed for so long between him and his own father. When they understood the position fully, he thought, they would feel that they deserved the rebuke he had given them. Cainsford therefore gave many details of the conversation he had had with George Littlejohn. In his earnestness he did not forget to mention Nora Dean, and in order to prove that the old gentleman at least trusted him fully, he showed them the check for $2,000.00.

The young men offered him warm congratulations, and now that peace was fully restored, Greggson urged Cainsford to accept his invitation to go to the shoot. Cainsford kindly refused, on the plea of business. Then he was asked out to have a drink. "Thank you, some other time," was the reply. They then passed out, after many protestations of good fellowship.

CHAPTER IV.

Evolution of a Vile Scheme

After closing the door of Cainsford's office, Greggson turned, and clinching both big fists, shook them furiously, as he hissed, "You d—— skunk, you self-opinionated blow-hard, I'll be even with you yet, and d—— you, don't you forget it."

Greggson's face at this moment was horrible to look upon,—so convulsed was it with hate, so cruelly vindictive.

As they went down the stair he said with a snarl, "Look-a-here, Teary, if I don't take the cackle out of that rooster inside three months, you may call Ance Greggson a d—— chump. I know him through and through. I'll teach him to threaten to throw me out of his d—— office, just because you and I did not say he was good and honest. Oh! I'll show him a trick, with a hole in it. Oh! yes. I tell you, Teary, I hate that fellow worse than h——. He broke my tooth, ten years ago; I swear to God, I'll be even, I'll break his proud heart. He respects old Little Jack, does he? Well, the old cuss won't respect him long after he finds his pretty lawyer to be a low thief. And the girl, I'd almost forgot her, Haw! Haw! I know the lovely Nora, she has crossed the ferry lots of times. Oh, Teary, but she is a stunner; and I'll make her hate the name of Cainsford as long as she has breath."

As Greggson had been pouring forth his tirade of threats and abuse, he and his companion were walking down Main Street.   They continued on their way for two blocks when Greggson suddenly grabbed Stancy by the shoulders and fixing him with his fiery eyes, said huskily, but gloatingly:

"I've got it, by —— I have got it," and he spelled the four words.

"If Ance Greggson does not make that honest lawyer weep, and wail, and gnash his teeth, he'll go hang; and Mr. Mark P. Stancy is going to help do it.   Yes—he—is—going to take a hand in and going to be $500.00 ahead at the finish.   It can't miss, no, it—can't—miss."

Again Greggson spelled the three words, while a sort of joyous light illumined his evil face.

"Why, what on earth do you mean, Gregg?" said Stancy earnestly.   "For heaven's sake, don't talk so loud, everybody is looking, be more moderate. Explain yourself, man."

"Moderate! did you say? moderate! and me with the happiest thought ever a customs officer had. Haw! Haw! Haw! but perhaps you're right; come over to Moore's, where we can be alone, and I'll explain, yes, I'll explain, and if Mr. Mark Stancy does not willingly fall to and carry out instructions, I will be under the painful necessity of informing a certain insurance company of what I know of the origin of the fire which occurred last fall in somebody's music store."

At the last words Stancy hurriedly brushed away a large tear, as he said fearfully, "For the love of pity, Gregg, don't.   I'll do what you want, willingly enough, don't fear, I haven't an undying love for your honest Cain, myself. Come on to Moore's and give me the cue."

They turned a corner, walked down a side street, through an alley-way, then entered a door in the rear of Mike Moore's saloon.

There were three or four pen-like apartments. They selected one farthest from the bar, seating themselves at a table covered with stained oil cloth. Greggson touched a bell which stood on the table. When the bartender appeared wearing a soiled linen coat Greggson ordered the best in the house. Then they drank and drank and drank. They whispered, they chuckled, they swore, and in that darkened room, while breathing foul air, plotted a vile scheme, that for low down cowardly meanness has had few equals. It could only emanate from the morally degraded, could only find lodgment in a brain diseased, or in a mind craving revenge.

We will not tire the reader by giving sordid details, suffice it to say the so-called scheme was born of hate, suckled on brandy, developed by lust, strengthened by greed, fondled by covetousness, and nourished in a place where the very walls appeared to exude evil.

*   *   *   *   *   *

After the two so-called friends had taken their departure, young lawyer Cainsford pondered long and earnestly. Suddenly he exclaimed, "Oh! if I could only cut out the cards, the drink would not bother me much."

He sat silent for a minute, then continued talking to himself.

"I cannot understand why I have such a craze
for play, the Lord knows it has cost me enough—with
all my winnings I am away in the hole. Then what
is worse, one night of it knocks me out for business,
then winning or losing, I want to keep on and on,
and on. I wish to goodness I was more like old
Frank,—he is always doing right, always helping
someone. By jove, if ever a man bore an appropriate
name, Frank Aligood is the chap. If he would only
come here and start practice, I believe I'd throw up
cards for good, and drop the whole crowd. The
talk with George Littlejohn was an inspiration. To
think it was marred by the coming of those two,—
like birds of evil omen. I did not like the look of
Ance Greggson when he pretended to laugh. it off.
How disagreeable he was, as his big grin showed
that gold tooth; I sometimes think he fairly hates me.
But to the deuce with him and his teeth, I must
get to work."

Cainsford looked at his watch, "Great Scott!" said
he, "I did not think it so late, I must deposit that
check before the bank closes. I wonder where the
mischief that boy is, off skating likely. Well, I
used· to like it myself. He took the check from his
safe, put on his hat, and locking the door, went out.

CHAPTER V.

A Customs Officer's Tool

When Cainsford returned he was accompanied by
a lad of about twelve or fourteen years of age. "Look
here, Tomkins," he remarked, "I do not want to be
obliged to lock this office during business hours. If
you cannot be here when wanted I'll certainly get
someone who can."

The boy hung his head, as he murmured, "I did
not think I was so long away."

Cainsford cut him short with the question, "Do
you know the man who is building on the corner
of Market and James streets?"

"Yes, sir," was the answer.

"What is his name?"

"Webster, Sir."

"That is right. Now listen. I want you to go
up there, find Mr. Webster, and tell him I can let
him have the money, the two thousand dollars, at
7 per cent. Do you understand?"

"Yes, sir."

"Then hustle, and come back at once with his
answer."

Tomkins hurried away, and soon reached the corner
where Mr. Webster was building. He did not find
him, however, and was informed that he had gone
to the country. Tompkins promptly returned with

the information. Then Cainsford instructed him to go again in the morning, and charged him to be sure to be at the office with Webster's answer by nine o'clock.

* * * * * * *

Tomkins got up earlier than usual the next morning. As he was on his way to Webster's, a coarse voice hailed him from across the street.

"I say there, Tomkins, I say, hold on, I want to speak to you."

Tomkins recognized the voice. It was a voice he did not like, and belonged to a man he was somewhat afraid of. Turning, he saw Customs Officer Greggson crossing the street. The latter's face was very red this morning, and his eyes bloodshot.

He slapped Tomkins on the back as he said gruffly, "Where in the dickens are you going in such a rush?"

"Oh! I'm on a message for Mr. Cainsford, and I've got to hurry. It's up to Webster's. He was away yesterday, and Mr. Cainsford seemed disappointed, so I must find him this morning."

"Is it a written message?" carelessly asked Greggson.

"Oh, no, just some business, something about two thousand dollars he can have."

"Who can have?" snapped Greggson.

"Why, Mr. Webster."

"Oh, I see, Cainsford is going to lend Joe Webster two thousand dollars, and where the devil did Cainsford get the money to lend? Eh!"

"I don't know," said Tomkins.

"Well, I do," snarled Greggson, "and he did not

come by it honestly. Besides, Webster does not
want the money now.   He borrowed it from a farmer
yesterday, and look here, Tomkins, YOU NEEDN'T GO
ANY FURTHER.   I know all about it.   What you've
got to do is, tell your boss that Mr. Webster said
he was much obliged, but that he had got the money
elsewhere.   Do you understand?"

"Yes,—but—but—he didn't say so, and Mr.
Cainsford will sack me if he finds out."

"He won't find out, booby.   You do as I tell you,
but if you value your skin don't mention my name."

"Oh! Mr. Greggson, I don't like to lie to Mr. Cainsford.   He was so kind to mother when Mamie was
sick," and a tear came to Tomkin's eye.

"Oh, shut your jaw," said Greggson, harshly.   "I
tell you he did not come by the money honestly, and
he is not going to lend it for a few days any way.
No, by ——, and look here Toney Tomkins, I want to
tell you something.   It's a secret.   Cainsford told
me himself."

At this point Greggson assumed a very mysterious
air.

"It is this.   He told me he got the money from
an old deaf man, and that he never gave the old man
even a receipt for it.   Now, Toney, what do you think
of that.   It's as true as there is a God in Heaven.
It's too d—— bad.   Do you think a lawyer has the
right to lend a poor old deaf man's money for which
he never gave a receipt?"

"Ah, no, Toney, certainly not, and say, Toney,
you and I have got to know what he does with it,
do you see."

Greggson now dropped the mysterious air as he

continued. "He's been kind to you, has he? Well, so have I, perhaps you have forgot the time I caught you smuggling coal oil across the ice with the hand sleigh. Oh, haw, haw, I see you remember it."

(At the taunting words Tomkins had turned pale).

"Well, so do I. I had to pour it out, but didn't I give you as much money as it cost you, didn't I?"

"Yes, sir," was the answer in a weak voice.

"Did I let you off and let you keep the sleigh? Well, I call that being kind, and generous too, and now I am going to be kinder still. Here take this."

Greggson thrust a silver dollar into Toney's hand.

"Now you can buy that pair of skates I saw you looking at in Mott's window, and all you've got to do is tell your precious lawyer that Webster does not want the money. And, listen, if anybody else comes to the office to borrow it, I want to know about it right away. Do you hear?"

"Yes, sir, but how could I let you know?"

Tomkins voice trembled, for Greggson's talk had mystified, and his threats had frightened him.

"Do you know where my office is?" the latter continued.

"Yes, sir, down at the dock," was the answer.

"Right, you just keep your eyes and ears open. If anybody comes to borrow money listen to all that is said. Make an excuse to go out, and run down to my office. If I am not there write your name on a piece of paper and drop it in the letter-box in the door? I'll know what it means and look you up, you may be sure, but don't for your life let on to Cainsford, or anyone else, that you know me. It's all for the sake of that poor old deaf man," and Greggson grinned and the gold tooth gleamed.

"If you do exactly as I tell you, the day Cainsford draws that money, and you let me know, I'll give you a five dollar bill. Do you understand?"

"Yes, sir."

"Well, it's a bargain, and if you don't keep it to the letter, I'll make it 'hot' for you over that smuggling, and don't you forget it."

As he made the threat he wore such an ugly look that poor Tomkins for the moment was terrified. As he felt the big round silver dollar in his hand, he mustered sufficient courage to promise weakly that he'd do the best he could.

"What time did Cainsford tell you to be at the office?" was Greggson's next question.

"Nine o'clock sharp," was the answer.

"Well, you'd better make a move then, you only have fifteen minutes; but hold on, what are you going to tell your boss about Webster?"

"That he is much obliged, but—but, got the money elsewhere."

"Right, you're O. K., here is 10 cents for candies. Now, light out."

As Tomkins rushed away Greggson watched him out of sight, and murmured, "there is one good spoke driven into the wheel that will roll my Bucko Lawyer to H——. Now for a good drink."

CHAPTER VI.

Victory in a Burglary Trial

Cainsford was not surprised when he received Webster's answer, for that gentleman had told him the day he applied for the loan that he required the money at once. He noticed, however, that his office boy Tomkins seemed somewhat disconcerted when questioned concerning his interview with Webster. He put it down to the fact that he had scolded him the day before, and thought nothing more about it.

Shortly before this Cainsford's services had been secured for the defence in a burglary case. There was strong circumstantial evidence against the accused. After hearing the latter's story, Cainsford believed in his innocence. This belief naturally awakened his sympathy. He then went to work in the prisoner's behalf, concentrating all the power of his keen intellect to bring about an acquittal. Weeks went by, the trial came on and awakened considerable public interest.

The prosecution had a very strong case, the evidence, though entirely circumstantial, seemed so complete and conclusive that the prisoner himself lost hope.

When Cainsford rose to address the jury he had the sympathy of the assembled crowd. He did not appear to have a leg to stand on, as the saying is.

Those present felt that an address to the jury under the circumstances was merely waste of time. However, when Cainsford's rich, mellow voice was heard it was listened to with marked attention. He dwelt at length upon the danger of relying upon purely circumstantial evidence when so much was at stake. He cited case after case where there had been a fearful miscarriage of justice, owing to the fact that jurors had accepted circumstantial evidence as conclusive evidence, and given their verdict accordingly; only to discover when too late that they had made a horrible mistake, and condemned an innocent man.

He enlarged upon and strengthened every point in favor of the accused. As he warmed to his subject his noble head was thrown back, and his powerful frame seemed to expand as his keen, magnetizing glance scanned the face of each juryman in turn. Every possible circumstance which could awaken sympathy for the prisoner was magnified. Every argument in his favor made so convincing that the listeners wondered why they had not thought of these things before. Then with a final burst of eloquence, while his large dark eyes flashed over the crowded court room, Cainsford appealed to their chivalry, and demanded for the prisoner a generous verdict, not only according to law, but on behalf of British fair play.

He sat down amid bursts of applause, which continued until the austere judge, in a voice of thunder, threatened to commit the whole crowd for contempt of court.

The jurors were not out for long. They filed in

slowly, and solemnly took their places. Then, amid profound silence, the foreman, who was a large man, rose, looked first at the judge, then at the lawyers, then at the jurymen to his right, turning his eyes on the prisoner's box, he fixed a steady gaze on its occupant, and his bearded chin seemed to tremble from the shock, as his mouth belched forth two words, "Not Guilty." The loudly spoken words were uttered with a ring of defiance in the tone, like shots fired in quick succession from an overcharged gun. As he sat down, there was a subdued cheer, and Cainsford noticed a wintry smile appear for a second on the foreman's hairy face as he gave two or three emphatic nods in his direction.

Mike Murphy's case was the last on the docket. At its conclusion congratulations poured forth upon Cainsford, indeed so surrounded was he upon all sides by acquaintances who seemed proud of his achievement, that he found it difficult to escape, and when he succeeded, felt immense relief to discover that he was alone in an obscure corner of the entrance hall.

It was not for long, however. He heard a hurried step, the rustle of a skirt, then two hazel eyes looked into his, whle their owner seized his hand and raised it to her trembling lips, as she said brokenly:

"God bless ye, sor, God bless ye, fer what ye done fer me and moin thish day I'll pray fer ye as long as Oi heve breath. Ave coorse ye knowed as well as Oi that Moik niver darkened the doore ave that house, nor the windie ayther, but some belaved he did, an that ould jidge wid his fierce vice and bald pate, belaived it too, an would hav sint Moik to jail, so he would, if ye hadent got up an made that grand, glorious spach. An och! if he had, what in the wide worruld would heve become of me an moy little wans, as luves their daddy so. I felt leike as if me poor heart would break, afore ye tould em all about how good an koind a lad me Moik was, aven if he did sometoimes take a droph too mutch. Ivery worred ye spoke so thrue too. Why bless yer koind heart, sor, Moik Murphy's that tinder, and sympathisin that he aven fades the poor wee burrds as comes to the back doore, cold mornins, when the shnow is so dape ther jist starved amost. Och! but it's a proud man he'll be thish day, an it's a grateful heart he'll be havin fur ye always, sor, an if iver ye nade a thrue frind, wid a sthrong arrum, an honest heart, and willin hand, Moik Murphy's the by fer ye. An whin ye hav a woife ave yer own, may she nivir know a sorrow, nor heve an achin heart. If she iver should Maggy Murphy's willin to sarve her, to the last droph av me blud, an I mane ivery worred I say, sor. But ther, ther, plase furgive me fer introodin mesilf, but I could'ent help thankin ye, no, I could'nt, an I'll tach me childern to pray fer ye as long as ye live, that I will, sor."

Here the tears again gushed and ra over the comely face, as with a final fervent, "God bless ye, sor! God bless ye, sor," Maggie Murphy hurried down the long hall.

CHAPTER VII.

"God Bless Ye, Sor"

For some time after Mrs. Murphy left him, Cainsford stood leaning against the dingy wall. The Irish woman had come upon him so unexpectedly, had been so earnest in her protestations of gratitude, so sincere in her assertions that she would pray for him, that he had been completely taken aback, and did not recover from his surprise until she had dropped his hand and disappeared. He blamed himself for his apparent apathy, and murmured aloud:

"Why the mischief did I not tell the poor woman that I had only done what was decent and right, and that the fact of winning the case was sufficient reward; but, no, I just stood there dumb as an oyster and let her cry over me, kiss my hand, and sing my praises, just as though I deserved and expected it all; pooh! it makes me sick."

Cainsford tried to pull himself together as he opened the door leading to the street; then for the first time he realized that he was both tired and hungry. He called to mind that he had been so interested in the case that he had entirely forgotten his lunch. Hailing a cab, he was at once driven to his boarding-house. After a bath and a good dinner he felt like a new man.

While leisurely sauntering to his office, an energetic

newsboy called to him, "Buy a paper, sir? all about the Murphy Trial."

Cainsford smiled as he read the big headlines.

When he reached his office it was nearly dark. He turned on the light, and seating himself read a graphic account of the trial and his address to the jury. As he read he could not help a thrill of pride. He felt that he possessed the ability to accomplish great things, and determined to do honour to his profession.

"Who knows, I may be a judge some day," he said aloud.

Then he sat and pondered long and earnestly. He recalled many things; his old home in Darkton; the many times his only sister Flo. had helped him out of difficulties. Why only last fall she had sent him a hundred dollars.

"Thank the Lord she did not know it paid gambling debts," he whispered to himself.

Then he called to mind the tender care, loving devotion and kindly advice, of his noble christian mother. His heart saddened as he thought of the many times he had grieved her by his wild ways and thoughtless acts. Many, many times had she shielded him from his father's just but stern reproach. Full as many times had she generously forgiven him, and prayed the more earnestly in his behalf.

The recollection that he had often caused that loving heart to sorrow brought a blush of shame to Cainsford's handsome face, as he sat there alone in the mellow light.

Was it not probable that at that very moment his mother was earnestly praying for him. Was it possible that his softened mood and present longing for better things was in answer to her prayers. "Yes, it may be," he whispered, "God knows that I have not been given much to it lately."

Then his mind reverted to his father. He remembered distinctly the last conversation shortly before the latter's death. He still had the book given him at the time. He remembered the very words spoken by his father: "Here, Chris, read this book with care, and make its title, 'Tact, Push and Principle' your motto for every day."

Then followed good advice and godly counsel, together with an earnest appeal for him to do the right; an appeal which could only come from a righteous man who had lived a pure and noble life. Then the parting scene, how vividly it seemed to pass before him. His father's shaking hand, as he gave him a well-filled purse with which to buy law books and furniture for his new office. He could still see tears in the kindly eyes as the twitching furrowed face was turned toward him. He heard again a sob as the trembling voice uttered the words, "Good-bye my lad, God bless and keep you, my boy; God bless and ——."

Ah! What is that? It seemed as though the words had actually been spoken close to him in his father's well remembered tones.

Cainsford was partly roused for a moment, but drifted away again into a dreamy wonderment of the possibility of departed spirits having the power to be near, and to know of the doings of their friends and relatives still upon earth.

"If it be possible," mused Cainsford, "father will not be displeased with what his son Chris has done to-day."

The events of the trial, just as they occurred, now passed vividly before his mind. He recalled the sudden appearance of Maggie Murphy. He again saw tears in her honest hazel eyes; felt again the burning kiss of gratitude on his hand, and heard the rich accents of her mellow Irish voice, as she seemed to repeat again and again, "God bless ye, sor."

A thrill of conscious pride surged through and through Cainsford, rousing him completely. He was filled with a satisfaction superior to that experienced when he had in three hardly contested rounds worsted the champion wrestler from Toronto, winning well deserved laurels for the Y.M.C.A. of L——, and plaudits of praise for himself.

Cainsford rose, and as he crossed to his desk, said aloud, "By Jove, I'll write to old Frank, there's a splendid chance for him here since Dr. Barker's death; he's too good a man to be buried in a back country village." As he seized the pen he noticed a small piece of paper upon which was written in a boyish hand, "Toney Tomkins was down." Cainsford carelessly threw it into the waste paper basket, then he started and continued to write, page after page, without pause, save for the time it took to rend one sheet from the pad in order to vigorously attack the next, without sound, save the scritch, scritch of the swiftly travelling pen, and the sche, sche, sche of simmering steam in the heating coils. For full an hour Cainsford wrote. At last he threw down the pen and exclaimed, "There you are, if that don't fetch him I don't know Dr. Frank Allgood."

As he leans back to light his pipe, if we peep over his broad shoulder we may read the last page written in a large bold hand:—

"There never was a better chance for a good strong man to work up a paying practice than here in this thriving wide awake town; and then it is so beautifully situated on the banks of the grand old St. Lawrence, with its thousand isles of beauty. Its boating, its fishing, its bathing. Why? I tell you old man it's big and pure enough for even you to plunge in and be made clean, feet and all. This should certainly be a strong inducement. Besides you are needed, very much needed indeed, by old, young, rich, poor, male, and female, especially the last mentioned, but the one who needs you most of all is Christopher Cainsford by name. He is willing to become your very first patient. Will gladly place himself in your skillful hands for treatment. Say Frank, I tell you honestly he needs a physician. He is diseased morally, sluggish mentally, and too beefy physically; so come out from among the backwoods, dear boy, and be ye separate, saith your old loving friend.

Chris. Cainsford.

The letter was addressed and as Cainsford smoked he mused and talked to himself, a habit he had.

"Yes," said he, "That letter should bring old Frank by the first train. Really there is a splendid opening for him here. I wonder how he's fixed for money. His last letter stated that he was kept pretty busy. I'll bet they don't half pay him, and if they do, the old silly, with his big soft heart gives the most of it away. He's sure to find folks that he thinks needs it worse than he does. He's got to come, hard up, or no hard up. If necessary I'll raise the wherewith myself. Bye-the-bye—I had almost forgotten Nora Dean's money lying idle so long, and I have never written a scratch to the old gentleman. It's a crying shame. That Murphy case knocked everything else out of my head, but here goes. Again the pen was seized and made to travel rapidly. The hastily written sheet was enclosed and the envelope addressed to Geo. Littlejohn, Smith's Corners. "I'll send him the paper too," said Cainsford, as he folded it up and addressed it," it will show him I have not been idle, and may interest him, because of his respect for the poor Governor.

Having stamped the letters and papers, Cainsford looked at his watch, it was nearly midnight. He hurried to the Post Office and dropped the missives in. While on his way to the boarding-house, he saw two men in earnest conversation under an arc light. He was almost sure they were Greggson and Stancy. In order to avoid meeting them he crossed the street. He had seen very little of either of them during the past weeks, and was rather glad of it.

Having reached his room, while undressing he thought what a busy day it had been. He felt at peace with the world and pretty well satisfied with himself, and determined to steer pretty clear of draw poker in the future. As he was dropping off to sleep he seemed to hear the tones of his father's voice. The voice seemed far away, but Cainsford caught the words:

"Let him that thinketh he standeth, take heed lest he fall."

Was it a premonition of coming disaster?

CHAPTER VIII.

TONEY SORRY, BUT AFRAID TO TELL

Ever since the morning Customs Officer Greggson
had intercepted the message intended for Mr. Webster,
Toney Tomkins had been a very unhappy boy. Oh,
how often he wished Greggson had not seen him that
morning. How he wished that he had refused the
silver dollar. He had never been really happy since
that morning. Even when he used the skates he
bought with the money, he did not have much fun, and
now the ice was gone and he could not use them.

We must say in Toney Tomkins favor that it was
more fear of Greggson than desire for money that
caused disloyalty to his employer. This fear, also,
caused him to report daily what occurred at Cainsford's
office. He tried to atone in a measure for his disloyalty by punctuality and close attention to duties.
He kept the office in apple pie order, was always on
hand when wanted; in fact had become such a perfect
model of an office boy that Cainsford raised his pay
a dollar a week. When this occurred it nearly broke
Toney's heart. He was naturally sensitive, and when
his employer praised him so highly, and spoke so
kindly, as he handed him his wages with an extra
dollar, he just about broke down. His eyes filled with
tears as he murmured his thanks, and he was on
the point of making a clean breast of it and telling the
whole story. (If he had, what a difference it would

have made in the lives of several persons). He did not do it, and why? Because of Greggson's horrible, cowardly threats.

And what had this officious officer been doing these past weeks? Very little to his credit, indeed! He had made an unimportant seizure or two; had watched the ferry closely, and caused its passengers as much annoyance as possible, in clawing over their baggage in search of something seizable. Now that the old St. Lawrence was open again his chance for spoil would increase.

We must not forget to mention a small purchase he made immediately after he and Stancy had arranged their little scheme. He bought two packs of cards exactly alike. He and Stancy spent their evenings using each pack alternately. The latter prided himself on being able to perform some very clever slight-of-hand tricks with cards. His long white fingers were peculiarly adapted for the purpose. There was one trick he practiced very frequently. It was to exchange the deck from his pocket for the one he was about to deal, without Greggson knowing it till the latter discovered that he held four aces. Then they would laugh immoderately, order the drinks, and as they drank, wish to —— he was there with the old man's money. Then Greggson would say, "Don't you worry, Stancy, all in good time. I know he's just hungerin' and thirstin' for a game this very minute. We'll accommodate him before long. Oh, yes, he'll be accommodated and don't you forget it. The only condition is that he carries the dough." Haw! Haw! Haw!

On the Monday after the Murphy trial there was

a. hurried knock at the door of lawyer Cainsford's office, and the alert Tomkins ushered in a short stout man. As he removed his soft felt hat the visitor handed Cainsford a sealed envelope. The latter opened and read the following note, while the fussy visitor mopped his perspiring face.

Customs Office, May 7th, 18—.
Friend Cainsford,—
The bearer, Mr. L. R. Pratt, is an acquaintance of mine. He has recently purchased the Perkins Mill up the line aways. He was bringing across some new machinery, and happened to mention that he wanted to get a loan of two or three thousand dollars. He said he didn't mind paying a stiffish interest if he could get the money quick. I thought of you, and sent him up.
Your old Schoolmate,
Ance Greggson.
P.S.—He can furnish gilt edge securities.
Gregg.

As he finished reading the note, Cainsford extended his hand to his visitor, as he said, "I am very pleased to meet you, Mr. Pratt."

"Spect you be, spect you be," said the latter in a shrill, jerky voice.

"I understand you want to negotiate a small loan," continued Cainsford.

"Right you are, sir, right you are."

"What amount will you require, and what security will you furnish?"

"Want a couple of thousand. Will give mortgage on the mill. Guess it'll do. Paid twelve thousand spot fur her, and made a whale of a deal at that; but

these pesky patent planers cost like fury, or I shouldn't
need a cent; but I do need it, and quick too.   When is
the soonest I can have the stuff?   Every minute that
mill is shut down means money, so you see I'm in an
all-fired hurry."

"Well," said Cainsford, "If I find everything all
right, you may have the money at seven per cent. and
I will have papers and money ready for you by Thursday."

"Can ye heve papers and witness ready, and money
here fur me Thursday morning, in time so I can ketch
the nine o'clock train fur Montreal?"

"Yes, I guess we can by straining a point."

"Strain a point, or no strain, the question before the
house is, Will ye do it?"

"Yes, I will do it, Mr. Pratt."

"That is O. K.   Here are deeds and papers to show
I'm no pauper.   Take good care of 'em all.   Now you
are down to business, and you can draw up your papers,
Mr. Lawyer, draw em up, and make it an X or a V,
as the old feller said when he and Betsy made up."

Then Mr. Pratt threw on his hat, rushed to the
door, flung it open, and shouted back in a shrill voice:
"Don't make no error fur I'll be on deck bigger 'an
a house Thursday morning at eight o'clock sharp.
So long."

As he ran down the stairs Mr. Pratt muttered,
"Ain't that lawyer feller a clinker to look at.   I don't
think he makes many errors.   No, sir."

CHAPTER IX.

On the St. Lawrence in the Yacht Idlewild

The two days following Mr. Pratt's call were busy days for Cainsford. He visited the Registry office, consulted Bradstreet, made some inquiries, and decided that Greggson had certainly told the truth when he stated that Pratt could furnish gilt-edge security. He also decided that it was kind and thoughtful of Greggson to send Mr. Pratt to him for the loan.

"I guess," said he to himself, "old Gregg is better than he looks. I must not bear him illwill.

Cainsford followed George Littlejohn's instructions implicitly, making out the papers in Nora Dean's favor. As he wrote her name he remembered the earnest words of praise her uncle had spoken, and wondered when he would meet her. (The meeting was much sooner than he expected, and was not prearranged). He had everything ready for Mr. Pratt by two o'clock Wednesday afternoon. Had spoken to a dentist who occupied an office next door to be present as witness. Now all he had to do was draw the money before the bank closed. As he was about to leave for that purpose, he said to Tomkins: "If any one calls tell them I have just gone to the bank, and will be back soon."

After his employer left, Toney Tomkins listened till he heard the down stair door close, then seizing his cap he slipped out, not waiting to fasten the office door. He appeared to be in great haste. Upon reaching the street he turned up Main to the corner of Broad, then down the latter toward the docks, as fast as he could run. He was breathless when he reached Greggson's office, which he found locked. He pulled a small piece of paper from his pocket and dropped it through the slit cut in the door to receive letters. Turning to go back he fairly ran into Greggson, who appeared suddenly from the freight shed.

"Well," said the latter gruffly, "what news?"

"He's gone to the bank. I think he's after the money for the man you sent," was the nervous reply.

"That is O. K. It's workin' out fine, and you're a regular amateur detective. I guess I'll be able to pay you that fiver to-morrow, and will likely know what has become of the poor old deaf man's money." Here the humorous side of something seemed to appeal strongly to Greggson, for he gave a loud haw, haw, haw. Then turning to Tomkins he said, "now, skin back."

As the latter gladly rushed away, Greggson hurried into his office, crossed to the phone and rang it desperately. He placed the receiver to his ear, and said loudly, "917, please."

Then, "Hello, is that Grand Central Hotel. Is Mr. Stancy there? Send him to the phone, please." After a pause. "That you, Teary? Is Ned there? Get a move on, BRING HIM ALONG, he will work in good. Everything is O. K. Meet C. at corner of Main and Market."

"Yes, if you hurry. Don't take no for answer.
Set Ned on."

"Yes, Dunk is aboard, and has steam up."

"Certainly, lying at lower dock."

"Yes, dead in luck, but for Heaven's sake, hurry.
Bye, bye."

Greggson hung up the receiver and left his office as
hurriedly as he had entered it. He walked briskly
along the dock to the east end, where was lying a trim
little steam yacht. She made a pleasing picture as
she sat there so gracefully on the bosom of the old
St. Lawrence, while gentle ripples seemed to fondly
caress her bows, upon which could be read the name
"Idlewild" in bright gold letters. Smoke was
issuing from her red funnel and she appeared ready
and anxious to glide away.

"Are you there, Dunk?" said Greggson, as he came
alongside.

A tall, dark young man showed himself, and Greggson continued gayly:

"Isn't this a peach of an afternoon for a run? I
expect my friends here very soon, and then we're off."

*　*　*　*　*　*　*

At the same moment that Greggson hailed Dunk,
two large men were vigorously shaking hands on
the corner of Main and Market streets, while a smaller
man stood looking on; a sort of gratified smile on his
face, and a sorrowful tear in his eye.

"By George, Chris Cainsford, I'm gladder to see
you than a gold mine," said the largest of the men.

"I'd most forgot that this was the town you had
adopted, till Gregg told me. My eyes, but you do look

bang up, not much like you did when I pulled you out from under the ice!   Do you mind that, Chris?"

"Mind it, of course I mind it.   How could I forget that you saved my life that time.   I'll never forget Ned Barlow, no, never; but you are getting an awful size Ned, you must weigh about a ton."

"Not quite, only 278 stripped," was the laughing rejoinder.

"Say, Chris, pawn my socks, I'm tickled most to death to see you.   How is the cold world using you anyway?"

"O, so, so, Ned.   I manage to get three meals a day, and clothes enough to cover my nakedness. How are you prospering, old friend?"

"I'm prime up with prospects, got a claim out West, sure to pan out rich.   Have had a good many ups and downs since I seen you, mostly downs though, till I staked this claim.   I'll tell you about it later.   Gee whiz Chris, I'm more than glad to see you! If it hadn't a been for Gregg, I believe I'd a never thought of you'r bein here."

"How did you happen to meet him?" asked Cains-ford.

"O, I was havin dinner up to the Central, and feelin kind of stupid, cause I din't know nobody, when who should walk in but Gregg and his friend here.   They sot down, and I didn't take no notice till I hears someone mention your name.   I took a good look and 'Holy smoke,' says I 'how are you Ance Greggson,' then Gregg smiled, and I see them purty teeth, and I knoo I was right.   I'd never make a mistake as to the owner of them teeth, no sir, not if I met em in Jericho; but say, Chris, I hed fish for dinner, and am dry as a Ciscoe, where can we go for a drink?"

"We can drop in to Moore's on our way to the yacht," spoke up Stancy.

"It's lucky we met you Cainsford, we were just going to your office.   Your friend Mr. Barlow was so anxious to see you, and Gregg and I want you to join us in a little run on the " Idlewild." Gregg told me to be sure and bring you along, and not to take no for an answer.   He's waiting at the lower dock. He just 'phoned me that he had steam up."

"I'm afraid, boys, you will have to excuse me, I ————.''

"Not a bit of it," broke in Barlow.   "Do you think I'm going pleasuring in a dandy yacht and leave Chris Cainsford behind.   No, sir, not on your tin-type."

"But I have business," insisted Cainsford.

"O, we'll be back early," urged Stancy.

"Now look a here, you just come along," said Ned. "I won't budge a peg without you.   You never was no spoil sport, and you're too old to begin spoilin' it now.   Why! I hain't seen you for nigh a lifetime, so won't ye come along, old man, won't ye?"

Cainsford could hold out no longer.   He remembered that this big, good-natured, careless chap had saved his life years ago.

"Alright, I'll go," said he, "and we'll get back early."

"Hurrah," cried Ned.   "To Moore's first, and to "Idlewild" next."

When they came out of Moore's there was a glint in Chris Cainsford's eye, not to be seen there when they

entered. The reader is sufficiently acquainted with
our young lawyer to know that he did nothing by
halves. Now that he had yielded to the persuasions
of Ned Barlow, he cast prudence to the wind, so to
speak. Before reaching the yacht, he was the
merriest of the party, and upon reaching it gave
Greggson a familiar slap on the back, as he said:
"Much obliged, for sending up Pratt, old man."
"Did you and he make it a go?" Greggson innocently inquired.
"Yes, siree, he is to have the money to-morrow."
"Is that so?" and Gregg grinned a satisfied grin,
and showed his gold tooth.
Then they clambered aboard. The "Idlewild" gave
a proud toot, toot, and away she skimmed, with
Greggson at the wheel.
It was a beautiful afternoon early in May. As they
sped along everybody felt joyous and light hearted.
Big Ned in particular was fairly beside himself. It
was his first trip on the St. Lawrence. He laughed,
whistled and sang, clapped his big hands and shouted,
first to one, then to another. "Oh! say, ain't this
glorious?"
Greggson first steered to Horrigan's Point, where
soft drinks could be had, and hard ones too, if you
carried the pass word, and knew the ropes. You may
be sure our party was well informed.
From Horrigan's to the Park is a short run, and was
made at top speed. "Idlewild" was not an appropriate name for the little yacht that afternoon. "Busy-
wild" would have been better. Her quick angry
puffs, and disdainful snorts were re-echoed from
shore to shore as she ploughed along. She caused

such a commotion that Old St. Lawrence seemed angry. The blue water sputtered, bubbled and frothed, til the diminutive boat was nigh out of sight. She left large rolling swells far behind. They appeared to be racing for each pebbly shore, and when they arrived, poured out a protest for being disturbed.

The merry party landed, and a pleasant hour was spent at the Park, one of the most beautiful spots on the Canadian side. Then our company crossed the river, and steamed away down to W——,a picturesque village on the American shore, where they visited different places of interest, not forgetting those where refreshments could be had. They enjoyed themselves to the full, and returned to L——, arriving there about dark, where they dined together, "on the best;" Ned Barlow paying the bill.

What then? Ned proposed going to the show. Greggson and Stancy opposed the suggestion, stating that the show was no good.

"I'll tell you exactly what we'll do," said Greggson. "The Royal Exchange has just been remodelled, its a swell place, with all modern improvements. On the upper storey there are rooms furnished on purpose for little parties just like ours, where we can go and enjoy ourselves just as we please, sing a song, tell a story, or have a nice quiet game of euchre, with no one to bother, and best of all, a dumb waiter to hand. All you've got to do is blow into a little tube, then whisper your little order, and up comes the VERY BEST THAT MONEY CAN BUY."

During this somewhat lengthy speech, Greggson had furtively watched Cainsford's face. It was somewhat flushed. The latter had had several brandies with soda during the afternoon and evening.   Greggson could see no sign of protest, and continued:

"For my part, I would like very much to hear friend Ned tell of his experience in the wild, woolly West.   Wouldn't you, Teary?"

"You may bet your bottom dollar," was the reply. "That would suit me down to the ground.   What say you, Mr. Barlow?"

"I say everything is bang up.   I want to be introduced to that dumb waiter, and dum quick. Ho, ho.   And I'll tell yarns that'll make your hair stand."

"Hurrah!   Chris, let's go.   I always take a drink to wash down good grub.   It sort of gives it a flavor, eh!   What?"

CHAPTER X.

Drinking, Gambling, Fighting, Flight

The party left the restaurant forthwith, arm in arm, Greggson and Stancy leading the way.   They were in great spirits.   They whispered and laughed as they walked along.   Greggson appeared to be giving his companion particular instructions.   When they neared the Royal Exchange he raised his voice a little, and said emphatically, "you do as I say, Teary, and you'll wear diamonds.   Leave the pack with the red string in the bar with Bill.   When we need 'em they'll come up by the dumb waiter, as innocent as lambs; cute as crazy Chris is, he can't tumble, no, by —— not if he had second sight.   An' say don't forget to tell Bill to put the bulge on the first few drinks.   You'd better be careful and not take too much though; not till we get it over.   Haw! Haw!   Oh, won't it be joyful?"

They pulled up at the Royal and waited till Ned and Cainsford came along, then entering together they passed through the rotunda, back to the wide stair, nodding good evening to numbers of men as they passed.   Having reached the landing of the first stair, Stancy excused himself, murmuring something about securing the room as he turned back.   The others climbed two flights more, Greggson leading the way.   "Here we are, my hearties, he exclaimed. "It's quite a climb, but it's finer 'an silk when ye land."

"How's this fur high?" saying which, he flung open the door of a large, low-ceiled room.   The gas was turned down, and Greggson turned it on, revealing the furniture.   A good sized square table stood in the centre, with four upholstered chairs surrounding it.   A couch, showing signs of wear, sat with its back to the wall.   Dark colored curtains hung at the windows, the lower panes of which were of frosted glass?   Opposite the table from out the wall projected a short tin tube, in the end of which was a bell like mouthpiece.   Close to the right was a small square door, and underneath it a narrow shelf. To the left of the shelf stood a small table covered by a spread, upon which were magazines, newspapers, etc.   At one end of the room was a low mirror, and a grey colored oilcloth covered the floor.   Altogether the room was well arranged for the purpose for which it was intended, namely, (we will just whisper it), *"gambling"*

"Allow me to test the dumb waiter first," said Cainsford, while crossing the room. As he blew down the tube, Stancy came in hurriedly.

"Now name your poison, boys," said Cainsford.

"B. & S. fur me," said Ned.

"Same here," said Stancy.

"Me too," said Greggson,

"Make it four, and done with it," he continued, "and cigars on the side."

The order was spoken into the tube, and soon a slight noise at the little square door announced an arrival. The door swung open, and there, close to hand on a silver tray, were four sparkling drinks, the soda still sizzing. Cigars too were in a tumbler on the side.

Ned Barlow seized a glass and as he held it aloft, shouted:

"Here's to you, Cain, old boy. May you never have trouble, and may your shadow never grow less. To you too, Gregg, for introducing us to such a peach of a place."

"Here's to Mark Stancy," said Gregg, "May he never shed another tear, or wipe his weeping eye," at which all but Stancy roared. He only tee-heed as a big tear stole down his pale face. Then the fun began in earnest. Ned told tales of Western life, both interesting and amusing, refreshing himself, after each, by a liberal drink.

Cainsford did not indulge so freely, but the boiserous way he sang a comic song gave evidence that his potations had taken effect, and that he was in a thoroughly reckless humour.

After the song Greggson carelessly proposed a little game of euchre. "That's the talk," said Stancy. "I wonder if they have a decent pack of cards here."

"Blow down and see," said Gregg.

Stancy complied, and as if by magic the cards appeared on the tray. They were tied about with a piece of red twine. The four young men drew up their chairs, and started the game, Stancy and Greggson playing partners. As Cainsford cut for deal, he remarked, "It is such a time since I've played, I've almost forgotten the feel of pasteboard, and I can't play long for I must be to business early in the morning."

They played for an hour or more, the losers sawing off after each game, to see who was stuck for the drinks. Cainsford seemed unfortunate. He· was stuck twice, the others only once each.

It was humiliating for Chris Cainsford to be beaten at anything, and Greggson had nettled him during the game by his big grin and belittleing comments, and the brandy he had taken had fired his brain. No wonder his dark eyes flashed, no wonder the mad desire for play was on him strong. It came Stancy's turn to deal. He offered Ned a cut, but the latter was fully three sheets in the wind. He had been drinking steadily, and playing so wildly, that Cainsford advised him to take the couch for a while. He was too obstinately drunk to comply, and when offered the cut refused, saying thickly, "No, hic—, run— em, jest as 'ey be."

Then Stancy hurriedly dealt. When Cainsford picked

up his hand he saw that he held the Queen of hearts,
three spot cards and the ace of clubs. Naturally he
was disgusted. In order to conceal his chagrin he
gave a fierce pull at the cigar he was smoking, then
as he removed it from his mouth, he caught such a
repulsive lear on Greggson's face that it startled him,
so much so, indeed, that his hand trembled, and for
a second he touched the burning cigar to one of the
cards he held. It happened to be the ace of clubs.
He noticed at once that the cigar had left a small
burnt spot on the face of the card. He was annoyed
at the time, and did not mention it; but played his
hand, and Greggson won out with a lone, scoring
another game. He haw, hawed, as he said, "I
guess it's my turn to buy." Going over he whispered
a quick order into the tube. When the tray appeared
it held a bottle of Hennessy, a bottle of syphon soda,
four glasses, and this written message: "Time to
close up."

Greggson quickly destroyed the latter, then opened
the bottle and served each with a drink, his own and
Stancy's mostly soda. Cainsford's and Barlow's
mostly brandy, after which he said provokingly:

"Perhaps, Lawyer Cain, you could play some
other game better? This is too everlastin,' dashed
slow for me, let's have a little draw. Will you go in
Teary?"

"With all my heart," was the prompt reply. "I'm
sick of this, but our friend Cain don't seem in luck
to-night, maybe he's afraid to risk it," and he winked
his dry eye.

"Afraid, did you say? Afraid," thundered Cainsford. "No, not a little bit, trot out your cards; by

the Lord, I'll play you for all you're worth. Dollar antey, and no limit, no limit, do you hear?"

"Yes, I hear," snarled Greggson, "and I'll trot you a heat to the finish. 'Twon't take long. No, by —— it won't take long. Here count the cards and be quick."

Cainsford did so, gave them a shuffle, and the three cut for deal. By this time big Ned was lolling in his chair mumbling a ribald song. The last big drink had paralyzed him.

Cainsford won the first pot, with two pairs, kings and aces, one of which was the ace of clubs. Again he noticed the burnt mark on it. Now the game became fast and furious. The crazy light was in Cainsford's eye, the brandy burned his brain. He became more reckless, and met with loss after loss. Again the hands were shown, and Stancy won, raking in Cainsford's last dollar, while the latter fumbled nervously in his pocket.

"Haw! Haw! clever one," laughed Greggson, tauntingly, "Suppose you're cleaned out? Oh! heavens but you're easy. I told you it wouldn't take long; but this is so allfired sudden, that it makes me sick. Here, blamed if I don't lend you a tener. Don't want to see a "brave sailor" like you stuck, oh, no," and he held out a ten dollar bill.

For a moment Cainsford sat perfectly still, gazing at Greggson's sardonic face. He saw the bright gleam of the gold-crowned tooth, and his face lit up with passion, as he said in a slow deadly voice:

"Ance Greggson, beware, not too many insults. Keep your money, for by the powers of Satin, you'll need it before you leave this room. Cleaned out did you say? cleaned out? well no, not quite."

He threw open his coat, unbuttoned his vest, plucked a pin from the top of the inside pocket, then shook twenty one-hundred dollar bills in Greggson's face, who sat watching every move with shining eyes.

He had quickly passed the cards to Stancy, accompanied by a meaning sign, while Cainsford was getting out the money. The latter threw down a one-hundred dollar bill, as he said fiercely: "There's my antey."

Gregg followed with his as he hissed. "And there's mine. Now, Stancy, deal."

Stancy gave he cards a vigorous shuffle, and while Cainsford was defiantly shaking the rest of his bills made a lightening-like movement, after which his long white fingers trembled, as he offered Greggson a cut.

"To H—— with the cut, run the cards," roared Gregg. Then turning to Cainsford a flaming red face, continued. "You want to lose more, Mr. Lawyer? Well, Ance Greggson can accommodate you. Oh! yes, your "old and tried friend" will do his best to oblige you."

As the taunting words fell from his lips, Gregg's face wore such a fiendish expression of exultant joy, that it sent a shiver of disgust through Cainsford, sobering him slightly; but as he looked at his hand, there was a gleam of satisfaction in his large dark eyes, and his face settled into grim determination, for he held the four "kings." As he started to whistle softly, Greggson said:

"Ho, Ho," then asked innocently, "are you in it this time, Teary?"

"No, thanks, not this time. The game is too strong for a weak hand, better luck bye-an'-bye, hee, hee, hee."

"Just as you like. I have such a regard for Cainsfords' courage, that I may succeed in bluffing a dollar or so from him on this little hand. Now "my Buco," bet."   And Greggson shut his square jaws with a snap.

"Five hundred." Said Cainsford as he placed the amount on the table. Greggson appeared to hesitate, as if afraid, then hauled from his pocket a large roll of bills. He counted out five hundred dollars, and said gruffly, "I'll be dashed if I don't raise you two."

"I'll go the two, and raise you another five hundred," said Cainsford, striving to quell the agitation in his voice.

Greggson gave Stancy a furtive glance, then doggedly counted five hundred dollars more, while the latter sat watching the growing piles with a green greedy glint in his watery eyes.

"I may not carry as much money as an honest lawyer," said Greggson, with a fierce oath, and an insulting sneer, "but Ance Greggson's check is good and here it is, and say just for fun, and to get the agony over, by—my—grandmother's ghost, I'll raise you eight hundred."

He produced a blank cheque, extracted a fountain pen from his pocket, and with trembling hand, filled it in, payable to bearer, for eight hundred dollars.

"Now, my learned friend, please put the rest of your hard earnings on that. Haw, haw, don't flinch, be a man, I said I'd trot you a heat, and I guess I've kept my word. Why the blazes don't you put up your stuff."

During this time Cainsford had sat silent, with a cold smile on his handsome face. He thrust his fingers through his damp wavey hair, then slowly laid the remaining one hundred dollar bills on top of Greggson's, check. The overloaded pile toppled, and Greggson shoved the money towards Stancy, as he said exultingly: "Hold her down, Teary, hold her down, till we see who owns her."

Then the two sat eyeing first their cards, then each other. On Greggson's face was a sardonic smile of contemptuous triumph, made more devilish by the bright gleam of the gold crowned tooth. On Cainsford's a combination hard to describe. It was quiet, deep, confident, with a suggestion of regret. In a smooth deadly voice he said:

"You brought it on yourself, Greggson. Show down your hand. I—HOLD—FOUR—KINGS." And he placed them face up on the table.

For several seconds Greggson held his cards suspended, then he hissed, like a serpent about to strike, "By heavens, the money is mine,—mine,—mine."

There was such venom in his voice as he mouthed the words, that the air seemed poisoned, then with a cruel gloating leer, while uttering horrid blasphemies, he spread four aces and the queen of hearts, on the table.

Cainsford was transfixed, the perspiration oozed from every pore. The veins rose on his temples, his large dark eyes were riveted on the four aces. The cards seemed to fascinate and also repel. One second his startled eyes seemed ready to devour each spot, the next ready to destroy. The fiery pupils would expand and contract, and the eye-lids tremble as if menaced by something horrible. He seemed under some frightful spell as he bent lower and lower still over the four cards, two with red spots, two with black. The background of each seemed to whiten and whiten, till his eyes were dazzled. With a gasp the spell was broken, he seized the ace of clubs, and held it aloft, while his powerful frame trembled from head to foot. Then, in a cold dangerously calm voice, he enquired::

"Where is the 'burnt spot' which should be on this card?"

The flame of battle flared in his face, as now in a voice of thunder he roared:

"Where is it, I say. Oh! you cowardly cheating thieves, I've found you out, you've changed the cards, you sprung a cold deck fixed on purpose to rob me. You're not fit to live, and by all the——." Here he was interrupted by Greggson, who jumped up, trembling all over. With a cry of rage Cainsford lounged forward to seize him, but missed, for he sprang behind big Ned, who sat sprawled there sleeping noisily like a great beast. Then followed an ominous click, click, and Greggson swung round with a revolver levelled at Cainsford's head. There was a murderous light in his small fiery eyes as he hissed through his strong teeth, "one—step—further —Cain—and by the Lord that made us, your a Dead——Man."

CHAPTER XI.

Crazy Chris and His Wild Ride

From the time Greggson placed the four aces on the table, till Cainsford's fury burst forth, he and Stancy sat as if frozen, and while unable to move, were compelled by some irresistible power to watch the battle of emotions as mirrored in Cainsford's twitching face and fiery eyes. When the final frenzy came upon him, Greggson, as we said, sprang behind big Ned, quaking with fear.

What about Stancy, what did he do? He was fearfully frightened, but oh, so busy—quickly—quietly—stealthily busy. What doing? Oh, just shoving the big piles of money into his clothes. He had made a clean job of it too when Greggson's fierce threat fell on his ear, then a joyous tear trickled down his gray face; and while the two stood glaring grimly, and facing each other, he snatched up his hat, and all doubled over, sneaked to the door. It was fast. With nervous haste he got it open, but trembled so that he dropped his hat. He did not attempt to recover it, but with one stealthy look backward, fled down the long stair, and as he fled he whispered to himself, exultingly: "I hope to heaven they'll kill each other, and I think they will. Yes—I do—I think they will, and if they do—oh—oh—if they only do, Mark P. Stancy is a made man; and will play at their funeral. He, he, he." * * * * *

When Cainsford looked into the muzzle of Greggson's weapon, and heard his mad threat, he paused with every nerve and muscle aquiver. Greggson seemed more like a ferocious animal at bay, than an armed man. Although he held the revolver pointed directly at Cainsford's head, and within a few feet of it, his fear was manifest.

The hat dropped by Stancy startled him. As he turned his head slightly, Cainsford made a sudden spring. There was a flash, a sharp report, and the latter stood swaying to and fro, like a tall tree in a gale. He felt a burning sting on his temple, and blood running from it. He was so stunned for an instant that he could not see, then through the thick smoke, he caught the glimpse of a devilish malignant face glaring at him like a fiend of hell.

The smoking revolver was still clutched in the large nervous hand, while Greggson's big round-shouldered form crouched, in seeming expectancy to see its victim fall.

With the spring of a tiger, Cainsford was upon him and before he could dodge, or raise his weapon, with the whole gigantic strength of his mighty arm, landed a crushing blow between the bulging, blinking, blood-shot eyes.

As that mighty blow descended on the upturned twitching face, Greggson went down with a crash, and lay like a clod on the floor, then Cainsford's fury abated somewhat. He had a dim sense of the calamity which had overtaken him. The discovery of the vile scheme, and the shooting had partly sobered him. He realized that he had robbed an innocent girl, and gambled the money entrusted to

him by a grand old man.   The thought was maddening.
Each moment his remorse grew stronger, causing
him to view his surroundings with greater loathing.
The foul air of the hot room, reeking with stale smoke,
and heavy with brandy fumes, seemed to send forth
a dull echo of angry voices and horrible oaths.
Then he noticed the broken glass, the torn and
scattered cards, the smashed chair lying where he had
thrown it when he first jumped at Greggson.   Turning,
his eyes rested on the disgusting sight of big Ned
lolling helpless in his seat, while maudlin tears crept
over the flushed flabby face, and mingled with the
stains thickly bespattering his torn shirt front.
Half way to the door is the hat dropped by Stancy
in his cowardly flight with the money. Near it
sprawls Greggson, his close-cropped head thrown
back, his distorted bloody face still wears a sort of
frozen sneer, and between the thick lips of the half
open mouth Cainsford catches the gleam of that
gold-crowned tooth which had proved such an irritant
to him the whole night through; but oh, as he looks
the jaws close with a snap and as blood oozes from
the mouth the head is jerked to the side, catching a
stronger ray from the dimly burning light.   The face
is so horrible in its bloody ghastliness that a thrill
of abject fear surges through Cainsford.

"My God, I've killed him," he cries. "I'm a
murderer, as well as a thief."

He sprang to the table, seized the brandy, and with
nervous trembling fingers filled a glass to the brim.
As he drinks it in great gulps the swollen veins stand
out on his burning throbbing temples, and great
beads of perspiration glisten all over his broad brow,

and mingle with the blood as it flows down and drops from his chin.

Once more he looks at that hideous face and sprawling form, then rushes from the room—where in one night he had lost money, manhood, honour, and very nearly life. Why had not the bullet taken his life instead of grazing his temple. Life was no good to him now.

He fled through the halls down the stairs to the street. As his feet struck the pavement he dimly realized that it was early morning. His eyes were filled with a mad light. They rolled and glared as he rushed along. A man he met when passing, shrank away from him, and with startled wonder watched him till he disappeared around the corner. There seemed an ever increasing pressure in his aching throbbing head; then voices seemed to whisper, "Crazy Chris? Crazy Chris? you killed him! you killed him!—you're a murderer!—you're a thief; you stole the young girl's money; you're guilty—"you're guilty." Then a bloody swollen face appeared to lear at him, and laugh in derision.

Oh! Oh! only to get away from the awfulness of it all. He is seized by a resistless longing to fly. He does not know how far, or in what direction he has come, but as he stops to quickly look about him, sees that he has reached the out-skirts of the town. A second later his wild gaze rests on a horse tied by the roadside, likely the property of an early rising farmer making ready for a drive to market; but there is no one in sight and mechanically, but with hasty fingers the rope halter is untied. It is new, and heavy, and stiff. As it is loosened the horse snorts and shrinks from him, and Cainsford notes gloatingly how big and powerful he is. Quickly knotting the rope he gives him a cruel jerk and attempts to mount. There is no stirrup, no saddle, just a bare glossy back. No one but an expert horseman can mount that tall horse from the ground. The first attempt fails. In a flash the nose is seized in a vice-like grip, and is held, while the bulging flashing crazy eyes of the man glare into the terrified eyes of the trembling horse. He yields, is released, and stands still, but shivers, as the man with a mighty spring is on his back.

Then, away, and away, on a mad race; a man trying to fly from a guilty conscience, which goads him, but not more cruelly than he goads the willing horse. He hears a shout away behind, probably the horse's owner. Chris Cainsford does not know. Crazy Chris does not care. His strong arm mercilessly swings the heavy knotted rope. Each vicious blow leaves a great welt.

"ON—ON—ON," shouts the crazy rider. On, on, on, flies the maddened horse. The wind has carried away the rider's hat and as it whistles by, seems to shout into his ringing ears, and re-echo in his brandy-charged brain, "Crazy Chris?—Crazy Chris?—you're a murderer; you're a thief; you're guilty, guilty, guilty, and you're on the road to hell!"

The horse appears to hear the voices too, for as his rider leans over his neck, to try and escape the awful din, the long ears lie back, and he springs away, and away, with such terrific leaps, that every strain-ing muscle seems determined to escape from the quivering, steaming foam-flecked body.

Flash! and they are passed a covered milk waggon,

with paralyzed driver and snorting team. Flash! and the flying hoofs thunder across a bridge, and the whistling wind seems to shout and shriek louder and louder—"Crazy Chris! Crazy Chris!—you robbed an innocent girl! You killed Greggson! You're Guilty!"—and a wail floats away with the flying foam bursting from panting nostrils.

Now a shrill whistle and indistinct rumble mingles with the wailing wind as the cruel rope descends again, and again, and again, on the quivering, shrinking side of the gasping horse. He tries by a more than mighty bound to clear the track before the swift coming train. Too late! A screaming whinney of agonized pain is heard above hissing steam and ringing bell as horse and rider are hurled through the air, and in the air, close to his, Cainsford sees a horrible swollen blood-stained face, leering and gibbering and gnashing a great gold tooth.

The unheeding train roars rushing away. Then all becomes still.

The sun peeps over the green hill, and the light comes glancing gladly, till it rests upon a poor bleeding horse all broken and torn, and on a man lying beside it, with black waving hair, then it shivers, and as the strong face whitens, it touches also a nervous hand, still clutching a knotted, bloody rope. A sigh comes from the gentle breeze; and glistening dew drops are shed by the grass blades while they Nestle—and Whisper—and—Creep.

PART II.

SCALEY JOCK QUIGGLEY

CHAPTER XII.

TWELVE YEARS BEFORE.

It was on a beautiful afternoon of early summer, in the month of June in the year 18—, when the sun had got about three-quarters of the way down his western ladder, that a horse, waggon and man appeared at the summit of a long hill on the York Road.

As the driver allows his beast to stop, they are strongly outlined against the bright western sky, making a singular, but not unpleasing picture. A stranger would be at a loss to guess what the long, black, coffin-like box, mounted on four wheels, was for. It is well and strongly made. The seat is so near the front that little space is left between it and the low dash-board. At the back end hangs a strong padlock, which secures the doubly hinged lid and door combined. It evidently, when locked, closes the only opening to the long, black dust-proof box.

Between the shafts, hitched well back, is a lean, black mare. Her appearance denotes age, experience, overwork and underfeed. The latter is exemplified by the hungry snap she makes at a tuft of grass by the wayside the moment her driver gives her a chance.

The latter is a striking contrast to his beast.   True, his appearance denotes age and experience, but it is of a comfortable sort.   He looks over-fed and under-worked.   Is round, fat, and pudgy, with drooping shoulders, thick neck and bullet head.   Coarse hair sticks out all around his well worn hat, and covers the most of his face.   The small portion visible is swarthy and sun-browned.   His eyes, partly concealed by over-hanging brows, are small and bright.   If we take particular notice, we will decide that these bright eyes have a decidedly fishy look.   Why shouldn't they?   If there is a pair of eyes in Canada possessing the right to look fishy, that pair of eyes belong to Jock Quiggley, the well-known fish pedlar.

There is not a road leading in any direction from the picturesque little town of Darkton unfamiliar with the black mare, black box, and brown driver. They are generally referred to as "Hungry Bess and Scaley Jock."

Now, Jock liked company, and liked to talk.   He was familiar with the family history of nearly everybody living within fifty miles of Darkton.   If he had no more appreciative listener, he would carry on a running conversation about persons and things in general, addressed to his black mare.   He also liked to sleep, and Bess could be trusted to bring him safely through; so, many were the sound snoozes he took while on the road.   The only advantage Bess would take of her master's inertness would be to try and get a bite to eat.   She was always hungry, could scent good grass quite a distance, and did not hesitate to cross a ditch in order to secure it. At such times Jock was liable to wake in very ill humor, and give Bess hard words and harder kicks. The kicks could be administered with less effort on Jock's part than blows, for he usually sat with one square-toed, heavy boot hanging over the low dash-board.

People said it was owing to the too frequent application of said boot that the hair was so thin on Bess' boney hips and bob tail. Be that as it may, the latter had only a few tangled strands left to protect its owner from the ever-familiar flies. The weapon was altogether inadequate, for no matter how desperately she weilded it she was seldom free from their buzzing and bite. They did not overlook Jock, but he did not mind them. Could sleep more soundly when surrounded by a swarm, and snore more contentedly while they played hide and seek in his whiskers. He was wont to say: "Flies is like cats, they like fish. Dogs doesn't. They sometimes snarl at and quarrel with me. Not so cats. They'll purr at, and faller me, if I just snaps my fingers at em. Its cause they likes fish, and so do I. I'd be a mean critter if I didn't, fer I get my livin out of em."

But Bess has had her bite and rest. Jock gives her a gentle boot-reminder, and they start again down the road. They have not proceeded far when Jock's ear catches the jingle, jingle of a bicycle bell, and before he can rightly turn, whiz! and a young fellow rushes by, mounted on a tall wheel. The road is smooth and down grade, so that rider and wheel are soon out of sight. Jock urges Bess along as he murmurs: "Great catfish, its a terror how them things can go when the're rid good. That seems a

purty limber chap. He went by so suddent, I didn't
have a good look; but I think its the same feller as
I see leadin a cow into Darkton tother day; and
when Bill Bush's dorg came yowlin out at her,
blamed if he didn't sort o' sit the cow onter the
humbly cur. Great snakes, didn't she make him
howl and huff it fer home; and her after him, head
down and tail up. I believe to goodness she'd a got
him too if he hadn't slipped under the bars, jes as he
did. When she couldn't git through, she clum up
with both front feet and glared over at him fiercer
an a fiend; an thet dorg jist slunk under the porch,
scarter an a fox. Great mudpouts, it was dreadful
funny."

Here Jock gave a hoarse chuckle, and continued:

"But I never seen a tamer cow than that mouse
colored one wus. When the young feller catched
up to her, he jist gave her two or three pats, and on
they went, quiet as lambs. I was too surprised to
find out his name."

"Hello, I wonder what's up with the wheeler.
Guess he's punktoord."

During the soliloquy, Bess had been jogging along
as fast as could be expected, and as she and Jock
turned a bend in the road they came upon the bicy-
clist, despondently leading his wheel.

"Good evenin, stranger," said Jock. "Had a
punktoor?"

"I rather think its worse. My chain is broken,"
was the reply.

"Too bad, you was makin good time when ye
went by me. Goin fur?"

"Quite a distance when one is obliged to walk

and lead his wheel. I am not very familiar with roads and distances in this part. I think, however, its about twelve miles to Darkton."

"So you're headin fur Darkton, be ye? I be too, so you best jist com alonger me. I'm goin by Merryvale. I allers suppers there after bein to market at Bridgeville. Bess generally feeds there too, whin I can git it handy."

"I'll take advantage of your kind offer on condition that you allow me to pay for our suppers and the mare's feed," was the reply.

"Alright, put ye're machine up here, top of this box; but I ain't no hog, an I'll look after feedin the mare meself."

As the conditions were satisfactory to both parties, the wheel was soon placed in position, but as the young man climbed up he got a strong odour of fish, and said:

"Perhaps the load will be too much, and your mare looks tired."

"No! no, we'er travillin light. Sold out my load of nigh a hundred. Nothin but a few scales left; cept one twenty pounder. Maybe if we stop to Jordon's I can sell him."

Jock had spread out the sheepskin cushion lengthwise of the seat. His passenger crowded his long legs as best he could in the narrow space. The driver clucked, the mare sneezed, and they were off for Merryvale, truly an appropriate name, for they had a merry time. There was enough of the serious intermingled, however, to make the outcome of that drive ever memorable to both.

As we said before, Scaly Jock was a great talker.

If he happened upon an appreciative listener he was happy, and his stories were limitless. He was in the humor on this occasion. He had had a successful trip. A good supper was assured him without cost to himself. His passenger was young, and best of all, a stranger.

"He must be some punkins or he wouldn't be ridin so fine a machine. They cost more 'an a horse,' thought Jock, as he said:

"That's a purty good bicycle, ain't it?"

"Yes, the Black Giant is considered a good wheel."

"Do it brake down ofen?"

"Oh! no, this is the first serious break I've had."

"Been ridin fur?"

"No, not this trip. I went to Bridgeville yesterday."

"Didn't you say you wus a stranger to these parts?"

"Yes, almost. My father moved to Darkton very recently."

"Ain't you the same chap as I see sit the cow onter the dorg tother day?"

Jock's passenger laughed a boyish happy laugh, and said:

"I didn't think anybody saw that, and I didn't exactly set her on; but that cow has a decided dislike for dogs and resents being interferred with. At the same time she will go around a block to avoid one."

"She didn't avoid Bill Bush's much tother day. Great Sturgeon didn't she make him streak it fur home! Wish she'd a got him. Meanist blamed cur on the York Road! My Bess hates him worse an pizen. He's allers sneakin out an snarlin at rigs. What would a happened if she'd a caught him?"

"I think his snarling days would have been over. She had not got over the trip down on the boat, and her dander was up."

"She seemed awful tame after. Is she ugly?"

"Not in the least, in fact she is a great pet at home. I have taught her a few tricks. Am a great lover of animals of all kinds, and as a rule they like me.

"Don't wonder they does." was Jock's mental comment, as he gave his young passenger a keen furtive look.

He saw a strongly-built tall lad of eighteen, or twenty years of age, black curling hair, heavy dark brows, and rosy face. The poise of the curly head, between well developed shoulders, gave him an air of manly independence, dash and fearlessness, which is the natural birthright of a true young Canadian.

After his hasty scrutiny, Jock continued:

"I likes animals too, ceptin dorgs; but I favors fish most, specially Lake Ontario whites and salmons. What did you say your name wus?"

"My name is Cainsford. I do not know that I mentioned it before!"

The passenger here gave Jock a curious look of inspection, as he continued, with a smile:

"Did you ever try to guess peoples names from their personal appearance'?'

"No, don't know as I ever did. How do you do it?"

"In the first place you look them over carefully, notice their color, age, clothes, feet, hands, etc. Then think of a name you imagine would best suit their general make up, at the same time making allowance for the general ware and tare of life. Of course, it takes a lot of practice to make a success of it. I feel quite convinced, however, that I could guess yours about right."

"Well, fire ahead, taint very common. What de ye guess it is."

Young Cainsford gave Jock a laughing glance from top to toe, and said:

"To the best of my belief your name is Jock Quiggley."

"Great—Swordfish! your right as a trout; but someone told you!"

"No, no one ever told me that was your name."

(He had heard of Scaley Jock before leaving his western home, however, and thought this must be he. He was sure never to forget it after their eventful meeting, and the doughty deed performed by Scaley Jock that evening, which added new luster to his already brilliant name.

CHAPTER XIII.

Hungry Bess Draws the Line at Shoepegs

When they arrived at Merryvale it was quite dark, and Cainsford had been persuaded to accompany Jock the balance of the way to Darkton after they got supper.

As they drove up to Jordon's hotel, Jock advised his passenger to go in and give his order, while he (Jock) put up the mare.

This Cainsford did and Jock drove Bess across the street to the hotel shed, selecting the darkest corner. It seemed odd, for already the lightest part was in deep shadow. After tying her, Jock removed the bit from the mare's mouth, then stood very still listening intently. He quickly slipped over to the nearest rig to his own, felt under the seat, turned back the cushion, and seemed to search diligently for something, more by feel than sight, however. He tried another, but without success. Then crossed to a third. It was a buckboard with a closed-in seat, forming a box. Jock removed the cushion, lifted the lid, thrust in his hand, and with a grunt of satisfaction lifted out a bag securely tied about a-third of the way from the bottom. He felt its contents carefully with finger and thumb, gave another little satisfied grunt, untied it, crossed quickly, and emptied its contents into the wooden trough in front of black Bess.

The latter gave a little whinnie as her master hastily unlocked his own box, from which he took some straw, forced it into the empty bag which he retied and returned to the buckboard.

Now that he had so carefully looked after Bess, Jock was ready for his own supper.

"Hope I'll have as good a one," he murmured, as he crossed the street. "Them's all-fired good oats, jedgin by their feel and weight."

He found his young passenger watching for him. They entered the dining-room together. Cainsford ate heartily, Jock ravenously, and kept it up without pause until everything eatable disappeared. He was still busy when Cainsford excused himself, and went to the proprietor to settle the bill, offering to pay for three. They were busy discussing the matter when a tall man with red hair came in and requested the use of a lantern, in a rich Irish brogue. As he disappeared with it, Mr. Jordon was called to the kitchen. He returned shortly, and resumed the interrupted conversation with Cainsford.

"Yes," said he. "It takes a lot to fill Scaley Jock, but I'll even up when I buy some more fish from him. Speak of the deal—here he is."

Jock waddled up with a complacent grin on his flabby face. "Nice evenin, Mr. Jordon," said he. "Much doin? This is a friend of mine, just from up West, (nodding to Cainsford). He's jist moved to Darkton. Great feller with animals. He's a trained cow he sets on dorgs"——

"Oi'll dorg yer," roared a voice. "Ye Scaley black thaif o' the worrld. Oi'll tach ye, so Oi will. Oi'll break ivery bone in ye'er fishy, fat carkas, Ye skulkin, scaley—son ave a sae sarpant. Oi'll larne ye te insult me perfession be fadin ye'er long, lane, stharvin, black carrin wid me louvily new shoe pigs, which Oi paid fur wid me hard arnins."

The big Irishman had seized Jock as he started his tirade of abuse, and fairly swarmed him round and round the place, emphasizing his angry words with angrier swats, first on one side, then on the other of Jock's bullet head. The onslaught was so fierce and sudden that everybody was astonished, and Jock most of all. The first furious shake rendered him powerless to do anything but gasp, and roll his fishy eyes. The swats made his head ring, and finally appeared to replace his astonishment with rage.

His little eyes shot forth flashes of murderous hate as he clutched at his hip pocket, and gurgled:

"Let—up—will—ye—ye—big—red—headed—over —growd Irish—er-r.   I—I'll—r—r—rip ye—up— quick--er—an—I'd—skin a bull—head.   Will—ye— let—up?"

Here he succeeded in lugging forth a big bloody fish knife.

"Ye'd drauth a knife on me, wud ye?   Ye murther-in, squirmin, mongril thaif.   Take—that—will— yiz?"

With the words, the Irishman aimed a terrible blow at Jock's head with his big boney fist.   It did not land, however, but was turned aside, and tore through space.   Before the Irishman recovered his balance, he was brought up standing, so to speak, felt a vice-like grip on his throat, and looked into a pair of black eyes with a peculiar commanding power in them; then a steady voice spoke in a passion-less, business-like tone:

"You must not maul Jock Quiggley anymore."

The voice was so cool, the eyes so fierce, and the face so boyish, that the Irishman was about as much astonished as Jock had been a moment before.

It was only for a second, however.   He tore him-self free from Cainsford's grasp, as he roared:

"Houly mother ave Moses, wud ye be afther layin hans on, an dictatin to Larry O'Ryan.   Ye'd throy to order ye'er betthers wud yiz?   Ye bare-faced, crain—shanked—foiry—oid spalpaen.   Ye'd take the part of yon, scaley black thaif, wud ye?"

Here the Irishman's fury became uncontrollable. He made a furious lunge at his young antagonist,

who instead of being knocked down and out, ducked
like a flash, caught Larry with his shoulder in some
unexplainable way and sent him flying clear over
his head. He came down on the hard floor with such
force that for once the fight was knocked clear out
of him.

In the meantime Jock had been prevented from
carrying out his murderous threat by Proprietor
Jordon, who was a large powerful man and had had
many a rough and tumble in his time, having been
a foreman in the construction of the Rideau Canal.
He rather liked a fight, and always wanted fair play.
As he saw Larry hurl himself at the tall lad, he felt
sorry, but was busy disarming Jock and could not
interfere. The result of Larry's mad rush both
astonished and gratified him.

"How in the name of goodness did you do that,
youngster? As big a toss as I iver saw a man get,"
said he, as he held the struggling Jock.

"Oh, simple enough," said Cainsford. "He did it
mostly himself, I only helped him. I've played foot-
ball a little. I am very sorry he came down so hard
though. Would you kindly help me carry him out.
A little fresh air will revive him, and then perhaps
we can discover the cause of the trouble."

"I'll help you if Jock here will behave himself!"
he replied.

"I will, sure, Mr. Jordon," said the latter. "I
niver touch a maun that's down."

They lugged big Larry out forthwith. He was
slowly recovering from the terrible shock, but was still
considerably muddled. Fresh air helped bring back
his wandering senses, however, and as he looked round

in a vacant sort of way, his eyes rested on young Cainsford who was calmly standing under a lamp post, his bright dark eyes following every move made by his late antagonist. He did not know how big Larry would act when he realized that he had come out second best in the scrimmage. He seemed prepared for any emergency, however, and Larry noticed it. At first his eyes kindled in angry recognition, then gradually mellowed, and a big shame-faced sort of grin appeared on his hairy face, as he said:

"Be the powers o' Killarny, that was the clainest, an quickest hump an thumble I iver recaived in all me born days. Begorra, me ois is blinkin, me lugs is singin, and I can fale mesilf goin yit. How in the name of all the saints did ye do ut onyway. Ye decaivin young mount-a-bank. Listen to me, will ye? Oi'll make a bargain wid ye, right here, now, on this blissed sphot! Oi'll make ye as foin a pair ave Sunday boots as iver was lasted, if ye'll tach me that thrick, jist 'aisy loik' ye know. Yis, bejabers, Oi'll do that same, as thrue as me name is Larry O'Ryan; besoids, Oi'll not dirthy me fingers ony more wid ye'er frind, that scaley thaif Jock, an Oi'll, yis, Oi'll parthon the dirthy nager fur fadin his starvin ould plugg wid thim louvily shoepigs. Oi'll lave it till all the bys if that same isn't a moity ginerous affer considerin the iverlastin larrup ye jist bin afther given me?"

A chorus of voices shouted "Right, Larry, right you are."

Young Cainsford at once held out his hand, and Larry gave it a shake and squeeze, that left an impression for an hour afterwards.

"Mr. O'Ryan," said Cainsford, "I certainly owe you an apology. I'm quite willing to show you the trick, as you call it, if you will kindly explain why you attacked Mr. Quiggley, and gave him so unmerciful a mauling. I will give you an order for the boots, and pay you your regular price. I am sure they will be superior in quality, coming from the hand of such a generous large-hearted man as Larry O'Ryan has proven himself to be on this particular occasion. With regard to the shoepegs and Mr. Quiggley's connection therewith I am entirely in the dark."

"Bedad an so's the ould black mare. Yiz wont be fer long."

"Mr. Jordon, wud ye be so koind as to lind us the loan ave ye'er lanthern. Troth I sae ould Scaley ferninst ye, bring him wid ye, and kim along all ave yiz and ye'll sae a soight that'll bring tares to the oys ave ivery mother's son, and lave a grane sphot in ye'er mimeries fur iver and iver, or me name's not Larry O'Ryan."

Quite a crowd had gathered and readily followed Larry, Cainsford, and the lantern, across the street to the big shed, Jock and Jordon bringing up the rear. It was beginning to penetrate Jock's thick skull that black Bess was in some unaccountable way responsible for all his trouble. True, he thought of the big feed of oats he had given her, but he knew her capacity, and felt sure they had disappeared utterly, leaving no sign, before Larry O'Ryan had come upon the scene at all, and even if they hadn't, what had they to do with red Irish's shoepegs? It was all quickly explained. Larry rushed over to the dark corner where black Bess was tied and said:

"Wud yiz, look at that now!   Did iver anny body sit oys on the loiks av that same!"

Here the shoemaker held the lantern over the feeding trough, revealing hundreds of shoepegs, here, there, and everywhere.   Black Bess had evidently been busy with them.   They were slobbered over and scattered in every direction, as if in resentment of the mean trick her master played her the mare had tried her best to destroy them.   The curious crowd gathered round, and with craning necks and bulging eyes took in the situation, then a unanimous roar of laughter burst forth, and made the old shed ring as never before.   Even stallid Black Bess was startled and dropped her draggled tail in nameless dread and terror.

"Hurrah! for Scaley Jock and Hungry Bess," shouted the crowd.   "Shoepegs forever."

"He'll be feeding her beeswax and peggin-awls next."

"Ha, ha, put him under the pump and wash his fishy fingers."

"Yes, give the scaley critter a duck.   It's not the first time him and his mare's gobbled other people's belongings."

"Do you mind the widow's oatmeal," shouted another voice.

"Let us duck him; water is the natural element for scaley things."

Three or four sturdy fellows started for Jock, half in fun, whole in earnest, to carry out the suggestion. He was nowhere to be seen.   Jordon, when the uproar was at its height had released him.

As the mistake he had made slowly dawned upon

him, and he heard the jeering threats, Jock hurried across the shed and hid himself, and while crouching under a waggon, gasped forth:

"Great Horney Days and Dogfish. Durned if thim oats wusent the infarnal shoepegs after all. Sufferin-eels, what'll I do!"

If Jock had been at hand, he would likely have received quick and cold punishment. Young Cainsford, who had laughed as loud as the loudest, now took advantage of the pause, mounted Jock's fish waggon, and his clear boyish voice rang out, with the laugh still in it:

"Gentlemen, and Citizens of Merryvale, I think it would be unwise to do anything to spoil the flavor of this very merry joke. Its about the funniest thing I have run across during my short life, besides, it is a very practical illustration of the truth of the words, "Be sure your sin will find you out." Mr. Quiggley has certainly been found out, but, gentlemen, allow me to say there are extenuating circumstances. In the first place he had no intention whatever of feeding his poor hungry mare with Mr. O'Ryan's shoepegs. It was a sad mistake I admit, but, gentlemen, we are any of us liable to make a mistake, and shoepegs are not very often found in a bag, in a buckboard, under a dark shed. No doubt as they are about the size and form, they felt like oats. I venture to say, if they had been the real article, oats, and not shoepegs, things would have been entirely different. Why! gentlemen, if Mr. Quiggley's famous mare had had anything like a fair chance, there would not have been a grain or husk left to tell the tale."

"Yes, begorra, there wud," interrupted Larry.

"It was the dirthy, scaley, fish-smellin sthraw, the ould omadhaun put in me clain bag, wus the dead give-away intoirly. Faith I could schmell that same the minnut I opened me sate to put in me buther. Troth, it was that sthrong its a wonther it hadn't a blowed me buckboord ta smithers, bad luck ta ut. Bedad, siz Oi te mesilf, some poor things crawled inte me vaical and doid. Thin I pulled out me bag ave shoepigs, but divile the wan could Oi foind. Thrue for yiz, it was narly fainten Oi wus, me surproize wus that great. It and the schmell. Begorra, ses Oi, Larry O'Ryan, its robbed ye are intoirly, as thrue as a pig the craythur has a curly tail, thin I sane somethin shoinin in the sthraw Oid took from the bag. It was a shmall bit of the outsoid ave a fish. That same, and the schmell, called to moind Scaley Jock. I took the lanthern, and wid it found this black craythur gnawin at, an droothlin over, me foine shoe-pigs, wid her ould wolf taath. Bad cess to the loiks ave her. Thin I went to foind that scaley thaif of the worruld, that's at prisent hoiden beyant there under the waggon. Yiz all knows how Oi succeaded, and if it hadent a bin fur this young garsoon here, comin bechuxt us there'd bin nothin lift ave the ould fish-monger besoids hair an scales, and there yiz are. Now, young spachmaker, go on wid ye'er argemints, its a holy terror yiz are intoirly. Arrah, but its a lawyer ye'll be bein, ahl out, go an wid ye, its glad we'll be to sthand furninst listenin till ye. Ishint that thrue, byes?"

"Right, ye are, Larry. Three cheers for him and Scaley Jock shoepegs. Hip! Hip! Hurrah!" and the old shed rang again. Then Cainsford's clear voice rang out.

"Thanks, gentlemen, on behalf of Mr. Quiggley and myself."

"Mr. Shoepegs you mean," said a voice.

"Alright, Shoepegs it is," laughed Cainsford. "By the way! I would like to reimburse Mr. O'Ryan for the loss he sustained by Mr. Quig— Shoepeg's blunder, and I am sure that gentleman under the circumstances will willingly make Mr. O'Ryan a little present, as a peace offering."

"Fur sure I will," came Jock's voice from the darkness. "I'll present him with the splendidest salmon trout that ever opened a gill, or wagged a tail; and say, lads! if ye'll promise not to duck me and say nothin, I'll pay the drinks fur the crowd, if it takes the price of me load."

"Hear, hear," laughed Cainsford.

"Hurrah, Hurrah!" shouted the crowd. "Where's the salmon?"

Jock waddled out of the gloom. His little eyes blinking at the light, while with trembling fingers he unlocked his fish box and drew forth a huge, beautiful salmon. Its long, smooth, glossy body shone like silver, while ice crystals as bright as diamonds dropped from it in a sparkling shower, as he handed it to the astonished Larry.

"There's the big beauty. He weighs twenty pounds an was playin' with his mate, in nigh a hundred feet of water, this time two nights ago, an he's been on ice iver since. Could ha sold him time an agin to-day, but hated to part him, fur I likes fish. Yes, I does, I likes fish."

Here Jock blubbered.

"But he's *yourn*, Larry O'Ryan, he's yourn.

Every inch of his silver body. By goldfish, there
never was a beautifuler wan brung to Merryvale.
No, never. Be good to him, Larry, and clean him
decent."

"Now, boys, come on, and I'll buy the treats, as
I said I'd do."

Again Cainsford mounted the box and proposed
three cheers for generous Jock. You may be sure
they were given with a will. As the echoes were
dying a voice shouted:

"A tiger for Shoepegs," and that is how Jock
Quiggley secured an addition to his name, and is
known to this day as Generous Scaley Jock Shoepegs.

The merriest place in Merryvale that night was
Jordon's. Everybody was merry, even Black Bess,
for Larry O'Ryan would allow no one but himself to
give her an overflowing peck measure of genuine oats,
saying as he did so:

"Ye poor ould broken-hearted bobtailed craythur,
its sorry Oi am fur ye thish noight. There, yiz are,
ate ye'er fill, be the swate-grain failds ave ould
Oirland, if it wusent fur ye, Larry O'Ryan wudent be
ownin the louveliest, swatest, pace offerin, that iver
waggled a tail."

CHAPTER XIV.

An Angry Ghost Demands its Teeth

It was late when Jock and his passenger started
They had ten miles to drive, but the road was good
and Bess jogged along willingly, well fed for once.
Jock's tongue wagged from the start. He had taken
a great liking to Cainsford. No wonder, for hadn't
he saved him from big Larry, and got him out of a
disgraceful mess. Jock appreciated the kindness,
and awkwardly thanked his benefactor, vowing,
again and again, to be his true friend for evermore,
and also promised to help him out if he ever got in
a scrape. Jock meant what he said, and eventually
kept his word.

He seemed anxious to justify himself, however, and
tried to do so, by telling of others who had to his
mind been guilty of far worse than feeding a hungry
mare shoepegs. He abruptly asked Cainsford if
he minded the man that shouted about the widow's
oatmeal. Receiving an answer in the affirmative,
Jock continued:

"That feller's the meanest, stingiest critter in
ten counties. His name is Eaph Cram. I'll tell
you what he done this spring, and you can jedge
for yourself. He come into Merryvale one mornin'
and went to Janson's store, where they sells everything amost,—groceries, drygoods, and liquors too.
After goin' in Eaph hung round for awhile, till he

sees boss Janson wa'nt busy, then went to him and said: "Day, Mr. Janson, do you keep darnin' needles?"

"Yes," says he.

"Well, my wife hadn't no change this mornin', so I brung in this here hen agg thinkin' I could buy a darn needle with it.   Could I?"

"Certainly," says Mr. Janson, and he gave him one.

"Eaph didn't go when he got it; jist hung round an' waited fur a good chance and then says to Mr. Janson, coaxin' like:"

"Don't ye ever treat your customers, Mr. Janson."

"Oh! yes, certainly, come down cellar," says he. Then they went.

"What will ye have, Mr. Cram?"

"Oh, amost anything, drop a good whiskey," says Eaph.

"Wouldn't you like an eggnog, Mr. Cram?"

"Don't mind if I do," says Eaph.

Mr. Janson got the same egg he'd got from Eaph for the darnin' needle, and broke it into about half a glass of whiskey.   It happened to be double yoked. Eaph drinked it all without a murmur, then they returned up.

Again Eaph didn't go, jist loafed round for an hour or so, enjoyin' the feelin' of the big drink he'd got.   When he see Mr. Janson goin' to dinner, he stopped him at the door and said pleadin' like:

"Sa— Say! Mr. Janson, don't ye think ye had otter give me nother darn needle, ye know there was two YELKS in that are hen agg."

Jock chuckled.

"As sure as suckers, that's true as my name's Quiggley.   Say! shoepegs aint a patch to that, be they?"

"Haw, Haw, Haw," roared Cainsford, then Jock continued:

"I think it seems meaner fur a rich man to be mean than a poor one. Don't you? I knowed one oncet. If ever a mean man left a mean memory after him, 'twas him. His name was Humphrey Hanner. They used to call him old Humph. He was awful rich, and made most of it foreclosin' and seizing things from folks what owed him and was short. One time he seized a hearse from an undertaker with a large family. When Humph tried to auction it, nobody'ed bid on the mournful black thing, so he stored it away, with a lot of other things he'd took.

"The poor undertaker had to leave town. He'd sort of lost his grip, not havin' right tools to work with, owin' to Humph seizin' on 'em; and that old hearse stood in the storehouse for years an' years, till the paint all peeled off, and the tires come loose. When Humphrey Hanner died, his son, John James, (he only had one), thought of usin' the old hearse for to bury his father in, but when it was brung out, it was too fur gone, so John James had to hire another. It went agin the grain, fur if anything he was saviner than the old man. I'll tell ye'r what he done, and ye can jedge fur yourself.

"Humphrey Hanner wore false teeth, and before he took sick had a new pair made. He didn't ware 'em mor'n a fortnight when he got so bad he didn't need 'em, and when he died, they was forgot an' wasn't put in. After the funeral, the dentist that

made the teeth, sent a bill to John James fur his pay.
John James had mor'n a hundred and seventy-five
thousand dollars, but he hated to part a cent.   When
he got the dentist's bill, he tried to sell the teeth to
a old woman as went round scrubbin'.   When she
tried 'em in, they didn't jist fit, was too wide in the
jawrs or somethin', then feelin' terrible disappointed,
John James took 'em to the man what made 'em, an'
wanted him to take 'em back, said they wus'nt wore
none to speak of, an' if he would take 'em back, he'd
have one of his'n filled, and pay him fur it.   The
dentist wouldn't."

"But the worst come later, and I was near scart
to death.   About three weeks after Mr. Hanner'd
been buried, me an' Bess was comin' home one night,
had bin away up to Knox and was all sold out. We hed
worked hard and was tired and hungry.   Somehow
I'd bin thinkin' of the Hanners' all the road down.
Afore we passed the Wentworth burying ground, I
felt terrible sleepy.   It had got darker than channel
cats, and drizzled rain.   All of a suddent Bess seemed
to stop and snort.   I couldn't see nothing, but was
terrible surprised, for it takes more than a "little"
to make Bess act up.   I clucked to her, but she didn't
budge, only trembled, fur I heerd the buckles shake.
I gave her a little kick, but she only gave a little
snort, and shook her tail.   By this I was gittin' a
little scared myself, and then, blueherrins! my heart
stopped, for a coarse solemn voice spoke and said,
seemin' close by, and yit fur away:

"Are—you—Jock—Quiggley—the—fish—pedler?"

"I am, ye're honor," says I, soft like, "but I
haven't a fish left, ye're worship, nare a wan, not even
a scale."

"I—don't—need—fish,—neither—do—I—require —scales,—but—I—must—have—teeth."

Then the awful voice, soundin' solemner 'an ever, spoke agin, an' said:

"I—bein'—the—spirit—of—the—late—Humphrey Hanner,—do—hereby—charge—and — command— ye—Jock—Quiggley—to—go—to—my — ungrateful —son,—John James,—and—tell—him—I — want — my—newest—teeth—placed—on—my—grave. Fur —woe! woe!—I'm—where—there—is—weepin',—an walin', and gnashin' of teeth—and I—have—to— gum—it. Woe!—woe!—woe!"

"He, he, he," chuckled Jock. "Haw, haw, haw," roared Cainsford.

Then Jock kicked Bess, and murmured:

"Say, shoepegs aint nothin' to false teeth, be they? and every word I've said about the Hanners is as true as trout, 'cept the grave part, and old Humph's ghost. They was brung about by me goin' to sleep and dreamin', just before Bess an' me got opposite to Wentworth buryin' ground, where old Mr. Hanner had been put. When I woke up, Bess was goin' for grass agin the grave yard fence, and Smokin' Sisco, warn't I sceered, the dream had part made me. I looked round best I could. It was darker than soot, an' my hair stood, when I see a dim pale shape, and heard a sort ave groan, all to wonst Bess hauled me an' the waggon right over to it. Guess she thought I was asleep yit, fur I hadn't moved hand nor foot, only me hat had riz. What de ye suppose it wus? Why nothing but a blamed yeller cow, munchin' her cud, and steamin' like smoke. The noise she made with her cud when I was sleepin' must ave minded

me of Humph Hanner and his false teeth, but squirmin'
mudpouts, I was awful scart, and I believe "yit,"
there was some TRUTH in what the coarse solemn
voice seemed to say that night in the dark, while
the—yeller—cow—munched.

CHAPTER XV.

A Scrimmage in the Snow.

After thirty-five years of earnest, conscientious
service, Rev. Jeremiah Cainsford decided to super-
annuate from the ministry. He determined to cease
cative work before there was a chance of his being
called an old fogie, and after giving the matter
much earnest thought he concluded that Darkton
was the most suitable place in which to take up
his abode. We will mention some of the most important reasons which led to this decision.

"The town was close to Lake Ontario. There were
a number of old and tried friends residing at Darkton, who urged him to come. There were good
schools. He had the opportunity of purchasing a
nice comfortable home, at a reasonable price. The
other members of his family were exactly suited with
both place and property, and urged him to make
the purchase. So it was decided upon, and he
and his family moved there in the early part of the
month of June, 18—.

Chris was delighted. Why do you suppose? Why? Because he thought he would be able to do the things he best liked to do, while living at Darkton, namely: fish, swim, skate, go out boating, keep a horse, a cow, hens, pigeons, and as many more pets as his father would allow on the place. If ever a lad liked pets Chris Cainsford was the chap.

The pets brought with them to Darkton were a horse, a cow, and some black Spanish fowls. The cow has already figured in this simple narrative in connection with the Bush dog episode. The reader may perhaps desire a better acquaintance, if so, here are a few facts:

She was purchased, when a heifer, from a young lady who had made a great pet of her, and gave her the name of Mousie. because of her peculiar color. Chris and Mousie liked each other from the start, and soon became great friends. They had a decided misunderstanding, however, about three months after Mousie became a member of the Cainsford family.

One winter's day, Chris thought it was about time to teach Mousie to lead. Of course she would follow him almost anywhere, but she was not halter-broke. Chris, therefore, bought a long piece of strong rope, arranged a slip noose in one end, and while saying kind words to Mousie, quietly slipped it over her horns, then he gave the rope a gentle pull and requested Mousie to come along. She did not comply, however, but shook her head and backed the other way, at the same time showing signs of great displeasure. Chris was a determined boy, Mousie a determined heifer, naturally a battle ensued. During the struggle and general mixup, they somehow got out of the yard, into an adjoining orchard where the snow was deep. Chris lost his footing, Mousie found hers, and away she went, head down and tail up, making a sort of snowplough of the lad at the end of the rope. Chris would not let go, no, never. He grit his teeth, and was dragged along. Of course, such strained relations could not last. Suddenly Mousie turned to avoid an apple tree, then wheeled abruptly, thus placing the tree between herself and her master, for now, master of ceremonies, Chris certainly was. He stayed on his side of the tree, and hung on like grim death. The tree proved an effective snubbing post, for Mousie turned a complete somersault, and came down with a great thud in the deep snow. She stayed there, too, for sometime after Chris regained his footing and recovered his breath. The lad had a red face when he clambered up, but it slowly changed to almost a snow color when he got a good look at Mousie lying there gasping, her eyes rolled back and tongue lolling out, and he was exceedingly glad when she straightened her eyes and winked. He was afraid her neck was broken. It was near it, yes, very near it.

When Mousie recovered the first thing she did was to get on her knees, and a more docile heifer never lived, for she was completely cowed. Did Chris tell his father? Oh, no, he decided to let it remain a secret between Mousie and himself. He thought he could trust the latter not to squeal.

A day or two later, Rev. Cainsford was surprised to see his son leading Mousie about the place with just a light cord.

From the time Mousie recovered from her summersault she regarded Chris as her lord and master. She would allow him to sit between her horns, would put up her foot to shake hands, and he could lead her with a piece of twine. She really appeared fond of him, and certainly liked his company. Sometimes Chris felt humiliated by a too public manifestation of her devotion. This was particularly the case after coming to Darkton.

Mr. Cainsford was unable to secure pasture for Mousie when they first arrived, and she was turned out on the road. She would not go any distance away however, and if Chris was sent down town on an errand, and this occurred frequently, she would follow him in spite of threats, or even punishment. Affection appeared to overcome fear. If he entered a store he would seldom have completed his purchase before he heard Mousie's familiar voice resounding. The bawls would continue till Chris rushed from the store to find Mousie with her head over the sidewalk, her ears elevated and her large luminous eyes earnestly watching the shop door. When he appeared she would moo-hoo a glad recognition, and start after him down the street, while the gathered crowd would roar with laughter, then shouts of badinage would follow them, such as, "Say, chappie, change your hat." (The one he wore was straw). Or, "Mr. don't you think your cow has too much rope?" or "The poor girl is jist dying fer love of ye." Chris received the banter very good-naturedly, but his face would become very red, and his eyes very bright, and in all probability, before they reached home the over-affectionate Mousie would discover that in some mysterious way, entirely unknown to herself, she had offended her young lord and master, and would become melancholy.

The black horse Sambo bore an enviable reputation. He also was purchased when quite young and brought up in the ministry, so to speak. We have not time to dwell upon his good points, or mention his bad ones. However, we are bound to make this statement. He always performed his duties as carriage horse faithfully and well, and it was said by those who were well acquainted with him, that black Sambo, the preacher's horse, knew more than some families.

CHAPTER XVI.

Dummy Wins the Sailing Race

Lake View Cottage, the name given the new home by Florence Cainsford, an only daughter, possessed two acres of land, roomy out-buildings, a thrifty orchard, lots of small fruit, a good garden, etc.

As we have said, the family came to Darkton in the early part of June, and as Chris would not start school till after summer holidays, he had considerable time for work around the place, and there was plenty to keep him busy. He was not averse to hard work, and believed that if a thing was worth doing, it was worth doing well, and always set about it with a will. During his busiest hours, however, he never forgot the promise Jock Quiggley gave him the night they drove home together from Merryvale.

Among the many stories told by Jock on that
occasion were some referring to the Darkton fishermen, and their work of capturing salmon, siscoe
and white fish from the depths of Lake Ontario.
The stories told by Jock were both amusing and
interesting, and when he promised to secure a passage
for Chris aboard some fast sailing craft, of course
the latter was delighted.

Lake View was a very appropriate name for the
Cainsford cottage. From his room window, Chris
had a grand view of the bay and lake. Nearly every
morning, if he was up early, he could see the fishing
fleet rounding the big lighthouse on their way out to
haul gill nets. Then again in the evening they could
be seen returning after the day's work was done.
They made a delightful picture while gliding along
so merrily over the blue waters; their white sails
gleaming in the gorgeous light of a summer's sunset.
Oh! how Chris longed to be on board. How he wished
he understood the sailing of such a craft. "I'll
learn and have a boat of my own," he said to himself
one evening after watching such a scene for an hour.
He forthwith went over to Jock Quiggley's who lived
but a short distance away. Jock received him very
graciously, telling him that he came in the very nick
of time, for he was going to the harbor next evening
to get his big load for Bridgeville.

The next evening came, and with it came Jock,
and away they went together, mounted on the
familiar fish wagon, Black Bess looking about as
hungry as ever. They arrived at the docks in time
to see the last of the fishing fleet just rounding Big
Light. Jock pointed out the second boat in sight
taking a stretch up the bay, and said:

"Do you see yon craft with a long streamer at her mast head."

"Yes, Mr. Quiggley," was Cainsford's reply. "You mean the one nearest this shore."

"Yes, that's her. The Widewave's her name. But look ahere, my young fren, I allers likes my chums to use my front name, namily, Jock. Jist plain Jock, pure and simple. I reckon you and me knows each other good enough not to want to stand on no ceremony, don't we? So fur my part I'd feel more to home if ye call me jist Jock, and me call ye jist Chris, see? Of course, I'd only stan it from my equals, though! I draw the line at wharf rats, and you'd better too, for you'll find 'em purty thick round here whin them there boats gits in."

"I am quite willing to accept and comply with your suggestion, Mr.—— Jock" said Chris. "But I do not understand about the wharf rats."

"Why, them's the barefoots, which hangs round to git a job unloading schooners and sich, or to take home a odd fish or so, when the fleet lands their load, havin' hed a good haul. There mostly a purty tough lot, but if ye do as I do, and stand on ye'er dignity some, they'll not bother none to speak of, and if they does jist give one of em a toss same as ye interdoosed big Larry to, and I calculate they'll not give no more trouble. No, siree, haw, haw, haw, it makes me laugh yit. Poutin catfish but didn't he come down kerplunk. Ho, ho, ho, ho," Then Jock pointed as he said:

"Look across to the other dock there. Them's a couple of wharf rats now, loadin' coal into the waggon with the sorel horse hitched to it, but look!

look! see how the 'Widewave's' layin' over. I believe to goodness gracious she's a goin' to git to
windward of the 'Pathfinder,' and if she do, she'll
beat her in, as sure as Bess has a bob tail. Can't
she more'n climb when she has a stiff breeze like
this here, and lots o' balast. I'll bet the old man
and Dummy's had a everlastin big haul, or they'd
not sock it to her so. Why! ivery blessed inch of
canvas she owns is on her, and pullin' like sin.
Oh! mighty, don't she handle purty? I don't believe ther's a better sailor in the whul crowd than
Dummy. Him and his dad has the best luck too,
that's why I buys their ketch, and it do keep me and
Bess a hustlin' to peddle 'em all, I tell yer."

As Jock's tongue had been running on, Chris and
he had been watching the swiftly approaching boats.
The wind was blowing fresh from the south-west.
The 'Pathfinder' which they saw first rounding the
Big Light, (situated about six miles away,) had kept
on the one tack, evidently intending to make the dock
without coming stays. In order to accomplish this
she was obliged to run very close to the wind. The
"Widewave," as Jock called her, was several minutes
after the "Pathfinder" in rounding Big Light. Now,
she was flying along at a great rate, and length by
length overhauling the foremost boat. She was to
leeward of the latter, however. It was quite evident
that the man at the helm was determined to take advantage of the freshening breeze. All at once, like
a thing of life, his boat came into the wind. Her
white sails fluttered, then away she ploughed on a
short stretch across the bay. Again she came
about, without losing way, and now with every

stitch of canvas pulling, having got to windward of the "Pathfinder," she foamed along like a race horse, the white spray flying from her bows as she lay over to the strong breeze, now almost abeam. She was certainly gaining, gaining, gaining, and Jock commenced to chuckle and clap his big brown hands. Cainsford stood almost breathless, trembling with excitement. It was such a gloriously fascinating sight. Ah! his heart almost stopped beating, and unconsciously he gave a shout of warning; a collision seemed inevitable, but just as the "Widewave" seemed about to plunge her bow into the Pathfinder, she luffed a trifle, just sufficient to miss her, then fell away, crossing so near the other's stern that she almost struck the projecting boom. Then amid cheers from the assembled rats and others, with a final swoop, she came into the wind, and her very sails seemed to roll forth notes of triumphant victory. Then she glided alongside the dock, and the water poured from her deck like a deluge of perspiration, as though produced by violent exertion. Now the pully blocks rattled, and swish, swish, swish, like magic she shed her white sails. As they were furled, Chris caught a glimpse of trays and trays, filled to overflowing with great gleaming, glistening salmon.

A loud cheer went up for Dummy Deacon and his dad, and a hip, hip, hurrah for the Widewave resounded from dock to dock, and shore to shore.

CHAPTER XVII.

Chris Cainsford had had earnest longings for a
chance to go out in one of the fishing boats. Imagine
what his feelings were when he saw them racing at
close range. He begged Jock to introduce him to the
Deacons, father and son, entreating him at the same
time to bespeak his chance to go out at an early date.

When the fish were removed from the Widewave
to the weigh house, and the crowd had dispersed,
Jock went about doing as requested with a great
show of importance. He first introduced Chris to
old Mr. Deacon.

"This young feller," said he, pointing to Chris, "is
an allfired particular fren of mine, with lots of grit.
He's got a trained cow, and wants to learn to sail
worse than to be an angel. I'll guarantee if ye take
him out he won't be no Jonah. No, sir. Like 'nough,
he'll teach Rhuban to *talk* fur he's great at trainin'
animals."

As Jock said this with a grin, the said Reuben rolled
up with his hands in his pockets. Jock seized his
arm, pulled his hand from the pocket, grabbed

Cainsford's, and placed one within the other, while with fearful contortions of his hairy face, he mumbled guttural sounds, then jesticulating wildly, he roared at the top of his voice: "James Reuben Deacon, your a shakin' hands with Christopher Calumbas Cainsford. Do ye hear?" Then Jock gasped for breath and Chris roared forth his rich Haw! haw! and the Dummy chattered with his jaws and laughed with his eyes.

He appeared to understand the situation exactly, and gave Chris' hand a grip that made him wince. The hand that steered the Widewave to victory in the recent race, was as hard as leather and strong as steel. It seemed as flexible as it was strong, for the moment he dropped the hand of Chris, he made some rapid signs, then as Chris seemed to understand and asked his name, using the single hand deaf and dumb alphabet, his round red face shone with pleasure, as his nimble fingers slowly spelled the answer. R....E....U....B....E....N D....E....A....C....O....N. Chris nodded and continued spelling. "You did well to beat the other boat."

The Dummy, (we will adopt the name used by every one), 'laughed his own peculiar laugh, while he complacently wagged his head.

When Jock Quiggley saw Chris talking the deaf mute languge, as though it was second nature to him, he was knocked cold, as the saying is. He stood in open-mouthed astonishment, and then fairly yelled:

"What did I tell yer, Joe Deacon? Aint he an
l round corn cracker? But poutin' suckers, how does
e know dummy lingo? I tell yer Joe, you'd better make up to him, all ye know, for if ye take him a sailin'

with ye, he'll bring ye more good luck than the old Widewave kin carry, and if he don't larn all about the hull business in three trips, my name's not Jock Quiggley."

Dummy Deacon was as much surprised as Jock to discover that this tall, fine-looking chap, was so well up in the deaf mute alphabet. He was more pleased than surprised, however, and from that time became Chris Cainsford's admirer and friend.

The fact that Chris could talk dummy lingo, as Jock called it, is easily explained. It chanced that a deaf mute who was travelling about soliciting subscriptions for the asylum at Bridgeville, stopped with the Cainsford family when residing up west. Chris and the old gentleman became great friends. The latter gave him some lessons, and left a book of instructions, which furnished a pictured alphabet of the different positions of the hand and fingers for the various letters, also signs, etc., in use for deaf mute scholars. Chris soon learned, and he and his sister Flo practised till they became quite proficient. You may be sure he was delighted to be able to make practical use of his knowledge in his association with Dummy Deacon.

Another thing which had a tendency to cement their quickly formed friendship was the fact that Reuben Deacon had spent two or three terms at the Deaf Mute Institute, for which Chris' former friend was travelling. The Dummy, an apt pupil, was taught the carpenter trade and became a good workman. One thing which he possessed in a very marked degree was the power of mimicry. When in the humor he could entertain by the hour, giving imitations of the character and style of different persons living in the town—from the preacher in the pulpit to the professional well digger. His impersonations were so perfect that he might have been envied by a Garrick. He gave Chris an example of his ability shortly after they met. It chanced that some reference was made to Jock Quiggley. Dummy at once performed a laughable imitation of that gentleman selling a large fish, not forgetting to give the imaginary steelyard a sudden jerk, then tipping it well back to secure every ounce of weight the fish possessed and a little more too, maybe. This was an accomplishment of Jock's which he practised every day. The impersonation was so ludicrously perfect that Chris roared with laughter, and as Jock himself, waddled up to inquire what tickled him so, and the former caught the merry twinkle in Dummy's eye, went off again, and peal after peal of laughter reechoed from dock to dock, causing more than Jock to wonder. When Chris recovered he informed Jock, if he would excuse him, he would prefer to walk home with Dummy.

It appeared like love at first sight with these two, and their liking increased when they came to know each other better. As they walk along side by side earnestly watching each other's flying fingers, we will briefly describe Reuben Deacon.

He was broad, round and squatty, with short legs and long body. His arms were short also, and looked muscular, even under his blue smock. He wore brown duck overalls, stuck into long legged boots. A round felt hat shoved well back on his head, made his jolly red face the more prominent. He had laughing grey eyes, light brown hair, a big dimpled chin, and wide mouth. The whole face indicated merry good humor; but he could become angry, yes, dangerously angry, as those who had tried to run on him or take advantage of his infirmity had found to their cost. Cainsford had an opportunity to discover something of this before they reached Dummy's home.

They came up to a load of coal stuck fast on the road. One hind wheel of the waggon had cut through a soft spot and was imbedded half way to the hub. Cainsford recognized the horse and waggon as the same he had seen at the dock, being loaded by wharf rats, as Jock called them.

The driver was a big, burly, round-shouldered young fellow of about Chris' age. He was busily engaged in thrashing his poor horse without mercy, weilding a great, heavy, black snake whip, and accompanying each cruel slash by a fierce oath. The horse made little spasmodic leaps, first to one side, then to the other, trying to escape the heavy lash, but was held prisoner by the strong harness, and unable to budge the heavy load.

Cainsford took in the situation at a glance, and was about to interfere, but was prevented by Dummy, who rushed up and seized the wrist of the arm about to fall with another vicious blow. The burly driver was so intent upon his cowardly work that he had not seen the approach of the Dummy and Chris, and was much surprised when he found that iron grip about his wrist. When the Dummy released him, he made a slash at the latter, but was too close for an effective blow. As the long lash wound around his legs, Dummy seized the whip handle and wrenched it from the other's grasp, at the same time giving him such a buffet that he was sent sprawling on the road. He clambered up, swearing like a mad man, but as he looked into Dummy's fearless eyes and noticed the resolute bearing of the latter's companion, he turned his tirade of abuse on the still trembling horse. Chris spoke kindly to him and offered to help him out. He replied roughly that he didn't want no help from that dashed Dummy. The former paid no attention to the angry words, but motioned to Reuben to bring a rail from the fence with which to pry up the sunken wheel. Dummy did so, while Chris petted the horse, looked into his frightened eye, and spoke soothing words while loosening the sweaty collar. The horse appeared to know he had found a friend, for as he was taken by the bridle and asked to come, he obeyed with alacrity, straining with all his power. The Dummy gave a great heave with the rail, and in a trice the wheel was out, and the load on solid ground.

As Chris gave the horse a final pat and stroked his nose, the poor brute acknowledged his gratitude by a soft whinny. Not so the surly driver. He seemed anything but pleased. He wore a hang-dog look, and when Chris handed him his whip, requesting him to use it with less vigour in the future, his lips parted sneeringly, as he said:

"I'll whail that d—— horse when I d—— please."

Chris scarcely noticed the nasty words, for the parted lips had revealed the most perfect set of beautiful white even teeth he thought he had ever seen.

The sorrel horse went off willingly, and turned to the right on the road to Darkton. As Dummy and

Chris stood watching, the former shook his head and spelled, making each letter with an emphatic snap of the fingers: "A....N....C....E.   G....R....E....G....G-....S....O....N."   Then followed the sign for bad, and a repeated motion of the front finger drawn rapidly across the lips, meaning "liar," "liar," "liar."

Chris Cainsford never forgot his first meeting with Ance Greggson, nor the very decided warning Dummy Deacon conveyed to him by his emphatic signs, with regard to his character.   It would have been better if he had "taken heed thereto."

CHAPTER XVIII.

A Schooner's Cargo, Cruise and a Fight.

It did not take Chris and Dummy long to arrange for their first trip to haul gill nets, but as this interesting and sometimes dangerous occupation has little to do with the leading events of our simple narrative, we will merely state briefly that Chris was on hand bright and early on the day in question, and his experiences were even more enjoyable than he anticipated.   On the way home he was allowed to steer the Widewave, bringing a climax to his pleasure. He took to sailing as a duck takes to water, and this was only the first of many days spent with Dummy Deacon and his father on board the Widewave.

Before the summer holidays were over, under the practical instruction he received from Dummy, Chris became quite an expert sailor, and bought a small sail boat of his own.   It required all his ready cash, a contribution from his father, and his revolver, to make the purchase, but he succeeded, and was about the happiest youth in Darkton. He named his little boat the Baywitch. She was well-named. Could skim along at a great rate, and did wonderful sailing for her size. The Dummy always maintained, however, that she was too small and light for safety.

About this time the leading church of the town decided to give its Sunday School a picnic. After much discussion, the officers and teachers accepted on behalf of the scholars the kind offer made by Captain George, who was a jolly old sailor, very popular with both old and young.

His offer was unprecedented. He proposed to take the whole school for a trip on board his schooner, the "Mary Taylor," away out to Nicholson's Island and back.

This island, of about two hundred acres, is situated about twenty miles due south of Darkton Harbor. On a very clear day it can be dimly seen from the shore, and our young friend Chris Cainsford had studied it frequently through a telescope from Lakeview Cottage. Of course, like every other member of the school, he was delighted at the prospect of going there as a passenger on board the famous "Mary Taylor."

After accepting the Captain's kind offer, the next very important matter was to choose a day that would furnish favorable weather conditions. Finally, all

agreed that it would be wise to have the worthy
Captain make the choice, as he was, perhaps, as good
a judge of weather probs as ever sailed the Lake.   It
did not take him long to decide.   He stipulated two
conditions, namely—to get up early and bring lots
to eat.

When the morning arrived, clear and bright, and a
gentle balmy breeze sprung up with the sun, there
were scores of glad hearts in Darkton, and Captain
George was pronounced the prince of weather prophets.
Scholars numbering about two hundred were conveyed with their baskets to the harbor in large bus
loads. Oh, what a jolly time it was! Then the
excitement of clambering on board the big schooner,
followed by the hoisting of sail, and the hoarse,
energetic "Heave Ho," "Heave Ho," of the crew, as
the Mary Taylor gilded gracefully away under the
fast increasing pressure of numberless yards of canvas
which was spread to catch the breeze.

It seemed no time till they were well across the bay.
The whole delightful scene was inspiring, and the
majestic gliding motion of the vessel possessed a
weird indescribable fascination only experienced by
those who have had the privilege of a voyage aboard
a large schooner on a beautiful day and a stiff breeze
blowing. The sturdy Captain gave the finishing
touch to the brilliant picture as he stood there
grasping the wheel with sinewy hands. He looked
exactly what he was, an ideal sailor man. His jolly
weather-beaten face was all aglow with joy and gladness. His iron grey hair and beard seemed to fairly
bristle with good nature. Now he uttered a quick
command, the wheel spun round, and as if in willing

obedience to his voice, the Mary Taylor, with awe inspiring dignity, swept slowly into the wind.   Do you wonder that the happy scholars cheered and clapped?   Do you wonder that a proud light shone in the good Captain's twinkling eyes.   For a moment the vessel's great white wings fluttered and shook in seeming indecision as the heavy booms swung slowly over, then as each white sail filled, she seemed to make a slight bow of willing compliance, and with gradually increasing speed made direct for the open water of the lake.   As she passed beyond Big Light, the breeze seemed to gladden, it hummed merrily through the rigging, singing a sort of welcome which appeared to put the Mary on her dignity, and the caressing waves were flung from her bows as if in disdain of their pronounced familiarity.

Captain George was certainly proud of his vessel, and had reason to be.   She had weathered many a fierce gale and brought him safe to port, when others of her kind became but dismal wrecks on sunken rocks or lee shore; but he never had been so proud of his Mary, or her cargo, as he was that beautiful day. And why should he not be?   Very few schooners have been so honored.   Her load represented the youthful, joyous, innocent beauty of a whole town, and they were not slow in sounding the Mary's praises.   Why they praised everything about her, from her topsails to her centre board, from her forechains to her rudder. Even her yawl boat received attention.   Their plaudits of praise continued till schooner and scholars neared the foot of Nicholson's green fringed isle.

As they approached, Chris Cainsford's rich baritone voice was raised in the grand old hymn, "Sweet Bye-

and-Bye!" then two hundred voices took up the refrain, and a great burst of melody rolled away, and away, over the dancing blue waves, and was re-echoed with wondrous sweetness from old Nicholson's rocky wave-washed shore. Then the great feast was spread under the beautiful green trees, and a more hungry, happy lot twould be hard to find.

They gave Captain George the seat of honour at the head of nature's table, for the cloths were spread on the soft green grass. Nothing was lacking to make everybody joyous, light hearted, and gay, and how they did eat with prodigous appetite, but at last were filled. Then followed races and games galore, also a tug of war, in which Captain and crew took part.

This being over, our friend Chris and a score other lads of about his age, started to explore the island. We will introduce a few of them. There was long Frank Allgood, noted for his big feet and kind heart. There was big fatty Barlow, whose right name was Ned. There was honest George Blisard, who was always called Cork, or Corkie, perhaps because of his color, for his hair, eyes and brows were as black as night. Be this as it may, he was an all round good fellow whom everyone liked, and respected, unless Ance Greggson. He did not appear to like or respect anything, or anybody, not even his own father. He was not a member of the Sunday School, but had taken advantage of the chance to visit the island. He had his cronies, of course but they feared him more than they liked him. He seemed by nature a vulgar, quarrelsome bully. He and Chris had met frequently since the day he was found beating his poor horse. He appeared to have taken a violent dislike to the latter, and every time they met it was made more manifest, by sneering taunts, and half concealed insults.   Chris had seen little of him on the way over, but after the games, he joined the exploring party. The young fellows started out in fine spirits.   Their pleasure was greatly marred, however, by Greggson, who seemed determined to make himself as disagreeable as possible.   Chris appeared to bear it all patiently, but if his companions had taken particular notice they would have observed a gleam in his dark eyes to which they were entirely unaccustomed.

When the party reached the upper end of the island, they found a lovely little cove, and someone proposed a swim. No sooner said than done.   There was a race to see who could undress first.   The bank was high and the water deep.   Corkie was in first with a great plunge, then followed the others.   They were all good swimmers, with the exception of Greggson, and he did not remain in long. Oh, what a time of splashing, diving, ducking, cheering, shouting, squealing, and all the other antics made by a jolly party having a good swim. Before the others came out Greggson was fully dressed, and appeared to find immense enjoyment in pelting them with wet sand as they climbed the steep bank. He singled out Chris as a special victim, and continued to annoy him till he was partly dressed and all the rest were out but Cork.   The latter was like a duck in the water, and seemed loath to leave it.   Chris had succeeded in getting his shirt, trousers and one sock on, when Greggson picked up his shoe and motioned as if to throw it into the lake.   Now Chris was particular about his footwear, and the shoe Greggson was swinging happened to be nearly new, and had only been worn on special occasions. No wonder he was vexed. He quickly pulled on the other sock, and said sternly:

"Ance Greggson, if you dare to throw that shoe in, you'll follow it, just as sure as you are alive."

The boys knew Chris meant exactly what he said, and all with the exception of Frank Allgood and Cork Blizard set up a shout of derision, followed by the words:

"Gregg darsent, Gregg darsent. Big Ance is afraid, afraid of a preacher's son. Ho, ho, ho." The derisive laughter and taunting shouts decided Greggson, and with an oath he hurled the shoe into the lake.

Cainsford had watched him intently, was aware of his decision, and before the shoe left his hand was prepared to spring, and it had not struck the water when with a mighty bound he was upon him like an avalanche. The strongest man could not have withstood the shock while in the position Greggson's burly form occupied at that moment. The shoe had not sunk before he went in headlong, with a floundering splash. The boys roared and laughed, of course, but it might have ended more seriously for Gregg than it did.

Cainsford's onslaught had knocked the wind out of him, and his clothes and boots weighed him down so that he was next to helpless in the deep water. If the alert Corkie had not swam to his assistance he would have had a hard time to reach the shore. He did reach it, however, owing to Corkie's help, who immediately after started to dive for the shoe.

The third attempt was successful, and he flung it ashore as Greggson climbed up the steep bank, looking worse than any drowned rat ever looked, and swearing such terrible oaths that the boys fairly shuddered. For a moment he stood still, then wrenched off his wet coat and vest and made a terrific rush at Cainsford, as he hissed, "By ——— I'll break every bone in your long carcass, you d—— reptile."

Chris was prepared for the rush, but was at a disadvantage owing to the fact that he only wore one shoe. Greggson showered in such a storm of blows, that he could not parry them all. One caught him on the nose with sufficient force to make it bleed, then for the first time, his companions saw Chris Cainsford in fighting humor. Oh, how his fierce eyes blazed. Even the furious Greggson for a second felt their power. That second gave Chris a chance. He struck out with fearful force. His opponent dodged, but as he did so, the blow caught him just below the ear. He staggered, tried to regain his balance, but ·missed, and down he went on the soft green sod. Chris calmly waited for him to rise, and the crazy light in his dark eyes gleamed as he watched his big adversary. Suddenly Gregg was up, and with a bound upon him, armed with the broken limb off a tree. It was about three feet long and a dangerous weapon. Gregg's strong arm swung a vicious blow aimed at Chris's head. If that blow had reached its mark, the Mary Taylor would have carried a corpse on her return trip; but Chris with the rapidity of thought dodged it, and his long arm shot out with terrific force, as he panted:

"*You'd murder, would—you,—there, take—that.*"

The blow landed fairly on Greggson's frothing mouth. There was a sharp crack, like the report of a small pistol. This time he did not wait to stagger, but went down with a loud thud, and lay wallowing, while blood, mingled with the froth, spread over his big face. The short, fierce fight was over; the fight which helped to fasten "Crazy" to Cainsford's other name.

When Gregg was pulled up, he put his hand to his bleeding mouth and discovered that one of the teeth he was so proud of was broken off close up to the gum. He gave a shriek of agonized rage, then set up a howl like a whipped cur, and uttering horrid blasphemies, swore to have revenge if it' took a thousand years.

As Chris stood watchful, still panting from his great exertion, he found the knuckles of his right hand all cut, bleeding, and swelling rapidly. He also discovered the gold ring his sister Flo had given him, to be all bent, broken, and one end almost imbedded in the bone of his finger.

Each combatant bore a mark of their first fierce encounter, to be carried to the grave. If it had been their last encounter, this tale would never have been told.

:   :   :   :   :   :   :   :   :   :   :   :   :   :   :   :

The schooner's return trip for the most part was as enjoyable as the passage out. The breeze freshened and veered around to the north-west, obliging the "Mary Taylor" to tack in order to reach the harbor. There was quite a sea running, causing the vessel to roll, and a number on board experienced the usual agonies of sea-sickness. These, needless to say, were not in a very joyous mood. There is a worse disease, however, than sea-sickness, namely, heart-sickness, and two of the passengers had an attack of this. One nursed a swollen and bandaged jaw, the other a swollen and bandaged hand. One sat in the darkest corner of the forecastle, breathing forth threats and muttering oaths. The other leaned over the schooner's stern, sad, sore, and angry, for what had occurred. In due time, however, the company and crew reached their home in safety.

The Mary Taylor and good Captain George are not forgotten. A spot on memories page still keeps green for both, for many recall that happy day with kindling eye and warming heart.

CHAPTER XIX.

HUNTING BLACK HEARTS—KILLING DUCKS

When school opened,Chris was on hand the first day. He had to run the gauntlet, as every spirited lad has, when he first becomes a member of a large school and had frequent misunderstandings with his companions, which brought the fierce light to his eyes, and established the name of "Crazy Chris," but he was generally liked, however, and made many friends. The two most familiar were Frank Allgood and Corkie Blizard. The three lads became great chums. Dummy Deacon, of course, did not attend school, but he and Chris were together very frequently.

During the winter there was lots of sport—skating, fishing through the ice, sailing ice-boats, etc.; but, as Chris and Frank had each chosen the profession they intended to follow, namely law and medicine, they studied diligently with this end in view. Frank Allgood's friendship and society were of great value to Chris. The former was a conscientious plodder, who would not let pleasure interfere with duty, and worked hard. Chris followed his example and a friendly strife developed, which had a tendency to produce rapid advancement in their various studies, which was necessary, as they had decided to go to college at the end of the next school term.

The winter passed, spring came, and with it an incident which brought Greggson and Cainsford together in a most remarkable manner. In order to understand how it occurred, it will be necessary to accompany Chris as he starts out about daylight on the 24th of May, 18—, a day which proved eventful in more ways than one. He had made arrangements with the Simmons boys, Jake and Pete, to accompany them to the Bluff, for the purpose of shooting Black-heart plover, which could be generally found there in large flocks during the latter part of the month of May.

The Bluff, a small rocky island, lies about half a mile off Picturesque Point to the west of Darkton Harbor. In order to go all the way there by water, a boat requires to travel twelve miles or more. Hunters, however, are in the habit of crossing the bay to what is called Long Cove, thence up the latter to its head, where the point is about an eighth of a mile across. Of course, it is necessary to portage this distance, but

as the point is very level, it is no great task unless the
boat be large and heavy.   The extra labor of making
the portage greatly shortens the distance to the Bluff.

On the day in question this route was followed, and
our party of three, in two boats, arrived there quite
early.   Having landed, they separated in search of
game, and they made a complete circuit of the island,
before they came to the conclusion that Blackhearts
were scarce, and searching for them extremely
hungry work.   A halt was called, fire built, and as
Jake prepared coffee, Chris and Pete examined the
game bags, finding that the whole party had shot
thirteen plover, not more than enough for a good
pot pie.

After eating a prodigious meal, a consultation was
held.   Chris suggested to start at once for home.
Pete and Jake declined, declaring at the same time,
that they were bound to have better luck in the afternoon.

Now, Darkton was noted at this time for fast horses.
A big meet was arranged for on this day, consisting
of running, trotting and hurdle racing.   As Chris was
passionately fond of this excitement, he determined,
when game was so scarce, to do his best to get back
in time for the contest between two famous running
horses.   He knew this race was expected to be the
event of the day and would not be called till quite
late in the afternoon.

When he quietly informed Jake and Pete of his
decision they merely laughed at him.   They were
not very well acquainted with Chris, and did not
dream that he would have the hardihood to attempt
the passage from the bluff to the beach, unaccom-

panied by their much larger boat. They were both experienced sailors, and already aware that the wind had greatly increased since their arrival, and that a heavy sea was running. They paid no further attention to Chris, however, till it was too late to prevent his going.

As he is preparing his little craft for the trip we will try to describe her. She measured thirteen feet keel, three feet six inches beam, and was eighteen inches deep, was well decked over at bow and stern, and had a running board six inches wide, inside of which a combing projected an inch above the deck. She had a three inch standing keel, a pair of short oars, and a good steering paddle. As there was only a narrow seat in the stern, she was half filled with dry marsh grass for the sake of comfort. Chris seldom used the oars. If there did not happen to be a breeze he preferred paddling. Indeed, the little craft was more like a monitor, or duck skiff, than a vessel intended to sail the rolling billows of old Lake Ontario. She was painted eight times before Chris could be satisfied with her color. The last achievement was as odd as it was pretty. The hull and running board were a rose pink. The wail and combing, a delicate blue. The scrolls, from the bow, were also blue, inside of which the name "Bay Witch" appeared in gold-leaf letters. She was built of cedar, and carried fourteen yards of snow-white canvas, cut for a sprit sail, which could be reefed. A pennant flew at her mast head with her name in blue. Altogether, she was like a beautiful toy boat.

When Chris proudly showed her to Captain George, the latter advised him to always keep her tied to the dock when he went for a voyage.   This, however, did not daunt the young sailor in the least.   He became so expert in handling her that fear never appeared to cross his mind.

Now, having made all snug, he left the Bluff from the east end.   As the wind was from the west he did not feel the force of it till he got well out.   He knew before starting that it was blowing very fresh, and therefore thought it wise to make the short run without hoisting canvas, particularly because of the chopping seas a west wind always produces, owing to the number of sand bars between the Bluff and beach.

When Pete and Jake Simmons discovered that Chris had actually started they beckoned frantically for him to come back.   It would have been very difficult to comply even if he desired to do so, for he was already out among great rolling white-capped waves.   All he tried to do was steady and guide his frail barque with the long paddle.   The fierce wind drove her from one great surging billow to another, with such speed that the bold little "Witch" seemed frightened and was doing her best to escape.

Chris Cainsford had plenty of nerve, but when he got among the angry waves raging and seething over the sand bars he needed it all.   He did not lose his head, however, but grasped the paddle, and with rapid and powerful strokes helped the Witch out of the trough.   It seemed to take a long time to get through the awful turmoil of waters, and the boat was tossed about every which way, like a dancing fairy.   Finally the last bar is passed, and now mighty rollers, assisted by whistling wind and busy paddle, hove the Witch shoreward, with ever increasing speed.

The next thing is to land without being filled or broken by the ponderous force of the huge seas as they break with an angry roar upon the sandy beach. It is well for Chris and his craft that no cruel rocks raised their deformed heads in menace along this part of the beach. If there had heen, the delicate ribs of the beautiful Witch would have been torn to atoms, and ground to pulp; but the time to land has come.

Chris quickly looks behind him, and sees a few boat lengths away, a mountain billow rearing its great silvery crest high above its fellows as it gathers force for its final fierce onslaught upon the shore. Chris shuts his teeth hard and backs water with all the strength of his strong arms and sturdy frame, and then as the little Witch is seized from behind and borne up, up, up, the wide paddle makes quick, vicious sweeps, and the trembling boat is carried high up on the beach, then, as the watery monster breaks with swish and roar, amid flying spray she comes down on her standing keel, and captain, paddle, and gun are rolled out on the sand.

Chris picks himself up with a great sigh of relief and a whispered prayer of thanksgiving, then looks back across the angry waters to the Bluff, and thinks he can dimly see Pete and Jake throwing their hats high in the air.

The next thing is to make the portage. The reader will know that the Witch must have been small indeed, when after arranging gun, paddle, basket and oars, Chris shouldered the load and trudged off to the head of Long Cove, only taking one rest on the way.

Having again launched his boat in the compara·tively still water of the cove, while quietly paddling

along on the look out for a chance shot, Chris is
suddenly startled by the whistle of wings, and the
quack, quack of a large flock of black ducks. He
dropped the paddle and seized his gun, and in his
excitement jumped up in the little boat and let blaze.
There was a muffled report, followed by a great splash,
and before Chris knew what had happened he was
struggling in twenty feet of water, and his little boat
bobbing serenely several lengths away. He still held
the gun, and managed to get alongside the Witch and
drop it in, then got hold of her stern and made for the
near shore, where clambering out he rubbed his
shoulder, shook himself, and stood draining and dazed,
wondering what had happened. One thing he recalled distinctly, as he pulled the trigger of his Indian
Chief gun, he, or she, kicked like a steer. The shock
was so great that he was sent out of his boat back-
wards with such force that she did not upset, but slid
from under him, so to speak. He examined his wet
gun and discovered that a narrow strip about three-
quarters of an inch long had been blown out of the
barrel just at the muzzle. He concluded that the
gun must have stuck its end into the wet sand, when
he and it were flung from the Witch as she landed
on the beach, and his painful shoulder throbbed a
strong argument in favor of this theory. He wrung
out his clothes as best he could, then shoved off.

Before proceeding on his way, however, he looked
around to see if anything besides himself had been
hurt by the shot. Oh, joy, there was one big black
as dead as a stone, and beyond it another poor cripple
swimming wildly about. He secured the one, and
made chase of the other. It could certainly swim like

a duck though trailing a broken wing, and Chris was thoroughly warmed after his cold bath, before it was captured and laid under the deck beside its mate. Then he paddled away with sore shoulder, heavy clothes, but a light heart. "I'll have the laugh on Jake and Pete," he murmered. "I wouldn't give that big pair for all the Blackhearts they bag. I'll sail across, too. I know its blowing a gale but the Bay is nothing to the Lake."

Having thus decided, he put two reefs in his little sail, hoisted it, and in a twinkling rounded Calf Pasture Point, and headed across the Bay without a thought of danger, for had he not weathered the giant billows of the angry Lake? Why, these were pigmies in comparison, but as the fierce wind got a chance the little Witch fairly flew, and her captain was obliged to climb her running board and lean as far to windward as his long body would reach. Even then she lay over so that he could see her standing keel, but it was glorious, even if the flying spray was hurled all over him and his plunging craft as she foamed along.

From the foot of Long Cove to Mrs. Ryan's boathouse is about two and a half miles, and was made in one stretch. As he neared the shore and dropped his sail, it seemed to Chris that the Witch never had sailed so fast, "Why I was tieing reef points only a few minutes ago," he said to himself, as he jumped out on the little dock and stretched his cramped limbs.

CHAPTER XX.

Chris and the Witch Save Gregg's Life

Chris had removed the ducks, and with a thrill of
pride was admiring them when Mrs. Ryan, a widow,
from whom he rented space in the boathouse, rushed
to him ringing her hands, as she shouted hysterically:
"Oh, Cainsford, Cainsford, that there cockle shell
will leave you in a watery grave yet, so it will, but
for mercy's sake look away down the bay! Do you
see that brown thing about the middle beyond the
lower dock?"

"Yes," was the reply, "I see something, but what
is it, Mrs. Ryan?"

"Oh, my God, it's my nephew, Ance Greggson,
what brought that old punt here last week, and he's
in it, with an old hop sack for a sail, and this awful
wind is blowing him right out into the lake where
he'll go to the bottom, with all his sins, for he's so
crazy drunk he don't know his own name. Oh,
Father in heaven, what will I do? I didn't think he'd
go out for he don't know how to sail. He never
would, only he's drunk and has a bottle. I begged
him not to go, but he just swore at me, took a drink
and shoved off. His father will blame me. Oh,
oh," and the poor woman sobbed and wrung her
hands.

Of course, Chris was astonished, but he took in the situation in a moment. There was no other boat in sight, and not likely to be, as the fishermen would be at the races. He knew that Mrs. Ryan's words were true. If the loggy, leaky punt stayed afloat long enough to drift beyond Big Light, (which was very doubtful,) she was sure to fill in five minutes, when caught by the huge seas of the lake. These thoughts passed through Cainsford's keen brain like a flash, and while Mrs. Ryan was ringing her hands he was hastily undoing reef points. He saw that his oars were in, and as he placed gun, basket, and game on the dock, noticed an old tin pail. On the spur of the moment he threw it aboard, then hoisted his sail and shoved off before Mrs. Ryan comprehended his intention. She wildly beckoned, as she screamed:

"For God sake don't go! Oh, do, do come back: come back!" You'll be drowned too! Oh, please ——My God, he's gone——"

Here she heard a shout above the roar of the wind:

"I'll do my best, but pray for us both."

The little "Witch" is now flying before the wind with all her sail spread, the strain is so great that she trembles from stem to stern, and at times almost buries herself in the foaming billows. Chris knew that if she did not fly as never before he would be too late, and Ance Greggson would be lost for sure. She carries on nobly, but her spar and boom creak and groan, as if in agony. How Chris watches every move of surging boat and straining sail as she rears and plunges through the spray.

If she jibes in this fierce wind Mrs. Ryan's words will prove true, and he will find a watery grave, but there is a resolute glow in his dark eyes as he kneels there in the shallow craft, grasping the steering paddle with tense muscles. All he can do is steady and keep her dead before it. He remembers his father's and mother's prayers, and offers up one of his own, asking for strength and guidance. As if in answer he sees the brown hop sack much nearer.

"Thank God," he exclaimed, "she is still afloat. I think I'll catch him before he passes Big Light."

He looked across to Picturesque Point, and found that he was between the triangle and the Grit Light. He had come nearly four miles.

Every moment the sea is becoming wilder, the waves more ponderous, and the surge more fierce, as the brave little Witch is carried from one gigantic billow to another,—but she is gaining,—gaining,—gaining on the wallowing punt and its drunken occupant. It seems a miracle that they are still on top the angry waters.

"I'll catch him yet," Chris cries, "but what then, what then?"

Now he sees with alarm that they are passed Little Light, and far, far from either shore. If they are carried another half mile, they will never return, no, never; but ah! he is almost alongside. What will he do? Will the Witch swamp if he runs her into the wind? Chris fears she will. Now he is passing, and does not look, but lets go his sheet rope. It flies away over the bow. The sail rolls and cracks in the breeze, as the boom swings and jumps from side to side. With trembling haste he frees the lower end of the sprit. It goes overboard and is seen no more. With a great heave he then hoists the spar from out the saddle. The sail nearly blows away, but with a frantic tug is pulled on board and quickly stowed.

As he grasps his paddle he looks for the punt. It is behind him. He gets the Witch turned head on to wind and wave, and a few powerful strokes brings him alongside. As he tears the hop sack off the oar, his glowing eyes behold a most repulsive sight.

The punt is nearly half full of water, and wallows deeper as a more stealthy wave than its fellows drops a small portion of itself over her side with a little vindictive splash. Partly on the high backed stern seat and partly on the old punt's slippery bottom sprawls Greggson. The discolored water laps greedily at his helpless form, while his large uncovered head lazily rolls from side to side with each sluggish effort of the water-logged punt as she tries her best to keep afloat. His wide-open mouth, and half-closed eyes add a demoniac horror to the red bloated face. One nerveless hand still rests on an empty whiskey flask. A gurgling snore issues from the thick lips and mingles with the chaos of sound all about the poor prostrate wretch.

The scarred weather beaten punt sinks lower and lower, and the froathing scum climbs higher and higher still inside her dingy hold, adding its dismal detail to the horrid picture of youthful sin and depravity making a hasty flight to perdition.

The unconscious passenger seems accompanied by a host of invisible fiends, shrieking and wailing in the fierce wind, hissing and gurgling in the angry water.

For several seconds Chris is held spell-bound by the revolting picture, but knows that every moment is precious, and he hastily make his boat fast to the punt. As they groan and scrape together, Chris sees that the delicate beauty of his darling Witch will soon be destroyed. He is tempted to cast loose and save himself, if possible. He knows that huddled heap there, when sober, hates him with revengeful, bitter hatred. Why not let the shrieking fiends have their prey. "Oh, no, no, God helping me, I will save him," he gasps, as he hurls pailful after pailful of cold water over the stupid Gregg, lolling his helpless length all unconscious of the deadly peril. Oh, how Chris begs him to waken and work for his life.

"Ance, Ance Greggson, your drowning," he cries. "If you don't bail you will be at the bottom in ten minutes."

It is true, any moment they were liable to be engulfed, and were drifting, drifting, drifting out into the Lake. The drenched Gregg comes slightly to himself, the cold water has taken effect. He seems to hear Cainsford's voice in the shrieking wind. He shuts his big mouth, and opens his bleary eyes. His hat is gone, and the water pours from him in all directions.

Chris hurls another half pail directly into his big bloated face with terrific force, as he screams:

"Bail for your life or you are dead,—dead,—dead, do you hear? Get down on your knees, where you can work, and for heaven's sake pray, for your time has come."

The consciousness of his deadly peril has at last penetrated Greggson's whiskey-charged brain, and he trembles like a leaf. His strong teeth chatter as he gazes with frightened bulging eyes at the flying foam and threatening waves. He goes to work awkwardly, but frantically, throwing water from the wallowing punt. Chris saw at a glance that it would be madness to try and get him aboard his frail craft. He is so frightened now that he would be sure to upset them both. The only thing possible is to tow him to shore. He noticed a piece of chain attached to the bow. He doubled his sheet rope, and made it fast to the narrow seat in his boat then cast loose from the punt, in order to attach chain and rope; at which Gregg blubbered pitifully, and begged Chris for God's sake not to leave him.

"Off with your coat and bail for your life," again roared Chris, as he fixed on his oars.

It was none too soon. As he swung his boat and headed for shore it looked as if their time had certainly come. A great roller broke all around them. The buoyant Witch was nearly submerged, and the water logged punt fuller than ever.

' Bail,—Bail,—for God sake, bail!" was Cainsford's hoarse cry, as he bent to the oars. Oh, how light they were for such a load. He strained and strained, and it seemed a hopeless task. The old punt was a dead weight, and scarcely moved. Oh, how he pulled and pulled. Oh, how his arms ached, and sore shoulder pained; but he kept the rope and chain so taut, he thought they would break. If that happened Gregg at least was lost. The latter saw this danger and tried with trembling haste to lighten the load. He was a powerful fellow, and his frantic fear redoubled his strength. He threw out barrels of water as he prayed, muttered, gasped and swore in his agony of fear.

Chris did not attempt to go up the Bay, but strove to keep the Witch and tow out of the trough and headed for shore. Would   he awful strain never cease? It seemed an hour since the tow-line tightened, and still they are far, far from shore, but are moving faster. Gregg's exertions are beginning to tell. The punt rides higher and takes in less water. Chris takes a moment's breathing spell, and is rejoiced to see that the punt gains on him, and the tow line slackens.

"Have you the other oar on board, Gregg," he hailed.

"Yes," is the hoarse answer.

"Put it on as soon as you can.   I am about done."

For some time Gregg continued bailing furiously.

Was it providential that Chris thought to bring that pail? It seemed like it, for now they are making much better time and the seas are less fierce. They have got out of the channel, and Gregg gives a loud cheer, and cries, "She's pretty nigh empty."

He put on the oars and rowed clumsily, but Chris felt gratified for he was just about exhausted. It is well they are near shore, for now the Bay is covered with a misty fog. Chris thought he heard a horn being blown away out toward Big Light.

"I'll bet it is the Dummy," he said to himself, "out in search with the Widewave," and halloed a reply, but he knew it could not be heard. They pulled more leisurely now, and at last the Witch touched the shore.

Chris staggered out, his legs all cramped and trembling, his hands blistered and swollen, his tired arms aching, and his right shoulder throbbing with pain. He had a grateful heart though, and as he flung himself on the damp shore, offered a fervent prayer of thanksgiving to the great Preserver for their marvellous escape.

After resting a while, they pulled up the boats and started on the weary tramp for home. They had landed six miles from Darkton. It was well they were picked up by a passing farmer, for Chris in particular was played out.

They reached the town some time after dark and sent a message to Mrs. Ryan, informing her of their safety. Chris discovered that she had given the alarm at the docks and Dummy and his father had gone out in search. They were late in starting, however, and missed the lads in the thick fog.

Very few people ever knew of that day's adventure, but Chris never forgot it, you may be sure. He informed the anxious ones at home that the very high wind had delayed his return, that was all.

Ance Greggson told Chris he was grateful, in a shamefaced sort of way, but never could be induced to talk of his narrow escape from a watery grave. He ceased to threaten Chris behind his back, however, and during the time the latter remained at Darkton tried to be friendly in a peculiar gruff manner. They even traded thoroughbred fowls, and Ance presented Chris with a pair of snow-white doves. They were accepted by the latter as heralds of Peace, but Chris did not know that away down deep in his Black Heart, Gregg still nursed undying HATRED, and longed for REVENGE.

CHAPTER XXI.

Dazzled by the Gamblers' World.

After their Matriculation, Chris Cainsford and
Frank Allgood left Darkton and started college
life. During the four busy years that have passed,
our two friends have been more or less intimately
associated, and now we find them occupying the same
boarding house. Frank still attending college, Chris
articled as clerk to a prominent law firm.

Although they do not move in exactly the same
set, their friendship is stronger than ever. They are
very unlike in general appearance and just as dis-
similar in general character. Strange that they love
and respect each other as they do. Frank admires
the handsome, impulsive, clever Chris. Chris admires the kindly, honest, homely Frank.

They each possess a justifiable admiration for the
other's superior qualities. Thus a generous envy
exists between the two—if we may use the term.

Chris is proud to introduce Frank as his intimate
friend. The latter is proud of the other's admiration,
but is altogether unassuming, and has a tendency
to depreciate himself. However, he can and has
frequently asserted his individuality, in a most telling
manner, when called upon to defend his principles
or stand for the right.

What is his personal appearance? Oh, I beg your pardon for not describing him sooner, for he certainly deserves marked attention. Frank Allgood is long every way. His head, face, body, arms, legs, feet, all are long, especially the latter. They are considerable trouble to him too, and often in the way, particularly if he chance to be in a drawing room, and is introduced to a pretty girl. At such time Frank has the habit of rubbing his narrow knees with his long fingers, while he tries desperately to conceal somewhere a portion at least of his great feet. They are so hard to hide, however, that the attempt generally ends in failure, which brings a blush to his freckled face. His companions sometimes call him "Feet," instead of Frank, or "Alllong." instead of Allgood. Strange to say he will answer to either, and laugh his large, quiet laugh, as though he considered the name appropriate. When standing erect on those feet, with no kinks in his long, slim body, and his red curly head upraised, Frank Allgood measures six feet three and a half inches.

To show that he is not foolishly sensitive with regard to their abnormal size, we will mention an incident which occurred shortly before Chris and Frank left Darkton, in which the latter's feet took part. Frank's father had built a new house, the plastering of which was not finished until quite late in the season and required artificial heat to dry it thoroughly. Frank was commissioned to keep on fires upon a certain night which set in cold. It was a lonely job, so he invited Chris to keep him company. Frank's brother called and chatted for a while during the evening; and before he left offered Frank his revolver for protection.

"Oh, no, thanks," said the latter, "if anybody comes to bother I'll show 'em one of these," and held up his feet. "If that don't scare 'em off, why—it —wont—be—no—great—trouble—to — stomp — em —to—death. Do you think it will, Chris?"

Then he laughed his quiet laugh at the little joke, and pointed one long finger at his two big feet.

Chris never forgot the occurrence, and sometimes reminded Frank of it when the latter least expected it, and generally when there were others present.

During the years of college life, the two friends have made rapid progress and learned many things, among others card playing. Frank played a little, Chris played a lot. The former, never when anything was at stake, the latter every time he got the chance, and had already developed a passion for "draw poker." Chris had also studied the violin, and made very marked progress under the able instruction of a German Professor, who considered him his most clever pupil. As they each loved music passionately they spent many happy hours together.

The house in which our two young men boarded was large and roomy enough to accommodate an average of twenty-five persons. They were mostly students, and a mighty jolly crowd, as the local police would inform you. Seldom a night would pass at Mrs. Pringle's boarding house without a little game of poker. The stakes, of course, were light, sometimes merely for matches, at other times for money, but more frequently they played for beer, thus forming habits which gradually grew stronger.

In Cainsford's case love for poker developed rapidly. He innocently entered the gamblers' world, and at once became dazzled. Like many, many others, before he saw the danger he was already caught. The passion for gambling when once aroused adheres closely to its prey, and like the tentacles of an octopus, binds its victim in adhesive bonds, NOT to be torn away. Its most terrible quality is its ability to lure and then hold. If a gambler attempts to remove the bonds he is generally the more SURELY bound, and the passion clings the closer.

This was Cainsford's case. Before he graduated in law he was a prisoner, so to speak, and before he started practice the passion was almost paramount. Frank Allgood had given him friendly advice, and set a manly example, not without effect. Chris would agree that his friend was right, and abstain from both drink and cards for a time. His bonds were stronger than he knew, however. He would relapse and after each relapse they clung the closer. Even during holidays when visiting the loved ones at home, the seductive monster, he carried about with him, would assert itself, and probably cause him to stay away all night in a vain attempt to satiate its greedy craving. The loved ones wondered and were sad, there was another who wondered and was glad. You, no doubt, could guess his name. Chris Cainsford called him friend, and addressed him familiarly as Gregg. It was with bounding, fiendish joy that this pretended friend discovered Cainsford's Mighty Weakness. He Strengthened it, Fed it and bided his Time.

The final result of his PATIENT WAITING, WATCHING, and CARE, was the EVOLUTION of the COWARDLY SCHEME, not only to ROB Chris Cainsford of money, but also to steal something MORE PRECIOUS,—his good name.

The reader is already familiar with the sordid details of Ance Greggson's scheme, and HOW FAR HE AND TEARY WORKED THEM OUT.

PART III.

SORROW AND JOY

CHAPTER XXII.

A Fearful Find at Sharp Curve.

With a fierce, prolonged hiss of air brakes, and a warning clang of her bell, "Old Firefly" stopped and stood quietly throbbing in front of the low-roofed station at Latchford. Her long, shining steel body gave forth a trembling shimmer of heat, while the angry rush of escaping steam told how impatient the great one-eyed monster was to rush on.

The driver of this hot, ponderous-wheeled horse signed his name Wm. Bonter, but was better known as "Lightning Billy," because of his well-deserved record for making fast time. He claimed that "No. 619" was the speediest engine on the Grand Trunk Road, and called her "Old Firefly," which was truly an appropriate name.

She had caused more than fire to fly as she roared along this early morning on her way down from the West. For once Lightning Billy was behind time, and judging from the uneasy sound coming from the engine's safety valve, had been trying his best to catch it.   The moment Firefly stopped her trainload of languid humanity, the driver jumped to the platform, and while carefully inspecting the front of his engine, evidently arrived at a conclusion, for he shook his head and hurriedly beckoned to the Conductor, who was just entering the station door.   When the latter was within hearing distance Bonter said in a low quick tone.

"I think a stray horse was put out of business up at Sharp Curve Crossing.   I know I struck something, but was running to make time, and the light was so hazy that I could not see very well.   All I know is that there was no buggy or waggon hitched to it, and it didn't even jar "Old Firefly."   Suppose we'll have to send in a casualty report though.   Will you look after it, George, and have Mike or some of the section men go up and see."

"Certainly, certainly," was the answer, and the conductor ran into the station, while Bonter returned to his post.

Very soon "All Aboard," was sounded, the bell clanged, the throttle opened, the wheels revolved, and with angry, disdainful snorts "Old Firefly" gladly rushed away, hauling the fast express.

Two passengers had got off and were now standing on the station platform.   One was tall, slim, and clean chaven, with red curly hair.   The other was short, stout, unshaven, with bristly brown hair.   They had stepped from different compartments of the train, and each noticed a drooping-shouldered man rush by carrying a huge valise.   He seemed excited and in

great haste. A slouch hat was pulled well over his
eyes, but as he looked furtively in their direction,
having climbed the steps of a second-class car, a
large tear could be seen stealing down his grey face.
Then face, form, and valise disappeared through the
doorway.

As the train receded from view, the two men gazed
about at their surroundings in a manner suggestive
of unfamiliarity. Thus they stood till the large blue
eyes of one were caught by the small brown eyes of the
other. Then both faces lit up with pleased recognition, and they quickly approached each other. One
with long strides, the other with short waddles. One
extended a long, slim, freckled hand; the other a short,
broad, brown one.

"Great Scott, where did you drop from, Jock
Quiggley?" exclaimed one.

"Gleamin' Goldfish, where'd ye spring from, Frank
Allgood?" wheezed the other. Then they talked and
laughed, as two old friends do, when they meet unexpectedly in a strange place. They ignored the
solicitations of both cab and buss drivers, and seating
themselves on a truck at the end of the station were
conversing earnestly when interrupted by these words,
spoken in a quick tone (the speaker evidently not
being aware of their presence.)

"You'll have to get a move on Mike, if you and Jim
pump that hand car up to Sharp Curve before No. 6
gets down."

"Bedad, that's thrue," came from a powerfully built
man in shirt sleeves. "But Jim's not here yit. Will
I go me lone? If Ould Foirefly, bad cess to the loiks
ave her, didn't stroik nothin besoids a sthray horse,

O'il nade no hilp.   Of coorse the mashane rins harrad wid oney wan at the handle ave her, but, begorra, jist whusper the worrud, and Moik Murphy's aff."

Dr. Frank Allgood and Mr. Jock Quiggley had been attentive listeners to the talk, and at this point the former stepped to the front of the station, and inquired:

"Has there been an accident on the road?"

"Oh, I guess not," said the agent disconcertedly, "but Bill Bonter reported that he had struck a horse, or something about two miles up the line."

"If I can be of any service I am quite willing to accompany your man Mike," said Dr. Allgood. "I am in no particular hurry to go down town, as people are not up yet."

"Them's my sentiments too," came from the ready Jock, "and as me frend here is a bang up corn-cracker of a doctor, if anythins hurt me and him'll be use- fuller than any Jim you've got."

The station master laughed as he said:

"We're not supposed to make these things public, but this does not amount to much, and if you wish to go, I do not object."

Without further loss of time the hand car was haul- ed to the track; Dr. Allgood grasped one handle of the propelling lever, Mike Murphy the other.   They bent their strong backs, and soon were under way.

"Bedad its tirrible tall cumpany O'm in this blessed mornin," said Mike, jerkily.   "So airly, and on- expected too.   Bejabbers, Docther! if you're as strang as ye'er lang its the proper pumper yiz are intoirely, and you and me kin bate only other two garsoons on the Ould Grand Thrunk."

Frank proved his ability to pump, for already they were rapidly rolling along. Jock said little, and worked less. It kept him busy holding on his new hat. Mike continued to gasp forth his Irish brogue between the ups and downs of the swiftly moving lever.

"Big parthon fur bain familiar, docthur, but them's a moity ginerous pair—ave—fa—fa—fate yiz—are the o—o—owner ave. Begorra, but their foin fur kapin a hand car stidy. No fare of her jumpin the thrack, bad cess to it, whin them pair ave fates aboord." And Mike chuckled, and his bare head and broad shoulders bobbed—down—up—down—up—as the noisy car rolled along at top speed.

"Hist! do ye hear yon whostle? Its No. 6. If we kape her goin loik this we'll be soonest at the crassin."

They pumped vigorously for a few minutes more, then Mike shouted:

"Arrah, but here yiz are, now aff wid the ould janglin craythur, quick."

The car was removed from the track in good time to allow a heavy freight to roll its long length past, with roar and rumble. When the flying dust had settled, our party looked about and found that the road bed at the crossing had been filled in several feet in depth, thus placing the track on a slight elevation of its own.

Sharpe Curve Crossing, as it is called, belongs to a side road, which intersects the G. T. R. track at a point two miles west of L——, and close to the crossing the line curves around a low rocky hill,

"Troth, I think Lightnin Billy was drunchk or dramin," said Mike, as he gazed around. "He tould us he struchk a horse, bad luck ta him, but divil the wan do Oi see. Whisht? Hould on! Bedad. What's yon rid thing lying beyant the fince, clost ta the himlock bush? Kim along wid yees, and we'll invistigate."

The three slid down the steep embankment, climbed a low fence and found ————. Oh! how they shudder as they look. How they tremble as they draw near. Two sprawling forms still lay where they had been hurled. Their only company, curious flies and broken glass blades.

The poor horse is a mass of broken, bloody horror. The man, ah— Dr. Allgood seizes a wrist, and the hand belonging to it reluctantly releases a moist, discolored, knotted rope. The shock and surprise of this awful unexpected find has set the doctor trembling like a leaf. He does not discover a pulse in the wrist, then the shirt is torn open, and hasty fingers lay bare a broad, white, still breast, to which the doctor places a listening ear. Ah!—he thinks he feels slight warmth. He thinks he hears a feeble, struggling heartbeat. Now with every sense alert he requests help to elevate the head, which is turned in such a manner as to nearly hide the face. It is covered by jet black wavy hair and is raised tenderly. As the face is revealed, blood creeps stealthily from the ears, the nose, the mouth. Even the half-open eyes are bloody, and as the strong men get a better view, a great, broken agonized groan bursts from them.

Their horrified eyes gaze into that white blood-dripping face. Then they cry out, one after the other, in accents of anguish:

"Oh, Lord God of Heaven! Alas, it is Chris," gasps Frank.

"Wirrasthrue! Wirrasthrue! Marciful saints, 'tis the lawyeer," wailed Mike. "The gran good lad what saved me. Och— Worra, worra, me poor heart's clane broke."

And great convulsive sobs shake the sturdy frame, and a shower of large tears drop upon the upturned face.

"O, Du lieber—Gott! O, Du lieber—Gott! The poor brave lad," gurgles Jock. "It's me own true fren, Chris Cainsford. What awful things happened to the one man I loves like a son. O, Weh! O, Weh!" and he wrings his brown hands.

For some seconds the three continue, with bowed heads and throbbing hearts, to sob quivering sobs, and weep scalding tears. The doctor recovers first, and again places his ear to the breast, and then whispers:

"Thank God, he is not quite dead. Is there any water near? "

Jock rushed away to a little stream which ran through the field, and while the doctor carefully examines the powerful limbs, Mike supports the drooping head.

"No bones broken," sighed the Doctor. "It is the head that is injured, probably a fractured skull."

"Blessed Vargin, de ye think he'll live?" moaned Mike.

"Och, the poor koind heart ave him, I wish 'twas mesilf as was layin bladin here, in place ave him. Arrah, but how in the worruld will Oi iver tell Maggie, as fairly worships the cliver lad, as done so much fur her and me. Achone!—Achone!—" and the big-hearted Irishman cried like a child.

When Jock returned with the water, the bloody face was washed and cleansed, the helpless head was bathed and bound—the bandages being hastily made from parts of Jock's white shirt, which he gladly tore up for the purpose. As they were being arranged, the latter asked brokenly:

"Oh, doctor, will he ever get well? If ye only save him, I'll be your fren for ever and ever."

"God helping me, I'll do my best," was the fervent answer, "but time is precious, if he does not lose more blood I think there is a possible chance."

Bushes, then garments were spread on the car, and with tender care the heavy body was laid upon them. Jock keeping the head elevated, as away they rolled.

"Fasht, or slow, docthur?" asked Mike.

"Fast, fast, every moment is precious," was the answer.

Then how Mike's mighty shoulders strained and pressed. How the doctor's long body flew up and down as the car rattled along with unaccustomed speed. No words were spoken, but the heaving chests, streaming faces and trembling forms told of terrific exertion.

As they slowed up at the station they were met by a curious crowd, but no time was lost. The bandages were again moistened, a cab secured, and the trio of faithful ones conveyed the friend they loved to the hospital, and as they bore the poor *unconscious burden* up the steps, they each whispered an earnest pleading prayer, to the *Helper* of the *helpless*.

CHAPTER XXIII.

Nora, the Golden-Haired Nurse.

As the inanimate form of poor Cainsford was being borne to a private ward at the lower end of the hospital, a golden-haired nurse, in snow-white uniform, stepped into the hall.   Her face paled a little as her large eyes rested on the helpless body as it passed, carried so tenderly.   She noticed with a sort of wonder that the face of each bearer gave unmistakeable signs of intense grief.   Strange, thought she, that three men so very unlike in personal appearance, should be associated thus, and each evidently suffering a sorrow too deep for words.   They certainly must love the poor man with a great love, and her eyes moistened with the thought.

As she stood irresolute, the house surgeon came along and stopped to say hurriedly:

"Very bad case, nurse Dean. Young lawyer Cainsford was struck by morning express while horse-back riding.   The horse killed, rider next thing to it. The tall man with red hair is Dr. Allgood.   He is an old friend of the injured man."

Having given this brief explanation the young doctor followed the others to the room which had been allotted, and while Jock and Mike waited outside, assisted to undress the patient.

After making a thorough examination, Dr. Allgood gave a great sigh of relief, as he said:

"Thank Heaven, there are no bones broken, and his pulse is slightly stronger."

Ice was applied to the head, heat to the feet. The doctor's anxiety and earnest effort infused his assistant, and they rubbed and chaffed the beautiful muscular limbs with untiring zeal. Their efforts at last were rewarded, for the pulse became gradually stronger.

There was a suggestion of hope in the doctor's tone as he requested the services of the best nurse in the hospital. Then he reported to the anxiously waiting ones. Relief and joy shone in the faces of Mike and Jock as they were informed that Cainsford had a possible chance to recover.

"He will probably be unconscious for days," said the doctor, "but careful treatment and good nursing mean a great deal. The result rests entirely with the Divine Healer. Let us pray for His help, boys."

When the doctor returned to his patient, the nurse already mentioned, turned from the bedside as she murmured:

"Poor fellow. How very sad, and he so young. My name is Dean, Miss Nora Dean. The house surgeon requested me to assist in this case. I understand you are Dr. Allgood," and she frankly extended her hand. As he shook it cordially the doctor felt a mysterious thrill. What a capable hand it seemed. What a magnificent specimen of pure young womanhood its owner was. As he gazed into the beautiful blooming face, and met the compassionate expression of her lovely eyes, he thanked God in his heart for sending such a helper. Then he said earnestly:

"Nurse Dean, I am indeed pleased to meet you, but very sorry that this terrible accident has brought it about. A letter written by my poor friend here was the cause of my coming to L——. To think of finding him as I did!" There was a quiver in the voice as he continued:

"I hope that with God's blessing, and your assistance, he may recover."

"I do hope so, indeed, Dr. Allgood," said the nurse. "This is the first time I ever saw Mr. Cainsford, but my uncle, who was a great friend of his father's, wrote me about him, and I read of his very clever defence in a recent trial, which caused me to admire his ability and evident good-heartedness."

"Miss Dean," and the doctor's voice was low and impressive, "a more clever, light-hearted, generous chap than Chris Cainsford never lived. We have been chums and friends for years, and when I see him thus, it completely unmans me. I think the skull has a slight fracture, and he is likely to remain unconscious for days, but while there is life there is hope, and we will do our best. Will we not, Miss Dean?"

"Yes, indeed, doctor. If I am capable of good nursing, your friend shall certainly receive it."

Miss Nora Dean, the nurse, was certainly capable, and kept her promise.

CHAPTER XXIV.

SCALEY JOCK VS. L. R. PRATT.

Shortly before eight o'clock, Thursday morning, May 29th, 18—, Mr. L. R. Pratt could be seen making his way down the main street of L——. Still puffing and perspiring, he rounded too in front of the lower entrance to lawyer Cainsford's office, which he found locked. Then an ominous frown appeared on his round red face.

As he looked about him he noticed a group of men and boys talking mysteriously, and pointing up at Cainsford's windows.

"Anybody know where the young lawyer feller is?" shouted Mr. Pratt, in his shrill voice.

The crowd turned on him a pitying glance, and one said:

"Hard to tell exactly. We've just heerd that he went clean crazy early this morning, stole Jim Sampson's sorel horse, run into the lightning express, and him and horse is smashed to smithers."

"Rats!" murmured L. R. Pratt. "Can't cod this here chicken. No, sir."

Then he rushed away on his dog trot, and did not slacken speed until he found himself in the midst of another small crowd in front of Greggson's office.

"Is he here yit?" asked Mr. Pratt, as he pointed towards the office door. Again he received a mysterious stare, and a coarse voice grumbled:

"No— and won't be for a while, I guess."

"Why?—Why?—how's that," squeaked Mr. Pratt.

"Well, we just heard that Greggson was murdered this **a.m.** He was found with his face smashed, lyin' in a pool of blood, and still grippin' a revolver he'd fired off at the feller what killed him, and they think they know the man. He's a big giant of a chap, and was seen with Gregg yesterday."

"Well, I'll be dog-gond! Has everybody in this blessed town gone clean crazy?" and Mr. Pratt with lowered head and swinging arms, steamed back up the street. As he turned the corner he was brought up standing, for he came full tilt against a round fat man, whose coat flew open, and hat flew off from the violence of the shock.

"By the livin' jehosaphat," gasped Pratt.

"O sufferin' eels," grunted Jock, (for it was he).

Then as they stood glaring and striving for breath, Mr. Pratt noticed that the man he had run into was short, dark, hairy, and also that he wore no shirt.

"I say, Mr.—— Mr. Tare-the wind, have ye time to tell me where's the Central Hotel?" inquired Jock. "I'm hungrier than a horney-day."

" 'Spec' you—'spec' you be," snapped Mr. Pratt, "and so be I. The Central is on up street, but if you're a goin' there to feed, I be goin' somewheres else."

And again he was underway heading for the Royal Exchange, as he murmured:

"I'll be durned if I'll eat grub with a hairy cuss like that, without no shirt. No, by jinks, never."

He reached the hotel entrance out of breath, as usual, and was about to open the door, when biff!

Bang! a huge form burst through it, closely followed by two policemen. Mr. Pratt was sent spinning, clear out into the street, where he sat down flop. When he had sufficient breath, he squeaked: "Jee—hos—a—phat."

Then filling his lungs, he burst out with:

"Well, I'll be dog-gond, if this here ain't the most mixed up mess of a hair-raisin sort of loonatic—asylem—darnnation—blamed—town, on this—green—earth's wide foot-stool."

"Jee-whiz! I always thought Kanada was slow and sleepy, but I've changed my mind, and it ain't took more than a century to change it nuther. I allow things have come, and kept a comin' so allfired fast and furious that I be trans-mografied if I know where I'm at, or what I'm a lookin' fur. Whether I be L. R. Pratt, er—er—er that there hairy, hungry sucker without no shirt."

Here Mr. Pratt shoved his hand under his vest and felt himself.

"No, thank goodness, I ain't that pesky critter anyhow. Blame my skin, I believe I'll take the ferry, cross over to Osswegotyee, and sort of cool off gradool, even if the Perkin's mill is shut down tighter an wax, and not earnin' a blessed, durned cent."

CHAPTER XXV.

After Jock Quiggley's collision, he buttoned his coat clear to the chin, and waddled up the street looking at store windows as he went. Gent's Furnishings, he spelled on one.

"Guess this is about the suitablest place for me," and he entered the store.

"Do ye sell shirts here?" he enquired of a clerk who was opening up for the day's business.

"Yes, sir," was the reply. "What kind and size, sir."

"Oh, a done-up one, ave course, with a big sized neck."

The clerk smiled as he opened box after box. Finally Jock made his selection, then asked with a broad grin, if there was any place out of sight where he could put it on.

"Ye see," said Jock "mine was used up on me poor fren what was run over by the cars. Do ye know him?"

The clerk stared at the speaker in blank astonishment, as Jock continued.

"By mighty! he was a terrible sight. Poor feller, and the very best fren I had too. I'd tare up a hundred shirts, and go to my girl's weddin' stark naked if it would cure him enough to know me, and call

me jis plain Jock Quiggley. But the poor feller
can't, and perhaps never will," and Jock heaved a
great sigh.

"What on earth do you mean? Are you crazy?"
asked the astonished clerk.

"No, not quite, but purty nigh," said Jock in a
husky voice. "Haint ye heerd about it?"

"About what," snapped the clerk.

"Why the dead horse, and the dying lawyer."

"Oh, you're off your base. I just came in and have
heard nothing but your delightful gab. Go in the
office there and put on your shirt. You can try
your fool talk on someone else that has more time."
And the clerk started sweeping furiosuly. Jock
looked at him reproachfully, then did as directed.

He appeared to have great trouble with his new
garment, judging by the grunts and smothered ex-
clamations which proceeded from the private office.

The clerk had completed his sweeping, when finally
his strange customer appeared still bearing an injured
air. "Look here, Mr.—Mr.—Quig—something," said
the former, "If you have anything to say that I
can understand, let us have it, but be quick, I'm in
a hurry."

"You'er allfired cranky, and don't deserve to know
nothin', but I don't want to feel mad at nobody this
sad mornin', so I'll tell yer. Now listen. It was
this here way. Me and Dr. Frank Allgood got offin
the early mornin' train. I come to go to my girl's
weddin', as lives down to Smith's Corners, and I
don't know what Frank come fur, but we was glad
to meet."

"Oh," groaned the clerk, "for any sake spit it out."

"You'd better respect your betters better,"

said Jock angrily as he started for the door.　The
young man called him back.

Although he could not make head or tail of his
customer's talk his curiosity was awakened and he
said kindly:

"Please do not be offended, but tell me really
what happened, as briefly as you can."

"You want it short, do ye?" grunted Jock.　"See
if this'll suit yer," then proceeded to gallop through
the following:

"This here happened.　Me and Mike and the Doctor found lawyer Cainsford, an' a dead horse, run
over by the cars.　The lawyer was nigh dead too
but we brung him down on a handcar and took him
to the hospital.　Me and Mike waited till they examined the poor feller; then Dr. Frank told us
that he had a fightin' chance; but didn't know
nothin', and wouldn't for days.　When we couldn't
do no more good we come away.　As we was leavin',
a big baby of a feller that they call Sampson come
awhinin' round for pay fur the horse he said
Mr. Cainsford had stole.　Mike was fur swattin' him,
fur he never onct ast how our poor fren wus, but
threatened he'd take the law on him.　I told him
if he'd shut his big jaw'r I'd pay him fur the dead
horse, if 'twas hisen.　Then he quit, and on the way
up, Mike tole me that poor Cainsford had saved him
from goin' to jail, and got him a job on the Grand
Trunk, and wouldn't take a cent fur all his trouble.
So he wants to help, and me and him is agoin' to
pay for that dead horse if it takes our last dollar,
and never let on to nobody; but it won't take nigh
all mine.　Oh, no, but if it did I'd do it, fur if ever

a livin' man deserves good frens, Chris Cainsford's the one, an—an—say he needs 'em purty—— Yes —Purty—Bad, this Sad, Sorrowful day." And the now sympathetic clerk noticed that the odd looking man's little eyes were very moist as he waddled to the shop door.

As Jock proceeded up the street towards the Central Hotel he was overtaken by two policemen, hurrying along with a large bare-headed man, who was evidently a prisoner. Jock was too much engaged with his own troubles to pay much attention, but he noticed that the big, red faced, wild-eyed man was hand-cuffed. He never for a moment dreamed that the prisoner was the lad he once knew as fatty Barlow, nor that he also was a devoted friend to the injured lawyer. Such was the case, however. The unfortunate Ned was indeed a prisoner, and charged with attempted murder.

CHATPER XXVI.

Ned Barlow's Arrest.

Ned Barlow's arrest came about in this way.
A chambermaid, while doing up her morning's work
at the Royal Exchange Hotel, heard a peculiar
noise in the large room on the upper flat, the door
of which stood slightly ajar. She pushed it open,
and caught sight of Greggson's sprawling form and
bloody face, then throwing up her hands she uttered
a piercing shriek, and fled from the room, down stairs
to the clerk, telling in frightened tones, that a man
had been murdered in room No. 9.

Her shrill scream partly roused big Ned, who was
sleeping off his night's debauch. He was still
muddled, but while peering round and wondering
where he was, his blood-shot eyes rested on Greggson.
He called to him, then staggered over to his side,
and was bending over the prostrate form, with
trembling hands and wondering eyes, when the clerk
and stableman rushed in. They as quickly rushed out
again, fastening the door behind them, and while
poor Ned was wondering what had happened, the
clerk telephoned for the police and started the story
that Customs Officer Greggson was murdered.

The police arrived, made some inquiries, then
entering the room with drawn revolvers, arrested

Barlow, taking no heed to his wild protests of innocence. He presented a pitiful sight as he stood there handcuffed and wild-eyed, vainly trying to explain.

Examination proved that Greggson was still alive. A doctor was sent for, and when he arrived, Ned Barlow was led down the stairs between two policemen. He pled earnestly for a drink to steady his nerves, and when gruffly refused he became angry. The fresh air was stimulating and when they reached the lower floor, Ned suddenly exerted his gigantic strength and hurled his captors from him as though they were children. He made a mad rush through the door, colliding, as we know, with L. R. Pratt, then away he rushed in the direction of the river. His wind only held out for a short spurt, however, he was obliged to stop, and was soon compelled to march through a curious crowd on his way to the lock up. Poor Ned.

*   *   *   *   *   *

The doctor having elevated Greggson's head, and forced some brandy down his throat, said that his was by no means a hopeless case. He discovered, however, that the nose was completely smashed, and unless very carefully looked after while healing, which no doubt would be slow, would prove a terrible disfigurement to the face.

Greggson was very weak from loss of blood, and could not, or would not, give any information with regard to his injuries. He was conveyed to his room at the Central Hotel and left in charge of the landlady. In the afternoon he seemed considerably stronger, and wrote a request to have Mr. Mark P. Stancy come to see him at once.

After a long delay the messenger returned with the information that Mr. Stancy was out of town, having been suddenly called away to visit his mother who was seriously ill.

Upon hearing this news Greggson appeared to go mad. He jumped from his bed, mumbling oaths and curses through his bandages, and while wringing his hands and tearing 'his hair, started his wound to bleed afresh. The frightened messenger called for help, and ran for the doctor. When the latter arrived he told his patient plainly that another such frenzied outburst might cause his death, and that as it was he was almost sure to be disfigured for life.

That night, as Greggson lay sleepless and moaning with pain, he fully realized the truth of the words: *"The way of the transgressor is hard."*

The next morning when the doctor called Gregg's face was so swollen he could scarcely see or speak, but managed to write with trembling hand: "Do you know if Cainsford, the lawyer, was at business yesterday?"

In reply, the doctor told him briefly of Cainsford's accident, that he was still unconscious, and lying at the point of death.

The effect of the statement startled the doctor. The visible portion of Greggson's swollen face expressed such malignant joy that the doctor was dumbfounded, and gravely shook his head, as he felt his patient's pulse. He would have been more astonished could he have read the vindictive wish of the burning brain, or heard the joyous throb of the black heart. As it was he experienced a peculiar thrill of repulsion,and leaving imperative orders, hurried away.

Shortly after his departure, Greggson was alarmed by the appearance of the Chief of Police, who having questioned him, was obliged to be content with nods and shakes of the bandaged head in reply. He then produced a lead pencil scrawl and handed it to Greggson, who read as follows:

IN JAIL, MAY 30.

For God sake, Gregg, tell this gent the truth, for I don't know anything about how you got hurt, so help me, God. They think I done it. Please, for Heaven's sake fix it, and let me get out, for I'm dyin' for a drink.   Your sufferin' comrad,

NED BARLOW.

P.S.—For the sake of old times, Gregg, be quick.

Greggson pondered over Ned's appeal for some time before writing a reply. He thought of accusing Cainsford of attempted murder and robbery, but was afraid if Stancy turned up with the money it might complicate matters.

The Chief's patience was about exhausted when Greggson reluctantly wrote the following:

CENTRAL HOTEL, MAY 30TH, 18—.

TO WHOM IT MAY CONCERN:

Ance Greggson, while in his right mind, does hereby swear emphatically on the Bible, that Ned Barlow had nothing whatever to do with my injuries. I do not accuse any-one; but would like to know where Mark P. Stancy is."

Signed in the presence of the Chief of Police.

ANCE GREGGSON.

It was fortunate for Ned that this statement was obtained. It was the means of securing his prompt release, and of course gave him the opportunity to quench his burning thirst; then he went to the hospital to inquire for his friend, Chris, whom he had heard was dying. Everything was a mystery to him. His astonishment was increased when he met Frank Allgood, who told him all he could, which was not much.

Ned left L—— by the first train, a sadder, but not much wiser man.

Possibly he was more sinned against than sinning, but like many, many others, Ned Barlow was his own worst enemy.

CHAPTER XXVII.

Confession and Faith.

Towards evening of the fourth day after his terrible injury, Cainsford's attentive nurse having lifted his limp hand gently, was feeling the wrist for his pulse when there was a quiver of the eye-lids. A faint sigh escaped from parted lips; another tremble of the lids, then the large lusterless eyes gazed up at the nurse, with vague inquiry.

This was the first sign of returning consciousness, and only lasted a few moments, till again he sank into his former stupor, but the nurse gladly informed Dr. Allgood of the occurrence.

From this time the flashes of returning consciousness became frequent, and were of longer duration. After each he would drift away again into semi-unconsciousness and murmur unintelligibly. This continued for about a week. Then the watchers' hearts were gladdened. One morning, as Dr. Allgood was quietly conversing with Nurse Dean, Cainsford languidly opened his eyes, turned his head slightly, and whispered in a weak voice: "That you, Frank, old man?" Then he endeavored to reach out his thin white hand.

"Oh, Chris, I do thank God to hear you speak once more," said the doctor earnestly.

"Why—what's—the—matter,—Frank?   Where—where am I?"   and a puzzled expression appeared on the wan face.

"Oh, you are in good hands, and doing well, I assure you, don't worry about it, and you will be yourself in a short time.

"But—Frank," said Chris feebly, "Why—am—I here? Who—brought me?"

"I brought you, because you were hurt. I'll tell you all about it as soon as you have a good sleep."

The same puzzled expression again appeared. He drew a long deep breath, raised his wasted hand to his bandaged head, and with a sigh dropped off into the most natural sleep since his accident.

From that morning Cainsford improved more rapidly; but during his waking hours, seemed always puzzling over something. Many, many times the nurse found the large eyes fixed on her face with such a wistful, pleading expression, that she felt a mysterious thrill, and in spite of her self-command, a burning blush would mantle her fair cheek. She would look away wondering why she felt this unexplainable something, so entirely new to her, but could not understand it.

One afternoon while Cainsford was sleeping peacefully she stood leaning over him, unconsciously studying the strong features of his pale face, when suddenly his large dark eyes opened and gazed into hers with such intensity that for the moment she was fascinated, and could not withdraw her glance. There appeared a new joyous light in his brilliant orbs, but it was gradually replaced by a sort of wonderment. The spell seemed broken, as he said with a gasp: "Oh, who—are—you? You are not Flo—nor mother? It seems to me you are an angel. Oh, yes, that is what you are, an angel," and he smiled wanly.

"No, Mr. Cainsford, you are greatly mistaken, I'm not an angel, just a plain girl. Nora Dean is my name."

As she told him, Cainsford started slightly, and whispered:

"Nora—Dean?—Nora Dean—." Again the puzzled expression appeared, and he evidently made a strenuous effort to remember. Then the nurse continued:

"You know your friend, Dr. Allgood, told you all about the accident, and my being appointed as nurse. Don't you remember? There, there, please do not try."

"But—but—" said Cainsford, and he reached out a trembling hand, "Please hold it. I think if you do it will help me to remember."

As she took his hand gently, he whispered softly:
"Nora—Nora—Nora—Nora Dean?—I remember
—yes—I—do—remember—Nora. I—wrote——."
As she listened to the soft tones, she again felt
that mysterious thrill, and her hand burned in his
feeble clasp, then their eyes met in a lingering irresistible gaze, and almost unknown to themselves,
during those brief seconds an undying love was given
birth.

Two days afterwards, Cainsford's mother and sister
came. Dr. Allgood had thought it better not to
inform them of the accident till Chris was out of
danger, as it would only cause them unnecessary
sorrow and anxiety. They could do no possible
good, while the patient was in the unconscious
condition which lasted so long. During the week
they were at L—— they visited him daily, and
their coming appeared to do him good. He became
gradually stronger; his appetite better; and his memory improved. Thus far, however, he could not
recall distinctly any recent events. He had a hazy
recollection, however, that some awful calamity
was in some unexplainable way associated with the
injuries he had sustained. That—was all.

* * * * * * *

The day Cainsford was taken to the hospital,
Toney Tomkins called and inquired for him. When
told of his employer's condition he burst into tears,
and sobbed as if his heart would break; saying
brokenly, that he was to blame. Dr. Allgood was
surprised at his evident distress, but could make
nothing of his mumbled words of self-reproach.
Toney felt that the man Greggson was in some way

accountable for all the trouble, and was nearer the truth than anybody else. He came again the following Monday, and was much excited, saying that a Mr. Pratt was waiting at the office for certain papers he claimed to have left with Mr. Cainsford. When Dr. Allgood questioned his patient, the latter could only say that he thought they were in the safe. Fortunately, however, shortly before his accident he had given his office boy the combination, and Dr. Frank, with Toney's assistance, was enabled to restore the papers to Mr. Pratt.

They were found in the safe, with a filled in mortgage of recent date. In carelessly looking through the document, the Doctor was surprised to find the mortgagee's name to be Miss Nora Dean. He was mystified, for he remembered that she had told him distinctly she had never seen lawyer Cainsford till the morning he had been brought to the hospital. He knew, however, any reference to the subject would only worry his patient, and concluded not to mention it.

At the end of three weeks, Cainsford was able to sit up, but was only the shadow of his former self. His hair had grown quite long, and to the surprise of doctor and nurse, the raven-black locks had turned silvery white at the temples, adding a new interest to the strikingly handsome face.

One afternoon, while sitting on the verandah enjoying the sunshine, Chris heard a brisk step approach; a sinewy hand was extended, and a mellow voice in earnest tones of sympathy, said:

"Why bless me—bless me, how changed you are. I'd scarcely know you."

Then a familiar trumpet was adjusted, and once more Chris Cainsford looked into the honest eyes of George Littlejohn. For a moment the former's face wore a puzzled expression, which had become almost habitual, then a burning blush of shame covered his pale cheeks, and a startled look, akin to fear, shone in his large dark eyes.

Chris Cainsford's truant memory had at last come back to him with overwhelming distinctness. He remembered now having gambled with the money entrusted to him by this kind old gentleman. The knowledge, which came upon him so suddenly while in his weak condition, was too much for him. He groaned, then sobbed like a child. George Littlejohn was, of course, surprised, but attributed the singular outburst to physical weakness entirely, and spoke words of sympathy in his gentlest tones. The words were so earnest and kind that Cainsford's shame and remorse became unbearable. He tremblingly motioned for the trumpet, and poured forth a piteous story of self-condemnation, telling of how, just when he was about to invest the money on splendid terms, he had been induced to gamble with it, and lost every cent. Now he was nothing but a miserable thief, and advised his astonished listener to have him arrested forthwith.

George Littlejohn was so bewildered that he thought of calling the doctor, believing that his niece, Nora, must have been mistaken in the report she had written, informing him that Lawyer Cainsford was nearly well. He thought his injuries had left him mentally deranged, but as the heart-broken recital continued, he concluded that it certainly was the outpouring of a guilty conscience, rather than the babbling caused by a brain diseased; for poor Chris, with his handsome face half hidden as he bent over the ear trumpet, continued to sob forth in trembling tones the sad story of the growth and development of his great weakness. The naturally proud, clever young man, presented a striking example of the tremendous power the passion for gambling has over its victim. It was pathetic in the extreme and wrung the heart-strings of honest George Littlejohn, as he sat with bated breath, striving to hear the broken words.

Then Cainsford's great form trembled from head to foot as he cried:

"Oh, Mr. Littlejohn,—I am truly a miserable man, and the fact that I realize fully my own degradation adds ten-fold to my suffering. For heaven's sake have me arrested. There is no palliation in the remembrance that I was cheated in the game. The seclusion of a prison cell may possibly destroy the mad passion which has destroyed me. Thank God father does not know that the son he loved, and did so much for, is a poor miserable thief." And great sobs burst from Cainsford's heaving breast, and tears of sympathy poured down George Littlejohn's ruddy face, as he said tenderly:

"Do not despair, it is never too late to mend. You come of too good stock to allow such a weakness to degrade you. You are young and clever, and can soon earn the money. Do not gamble any more. Your father's God is able to deliver. Put your trust in him, and go to work, remembering the words of the psalmist: "Thou has delivered my soul from death. Wilt not Thou deliver my feet from falling? What time I am afraid I will trust in Thee." Do it, my dear lad, trust him fully, and let the loss of the money remain a secret between Jeremiah Cainsford's son, and Jeremiah Cainsford's friend."

"But your niece, Miss Dean," groaned Cainsford. "I feel that her devotion has saved my miserable life, and I love her. Oh, I love her with all my heart. How can I look into her pure face, and beautiful eyes, knowing that I robbed her. Oh, Mr. Littlejohn, my punishment is greater than I can bear."

Convulsive trembling followed, then silence, finally broken by the voice of Mr. Littlejohn, in his brisk, business-like tone:

"Look here! I'll tell you what I'll do. I'll place the amount you lost to Nora's credit in the bank. You can consider it a loan to yourself at six per cent until you pay the principal. If you do not gamble, and work hard, it won't take long, and in this way she will be the gainer by two or three per cent."

Cainsford looked at the old gentleman in bewildered astonishment. The expression changed, and the pale handsome face shone with a great gratitude. He seized the other's hand and in tearful tones, spoke into the trumpet.

"I'll—never—never—forget your kindness. Thank God for such a friend as George Littlejohn."

CHAPTER XXVIII.

"I Love You, Nora, With All My Heart."

From the day of George Littlejohn's visit, Cainsford improved rapidly, and was soon able to take long walks. Dr. Allgood had established himself permanently at L——, already he was a general favorite, and had secured quite a practice. He looked after Cainsford with assiduous care, and at last consented to allow him to return to business.

As Cainsford was about to leave the hospital, the doctor called Nurse Dean and requested her to bid their troublesome patient good-bye. Then laughing his quiet laugh, hurried away with great strides, leaving nurse and patient alone and facing each other. As their eyes met, Cainsford's face flushed, then grew pale. His large eyes filled with the light of a great love, then dropping his noble head, he trembled like a leaf. When Nora looked into his eyes, her beautiful face flushed with a burning glow, yet the violet lustrous eyes never wavered till he lowered his head. Then she whispered softly: "Good-bye, Mr. Cainsford, good-bye."

As the meaning of the gentle words found lodgment in Cainsford's brain he lost control of himself, and held out his arms, as he said with trembling lips:

"Oh, Nora—Nora—, I must speak. I am not worthy, but I love you. I love you with all my heart."

The burning words thrilled through Nora like an electric shock, and a great joy shone in her lovely face, almost unconsciously she came closer to him and murmured in low sweet tones: "Oh—Chris, Oh, Chris."

The softly spoken words filled Cainsford with such joyous delight, that he cast restraint to the winds. His long arms encircled her shy graceful form.   He drew her to him, looked into her violet eyes, and as he met their glance, and felt her soft arms about his neck, he kissed her golden hair, her flushed brow; and as he whispered: "My heart's darling," their lips met in a burning, lingering kiss of thrilling ecstasy.   Then as he held her from him and gazed into her blushing face, Chris said in low intense tones:

"Oh, Nora, darling, this is the happiest day of my life.   I am not worthy, no, no,—not worthy to hold you thus, but God helping me I will become worthy, darling.   I only ask you not to forget that I will always love and live for you alone."

Tears gushed from Nora's luminous eyes, and the long dark lashes trembled, as she whispered brokenly:

"Oh, Chris, my love, you know I never, never will forget. This seals my promise," and with shy bewitching grace she pressed her trembling lips to his.

Then for a while was silence only broken by low sighs of love.   At last, gently releasing his enfolding arms, she whispered, each word dripping o'er with a joyous tear:

"I know you will be good, when I love you so."

"Oh, my darling you are so pure and I so unworthy, I do not deserve your love, but heaven helping me, I will."

He raised his arm aloft, and again whispered earnestly:

"Heaven help me from this hour to do the right."

"Heaven will help you. Now, good-bye, and God be with you."

Having uttered these short fervent words, with the light of a great love shining in her beautiful eyes and tear-stained face, Nora glided from the room.

* * * * * * *

As Cainsford walked briskly to his office he felt that he was certainly the happiest man in the world, and oh, what a beautiful world it was. Never had the sunshine seemed so bright. Never had the trees and grass looked so green nor the sky so blue. The balmy breeze seemed to murmur, "Nora loves, Nora loves you." The rustling leaves seemed to whisper the same sweet secret, and the birds to have heard it, and were glad, for their warbling was charged with notes of light-hearted joy. As they trilled in wild sweet tones, Cainsford thought he could hear through the refrain, "Nora loves you, Nora loves you. Oh, beautiful Nora."

No wonder his face shone with happiness. No wonder the light of a noble resolve was in his eyes; a resolve to do the right at any cost. He determined to win back his good name and to earn the lost money, feeling that he could accomplish anything, or be anything, for the sake of the beautiful girl who had given him her love. It certainly was a powerful incentive, and he set about his work, concentrating all his energies to accomplish the end in view.

: : : : : : : : :

No one knew how glad Toney Tomkins was to have his employer back. He was somewhat startled, however, when the latter asked him if he knew anything about Customs Officer Greggson. Toney hesitated, then produced a local paper of recent date, and pointing to an item, headed "MISSING," handed the paper to Cainsford, who was astonished to read as follows:

"MISSING"

" It was reported in this town today that when a government official endeavoured to interview Customs Officer Greggson he was not to be found. Rumor has it that the substitute who was sent to relieve Greggson at the time he was laid up, after receiving the mysterious injuries (already mentioned in our columns) the former discovered certain letters in the safe, purporting to come from persons engaged in smuggling on a large scale. The contents of these letters led to the conclusion that Officer Greggson has been in league with a gang of smugglers, and has taken advantage of his position to defraud the government for personal gain. The fact that he is missing certainly suggests that he must be afraid to face an investigation and his sudden disappearance seems like a tacit acknowledgemen of guilt. A singular thing which may have some connection with the Greggson case, is the fact that M. P. Stancy, Church Organist, has never been seen in L—— since the morning Greggson was found lying unconscious in an upper room of the Royal Exchange. The cause of Greggson's condition at that time remains as great a mystery as ever. The two men were considered great friends."

While reading the above article, Cainsford's face hardened, then a bitter smile appeared, as he re-read it.

Up to this time he had had a faint hope that there was a chance of getting back a portion of the money he had been robbed of. What he read in the paper destroyed this hope utterly. He tried his best to forget it, and set to work in earnest, sorting papers, and looking into affairs.

:　　:　　:　　　:　　:　　　:　　:　　:

From the day he left the hospital to take up the routine of business, Cainsford's efforts met with unalloyed success. Fortune seemed to smile on him, and at the end of eighteen months, came the crowning event of his life, namely, his marriage to the beautiful Nora Dean.

Just before the ceremony, in the presence of her Uncle George, Cainsford handed Nora a beautiful little case, which contained securities in her own name for two thousand one hundred and eighty dollars. The case also contained a perfumed note on which was written:

Dear Nora;

Receive the enclosed as a token of the esteem in which you were held by your loving cousin,

JERRY LITTLEJOHN.

Before she had time to open the case Chris produced a check already filled in for two thousand and sixty dollars, and requested Nora to sign it. She complied wonderingly, and handed it to Chris with a shy blush. The latter gave the check to Mr. Littlejohn, as he said:

"This is yours, my dear friend, and with it accept my heartfelt thanks for your great kindness to me, the day I needed a friend so much."

Tears were in his honest grey eyes as the old gentleman said brokenly:

"I knew you would do it, my lad. I knew you would do it. My prayers have been answered, and I am a happy man this day."

As Christopher Cainsford, barrister, and Nora Dean, nurse, stood up to be joined in the holy bonds of matrimony, there was a subdued murmur of admiration from hundreds of well-wishers who thronged the crowded church; and while walking down the long aisle as husband and wife they were followed by scores of admiring eyes, for a handsomer couple could not be found.

While boarding the Steamer "Rosthey," known as the grey hound of the St. Lawrence, showers of rice poured about them, and a great cheer went up, as they steamed away on their honeymoon trip, o'er the blue waters of "Old St. Lawrence."

CHAPTER XXIX.

Dr. Allgood and a Happy Home.

Time rolls on, and we will now ask the reader to accompany Dr. Frank Allgood, as he hurries down the main street of L——. It is the evening of the fourth anniversary of Chris and Nora's wedding. Little change is noticeable in the good doctor's appearance. He is a trifle less gaunt, perhaps, but his strides are just as long, and his feet just as large as they were four years ago, when he wishes God's speed to the handsome couple as they sailed away. He has just returned from a two weeks' visit to his boyhood home, and his face wears a happy expectant smile as he turns up Church Street, walks half a block, and stops in front of a tasty cottage, the verandah of which is half concealed by clinging vines.

As the doctor pauses before this cozy house, which is the Cainsford home, the sound of music and childish laughter greets his ear, wafted by the gentle breeze through the open window. He rings the bell, but before a trim little rosy-cheeked maiden has time to open, he is through the door and in the hall. She smiles and gives him words of welcome, in soft tones, with an Irish accent.

"Yes, sor, Mr. Cainsford is in," she says in reply to a question. "And they are having great fun wid Pilot."

Then as the drawing-room door is swung open, he hears clapping of little hands, and shouts of childish merriment, mingled with the musical notes of piano and violin.

So intent on the pleasure of the hour are the group before him, that they fail to notice the tall form in the doorway, and he has sufficient time to observe the details of a most pleasing picture. The central figure is a large, loose, long-haired, sienna-colored setter pup, or young dog, if that be more respectful. For if we watch him perform, we will at once say he is deserving of both praise and respect.

With head up and tongue lolling out, he swings round and round the room, and while holding his long length erect, moves his big hairy feet in perfect time to the sweet waltz music. While listening we are convinced that the players are accomplished musicians.

As the long-limbed Pilot continues to waltz we notice that his rich brilliant eyes are ever directed toward the violinist, with a blinking glow of love and adoration in their luminous depths, and we feel like joining the little girl in her glee and hand-claps, as she toddles after the revolving mass of shining tawn-colored hair, while shouting shrilly: "Dear, dood, dog Pilo! Dood dog Pilo."

The music becomes faster, and the tall man at the door knods his curly red head, while every lineament of his clean-shaven face expresses proud delight, then as with a grand crash of melody, the music stops, and with a final flourish of the bushy tail, the panting dog comes down on all fours, the doctor does clap his long freckled hands, and shouts in a rich deep voice: "Well done, boy Pilot. Well done all."

At sound of the great voice, glad surprise is seen in the happy faces of the little group. The musicians seize his hands, and shout boisterous words of welcome. Then the little girl rushes to his out-stretched arms, and as he seats himself, nestles in his lap, while Pilot barks joyous notes of recognition.

"Oh, doctor, we are so delighted to have you back," says Nora. "Our anniversary would not be complete without you."

"That is a positive fact, old man," says Chris.

"I's dlad too, Dodo," coos the little girl.

As he answers and asks numerous questions, Dr. Frank looks as though he was certainly as glad to be present, as his host and hostess are to have him. He looks into the face of each, and considers it an honor to be called their friend. Nora's full, beautifully rounded form, is more matronly than it was four years ago, and there is an expression of tenderness and subdued joy, only to be seen in the face of a loving, devoted wife and mother. Her golden hair in shining waves, gives a sort of halo to the rounded beauty of rosy cheeks and dimpled chin. The long dark lashes and arching brows are in striking contrast to the gleaming color in her rippling hair, adding to the luster of her violet eyes, and increasing the fascinating charm of her expressive face.

The face reflects a pure soul, a glad heart, and contented mind, and suggests strong individuality, and noble character; character that would remain steadfast and true in the hour of trouble or adversity, and if called upon would be capable of heroic acts of self-sacrifice for, and unwavering faith, in those she loved.

These were the impressions Dr. Frank Allgood received as he studied Mrs. Chris Cainsford on the evening of the fourth anniversary of her wedding day.

What about her husband? Has four years of married life changed Chris Cainsford? No, not much. He is more comfortably corpulent, and the hair at the temples is, if anything, whiter, but he seems as young as ever, and is certainly a remarkably handsome man. He has been almost a model husband. Only twice durng the years has his passion for play got the better of him, and at each time the seductive demon was vanquished by Nora's forgiving care and tactful kindness.

There are three members of the Cainsford home with whom the reader is but slightly acquainted. They require a brief description, and we will begin with the smallest.

Little Helen Cainsford has just passed her third birthday. She is the constant joy of the household, and beloved by all who meet her. She bears an undefined resemblance to both parents, and still does not look very much like either. Dr. Allgood calls her "Sunbeam." Truly an appropriate name, for she scatters joy and brightness wherever she goes. Her old-fashioned sayings and sweet ways are perhaps more to be admired than her cherubic beauty.

She is idolized by her father, cherished by her mother, worshipped by the doctor, adored by Maggie, watched over by Pilot, and fondled and petted by all. She seems to possess a God-given gift for music. Her ability to pick up and remember the air of any piece she hears is phenomenal; and she goes about singing all the day. Her favorites are two familiar sacred songs, namely, "Into a Tent where a Gipsy Boy Lay," and "Papa Come this Way." Her mother has taught her the words of these, and if, as is often the case, her father accompanies the sweet childish voice by mellow chords on his violin, the effect is most pleasing and pathetic.

The fact that little Helen cannot speak the words plainly, only gives an added charm of plaintive tenderness to their meaning. She has been told the story of the fisherman who, being lost in the fog, was guided to safety by the voice of his little child calling from the shore. "Papa! come this way." Remembering the story, when she sings the song which bears that name, she does it so earnestly, that one would think she understood the meaning of every word. Then as she starts the chorus, she will invariably fix her large trustful eyes on her father's face, and sing with angelic sweetness. "Papa!—tome—iss—way. Papa!—tome—iss—way. A lil voice—talls—from—at—shoea. Papa!—tome—iss—way."

At the conclusion of the song Cainsford usually showers kisses upon the little sweet-faced singer, and the watchful Nora sees moisture in her husband's dark eyes, as he whispers tenderly: "Now sing the "Gipsy Boy" for papa. Will you, Sunbeam?"

The next member of the Cainsford family we will endeavour to describe, was given the name of "Pilot" the day Dr. Allgood brought him as a present to little Sunbeam, about four months previous to the evening in question. His master had given him careful training during this time, and now he cannot only waltz to music, as we have seen, but fetch and carry, act soldier, play leapfrog over chairs, sit up, nod yes and no, bow, and do many other tricks too numerous to mention.   He is perhaps the happiest inmate of the happy home.   His father was a thoroughbred Irish setter.   His mother a thoroughbred English setter. The man from whom the doctor purchased him claimed that he was half-brother to the famous trotting dog "Dock," although that illustrious setter could number his friends and admirers by hundreds of thousands, and was deserving of greatest praise from all—still he might well be proud to own relationship and call Pilot brother, for a more clever, faithful, steadfast friend than he proved himself to be, man nor dog, never had.

What does he look like?   Well, as we have said, he is long, loose, tall, with powerful limbs.   His honest face and broad brow has a narrow strip of white running from his black muzzle back between the long silky ears, terminating in a band of soft silvery hair which encircles his neck.   Paws and forelegs are white half way to the knee.   White hair also divides, in shining waves, from the centre of his broad breast, and tips his bushy tail.   The muscular form is covered by masses of rich, sienna colored glossy hair, which reflects a golden glow when in strong light. His eyes are beautiful, but hard to describe.   They are deep, true, trustful, with a touch of mystery in ethir luminous depths.   His varying moods cause them to sparkle, glimmer, or burn, in ever-changing color.

As he gazes into his master's face after the waltz, they are filled with an expression of adoration, and the silken ears are raised in seeming expectancy,then as he hears these words of praise, "Good lad," "Well done, Pilot," he wags his silver-tipped tail in proud delight, and licks the hand of the man he loves. His greatest joy is to be with his master, but if left in charge of little Sunbeam, he accepts the responsibility with knightly grace, and never lets her out of his sight.

We will refer briefly to one other member of the Cainsford home. A trim comely little maiden, of about twelve summers. Her good qualities are many, and can be summed up in a few words. She is generous, kind-hearted, witty and clever. An ideal little servant who was taught to love and reverence the name of Cainsford before she ever saw the man who bore it. Her parents, Mike and Maggie Murphy, are proud of their daughter, and proud of the place she occupies in the Cainsford home.

CHAPTER XXX.

An Operation Saves Pilot:

You may be sure Dr. Allgood did not come empty-handed on that anniversary evening, but brought presents for all. Among the many was a large, clear, glass allie. In its centre, with extended wings, was poised the form of a white dove. This allie seemed to please Helen most of all, and it was a mystery to her how the dove got inside the glass. After asking many questions, she started to roll it across the carpeted floor; and while her parents and Dodo, as she called her tall friend, are talking of old times, she and Pilot are doing great things with the allie.

"Now do det it, Pilo," she would shout, as it rolled away, hurled by her chubby hand.

If the willing dog did not drop it at her feet, she would thrust her little paddie into his capacious mouth, and haul it out, while she gabbled: "Oo'r a dood doggie, lil Pilo. E'll done lil addie."

Then again she would roll the allie. As this continued, Pilot became excited and let the slippery thing fall frequently. Cainsford noticed this, and in a tone of reproach said: "Pilot be more careful. Shame on you, lad."

The sensitive dog had just secured the round, heavy, illusive thing as his master spoke. It evidently rolled in his mouth, and in his eagerness to hold it, he made a sudden snap, and the allie was gone. Pilot gulped and licked his chops in bewildered astonishment, then turned his honest face, and looked into his master's eyes with a mute inquiry:

"By George, Frank, as I live, Pilot has swallowed your present."

"Surely not," said the doctor, and a slight shade of anxiety appeared on his strong face.

"He has, indeed. Will it hurt him, do you think?"

"Hard to say. The allie is large, but a dog's stomach can handle almost anything that enters it, and I think Pilot's will succeed in this case."

Little Helen scolded Pilot for eating Dodo's present, and for a time was quite vexed with her hairy playmate, but before going to bed made it all up and was as merry as ever.

As Dr. Frank was leaving for home he asked Chris
to watch Pilot carefully, and if he noticed signs of
distress to let him know.   For three days the setter
seemed about as usual, with the exception of a partial
loss of appetite.   On the morning of the fourth, however, Cainsford wondered to find that he did not come
from his bed in the shed with his usual alacrity—on
the contrary, he came with drooping tail and staggering steps, but managed by a great effort to reach his
side and lick his hand; then crouching at his master's
feet, lay his head along his paws, fixed pain-stamped
eyes on his master's face, and whined pitifully.

An urgent message was at once sent to Dr. Allgood,
who was soon at hand.   He made a hasty examination, and gave Pilot a powerful emetic, which brought
on violent vomiting.   It did not relieve the suffering
dog in the least, however.   Then injections were
resorted to with no better result.   For two hours
the sympathetic doctor and anxious master labored
to relieve the misery of poor, patient Pilot, but without avail.

During this time the dog's wistful pleading eyes
scarcely left his master's face.   It was pathetic in
the extreme, and wrung Cainsford's heart.   Pilot's
agony was so great that his tawny coat quivered, and
his powerful frame was doubled up in convulsive
throes.   After each of these, he would raise his honest
face, fix soft lurid eyes on his master, with an unspoken prayer in their rich hazel depths, then moan
plaintively.

"Oh, for heaven's sake, Frank, can nothing be done
to relieve his misery," said Chris with trembling lips.

"I think the only thing is to perform an operation,"

was the doctor's reply. "Symptoms indicate that the allie has passed through the pyloric end of the stomach, causing an obstruction, which, if not removed, must prove fatal."

As Cainsford heard the words, his face became set and grey, and he asked brokenly:

"Can it be removed, Frank, and will the operation save his life?"

"It is certainly a very serious operation, and much easier said than done, but if gangrene has not already set in, and we are extremely careful, the operation may possibly save the poor chap's life, but we will require to act promptly. You notice he has lost the use of his hind legs entirely. Oh, how sorry I am for bringing Sunbeam that treacherous allie. If Pilot dies, it will just about break the poor lamb's soft little heart. She loves him so."

"Then for heaven's sake let us save him. I love him too, yes, I do," and Cainsford sadly shook his head.

"At present he is suffering terribly," said Frank. "I think a hypodermic injection of morphia will deaden the pain and keep him quiet till I can get my instruments."

While speaking the doctor proceeded to carry out his own suggestion. Then, having administered the morphia, he rushed away.

After his departure Pilot tried to drag himself a little closer to the man he worshipped. He gazed for a few moments on Cainsford's anxious face with an intense look of love and devotion; then seemingly the morphia stupified him, for the trembling lids closed, and with a moaning whimper the dog dropped his head and lay powerless, breathing heavily, while his master sat in heartfelt sorrow watching Pilot's struggles for breath, and anxiously listening for the doctor's returning footfall. It seemed hours before it came, and oh, what a relief.

The latter set to work with careful haste. His deft fingers formed a cone, using a newspaper for the purpose. Having moistened a sponge in warm water, he wrung it out, and inserted it into the cone, at the small end of which was left an opening to allow the passage of air. The doctor was careful to see that the sponge was well up before pouring chloroform over it. It was necessary, of course, to leave space for Pilot's long nose.

In the meantime Cainsford had succeeded in arranging a muzzle, by placing a strap around the dog's jaws, and carrying it behind the ears. It was a wise precaution, for when the chloroform had partially taken effect, Pilot became like a mad dog, and struggled so fiercely that plucky Maggie Murphy was called to assist. His frantic craze did not last for long, however. The spasmodic wriggles gradually ceased, till with a low whimper, he lay still in complete unconsciousness.

No time was lost. With steady hand Dr. Allgood made an incision beginning at the ensiform cartilege, or at lower end of breast bone. His long flexible hand was then thrust into the opening, and soon located the allie. It was about six inches from the pyloric end of stomach, and slightly to the right, in what is called the duodenum. This was carefully drawn to the opening, and dressing forceps adjusted at either side of allie. Then the skillful operator with quick-moving deft fingers made a longitudinal cut, and the cause of all Pilot's suffering was revealed and quickly removed.

"Thank God," said Cainsford, who had been a sorrowful, but greatly interested assistant, during the delicate operation.

"We are not through, yet," said the doctor, as with supple, firm fingers he began sewing up the opening. The strain of concentrated effort was quite manifest in his strong face and perspiring brow. How very, very careful he was, in closing the slight cut he had made so quickly, and well he might be for a noble dog's life was at stake. However, it was soon finished. Every stitch examined carefully, and forceps removed. Then followed the closing and sewing of the external opening. This done, with a great sigh of relief, the doctor wiped his streaming face, as he said earnestly:

"There, Chris, I have done my best for the poor brute, and if he is not allowed to have anything but liquids for the next ten or twelve days, I have every reason to believe he will recover, for dog-life is very tenacious."

When the doctor had washed and carefully put away his instruments, Cainsford grasped his hand, and said earnestly:

"This is only another addition, Frank, to the huge debt of gratitude I owe you, which, I fear, I will never be able to repay."

"Do not for a moment think of it," replied the doctor. "Why, Chris, if Pilot comes round all O. K. I will be repaid a hundred fold, and it will be a feather in our caps well worth publishing. I never before had the opportunity of performing so delicate an operation, and think of the pleasure it will afford to know that we have saved a good dog's life."

While the friends were speaking Pilot showed signs of returning consciousness,and in one hour and fifteen minutes from the time the hypodermic injection was given, he was able to again lick his master's hand and gaze into his face with an expression of everlasting love and fidelity in his soft honest eyes.

We are glad to be able to tell you that he recovered fully, and became the more devoted to his friends and master.

CHAPTER XXXI.

Music, Women and Wine.

About six months after the occurrences recorded in the last chapter, lawyer Cainsford won a very important suit in which certain American capitalists were deeply interested. For weeks previous to the hearing of the case Cainsford had been so absorbed by it that he worked almost day and night. Of course, the mental strain was very great. When at length the law suit was brought to a termination, and he won a decision in favor of his American clients, the young lawyer was much gratified.

During the four and a half years of married life his business had developed and prospered exceedingly.

However, he felt that the victory won in this important case was the crowning effort in his professional career. He was justly proud of the achievement. Not only because of the substantial amount he received for his services, but also because of the far-reaching advantages which would naturally accrue from the fact of winning, against odds so to speak, a case which awakened so much public interest.

After it was won and the strain removed, there naturally followed a mental collapse, and Cainsford felt the need of change and rest. No wonder he was pleased to receive an invitation from one of his clients, urging him to bring his wife and little girl to visit him at his home at Rochester. It so chanced that a day or two previously Nora had written her Aunt Nellie Littlejohn, that Helen, Pilot and herself would visit her girlhood home for a couple of weeks.

Considerable discussion followed, in which Nora urged Chris to accept the invitation to visit Rochester. while she went to the country. Affirming that she would much prefer it to going among strangers. "Besides," said she, "Aunt Nellie is very lonely, and will be so disappointed if little Helen does not go out to cheer her up."

At last Cainsford somewhat reluctantly consented to comply with Nora's strongly expressed wish, and three days later bade his loved ones good-bye.

*   *   *   *   *   *

Upon his arrival in the beautiful city of Rochester, he was met by his friend Mr. Frederic Allen, who drove him to his palatial home and at once introduced him to his wife, who was a very beautiful woman and a leader in Rochester's fashionable society.

It was quite evident that Mrs. Allen was both surprised and impressed by Cainsford's distinguished appearance.   The silvery white locks at his temples, in such striking contrast to the balance of his hair which rolled back in raven black waves from his face, could not help but attract attention.   His brilliant dark eyes also added their quota to his appearance of striking individuality.

Mrs. Allen noticed these points with one glance of her soft eyes, and her effusive words of welcome were accompanied by a look of decided approval.   "This green Canuck that Fred said was coming turns out to be about the handsomest man I have ever seen," was her mental comment, as she gracefully extended her shapely hand.

Her husband, Frederic Allen, was an off-hand, generous, cultured, wealthy American gentleman, with strong likes and dislikes.   He had taken a great fancy to our handsome Chris at their first meeting. His friendship was cemented by the masterly way the young lawyer handled the recent case.   He was aware that his wife, (who was a New York belle before her marriage), had an undefined prejudice against anything Canadian, probably owing to the fact of her absolute ignorance of either country or people.

He thought to give her a little surprise, and had consequently left the impression that Cainsford was merely a struggling lawyer he wished to encourage. Mrs. Allen, of course, drew her own conclusions, and expected that their coming guest would naturally seem out of place in society, and of course show greenness and the lack of culture and breeding.   Her husband evidently enjoyed the surprise Cainsford's appearance gave, and during the conversation which followed did his best to draw the young lawyer out, and make him feel that he was indeed a welcome guest.

Cainsford's coming was the prelude to a round of pleasure in which, backed up by the esteem he was evidently held by the influential Allens, and his own superior personality, he soon became the lion of the day and was made much of. Mrs. Allen appeared proud to have him for escort as she took daily drives among the elegance and fashion of her home city. She even had the temerity to inform her good-natured spouse, that it was well for him that he had secured her before she met this noble, handsome Canadian Knight.

Her admiration for Cainsford was perhaps increased because of the fact that he, although always kind, courteous and brilliant company, never indulged in the exaggerated flattery Mrs. Allen's numerous gentlemen friends usually showered upon her. Possibly she felt a slight tinge of womanly pique because of his apparent lack of appreciation for her great beauty and fascinating charms. If she had had the power to peep into a capacious drawing-room belonging to a commodious Canadian farm house at Smith's Corners, she would probably have guessed the cause, for she could have seen a beautiful golden-haired woman enjoying the antics of a large setter, as he romped and played in proud protecting delight with a lovely little girl of about four years of age. Mrs. Allen could not see this beautiful picture, but what she did see and had noticed frequently, was the fact that Cainsford abstained entirely from the use of intoxicants. It seemed odd; for to her a dinner was not complete without a glass of wine.

The good lady determined that some time she would test him and possibly discover the reason.

Upon a certain disagreeable afternoon, Mrs. Allen persuaded the gentlemen to remain in after luncheon to help entertain her niece and another friend from Buffalo, promising them a musical treat, as her niece was an accomplished vocalist as well as pianist. The gentlemen willingly consented, and were not disappointed. Miss Howard possessed a pure soprano voice of wondrous power and sweetness. The singing was a rare treat for Cainsford, and he was profuse with words of praise.

As the dark-eyed singer accepted his compliments, she said quietly: "I think, Mr. Cainsford, you must certainly be musical yourself. Will you not favor us?"

"I am passionately fond of music," said he, "and I have an old violin at home which I sometimes try to play, but even if I had it here, an effort on my part would seem very tame indeed following the rare treat you have just given us."

"Oh, I do love the violin," said the vivacious Miss Howard, "and really I envy those who can play it."

"By the way, Uncle Fred, have you not a violin famous for its age and tone?"

"That I have, Miss Howard, and if friend Cainsford can play upon it as successfully as he plays upon the hearts and minds of judge and jury, it will only add to the old fiddle's fame to have him draw its bow."

Having delivered this very pronounced compliment, with an elaborate bow, Mr. Allen left the room.

He soon returned, and with another bow, placed a worn violin in Cainsford's hands. At first the latter seemed abashed, and tried to excuse himself, but as he did so, almost unconsciously tuned it, and knew at once that the old violin possessed a tone of marvellous quality. Unthinkingly he drew the bow across the strings with a lingering sweep of his long arm. The melody produced thrilled him with such delight that he was compelled to continue, and as he played he appeared to become entirely fascinated, and produced such soul-stirring chords that the listeners were spell-bound, and the player apparently lost in a delicious oblivion. Then a quavering, swelling melody rolled from the violin, as if the common-place looking instrument possessed some hidden witchery, never before discovered.

Never had Cainsford held such a violin; never had he produced such music. He was completely carried away by it. He forgot himself and his audience. His handsome face shone with a sort of indescribable inspiration. His broad chest heaved. His dark eyes glowed and sparkled in varying hues as the intoxicating melody rose and fell in bewitching notes of harmony. When at last he ceased, the air of the room seemed to still vibrate and re-echo with sweet cadence. Then followed moments of silence, broken by Mr. Allen, who said admiringly:

"By Jove, Cainsford, you are a wonder. I have heard music before, but never anything so bewilderingly captivating. When law fails, you have a fortune at your finger tips, if you can play in public as you have played for us. Where in the world did you study?"

"Only in Canada, my dear sir, with a German professor; but I do not deserve your praise. You forget the violin.   Why, I never drew a bow on anything like it.   It is almost capable of playing itself, and fairly bewitched me."

While Cainsford was speaking Mrs. Allen's beautiful eyes rested on him with absorbing interest, as she said tremulously:

"Oh, Mr. Cainsford, if the violin bewitched you you certainly bewitched your hearers.   You are certainly a wonderful performer."

"Yes, indeed," said Miss Howard.   "I want to thank you for the unexpected pleasure you have given," and she extended a soft white hand.

Here again Mr. Allen burst out with: "By George, Cainsford, I'll crack a bottle of my best champagne in honor of your performance."

While he was giving an order to the servant, Mrs. Clair, the Buffalo widow, extended a fleshy hand, and said patronizing:

"Your playing is very fine, for sure, but as you say there is a great deal in the quality of a violin. Of course, all musical instruments made in the United States are considered superior."

"And so are American ladies," said Cainsford, with a smile to Mrs. Allen, and a bow to the red-faced widow.

Just then the wine was brought in, and Mrs. Allen rose as she said:

"Allow me to have the honor of serving the illustrious violinist," and she poured out a large glass of the sparkling wine and handed it to Cainsford, who hesitated before accepting, and said falteringly:

"I very seldom indulge.   Will you kindly excuse me this time?" and he returned the untasted glass to the tray.

"I do not believe I can," she said somewhat re-proachfully, as she looked at him with a dreamy admiring radiance in the hazel depths of her lovely eyes.

"I want to again congralutate you, and drink your health. How exquisite it will be to have such music as you can furnish on board the yacht, but I forgot you have not been informed. However, you will be soon. In the meantime (again she handed Cainsford the wine) please drink success to the voyage of the Gladys, the yacht my husband named after me."

While Cainsford still hesitated, Mrs. Clair said, with a suggestion of mockery in her tone, "Perhaps Mr. Cainsford is not altogether familiar with society customs. Perhaps they do not drink wine in Canada, or perhaps he is a teetotaler," saying which she smiled broadly.

"Oh, Mrs. Clair, I am sure you are entirely mistaken," spoke up Miss Howard. "I know one who plays the violin so divinely is not afraid of an innocent glass wine."

"I am sure," said Mr. Allen. "If you ladies will but give the poor man a chance, he will gladly drink my wife's toast, when he knows that the proposed trip to Alexandria Bay is gotten up in his honor. Besides I only offer a glass of this famous vintage to very particular friends."

Cainsford felt that it would seem boorish to offer further objection. He rose and with a graceful bow touched Mrs. Allen's glass, as he murmured earnestly:

"May our anticipated voyage be all joy and gladness and Mrs. Allen's voyage through life be ever the same."

Then raising the wine, with a burning blush, Cainsford drank almost greedily. As he replaced the empty glass, he felt a thrill of shame and knew he had fallen; knew that the promise made to his beautiful, trusting, loving Nora was broken.

Oh, why had he not been man enough to explain and tell them that it was dangerous for him to drink even one glass of wine? For five minutes he despised his own weakness. Then, as he felt the effects of the seductive beverage he wanted more. The unspoken desire was so manifest that Mrs. Allen replenished his glass, as she said merrily: "I thought its flavor would warm your heart."

"It could not do otherwise, coming from so fair a hand." And Cainsford's brilliant dark eyes looked into hers with a new sparkle in their dusky depths which caused the lady to blush vividly.

A short time afterwards when Mrs. Clair proposed a little game of her favorite draw bluff, there was no dissenting voice, and Cainsford joined the game with such marked avidity that Frederic Allen smiled and murmured to himself. "This young handsome Canadian is not so refreshingly innocent AFTER ALL."

CHAPTER XXXII.

Cainsford quickly discovered that his tenacious enemy, "*Passion for play*," had only been slumbering. No sooner had his strong armour of total abstinence been removed than it came upon him. The tempting sparkling wine had disarmed him, leaving him helpless before the fierce onslaught of the treacherous monster, which was now wide awake. It surged through and filled him with an irresistible craving which carried all before it. He could not rally his forces to offer even a weak resistance before he was down. It seemed as though, during the five years of his enemy's comparative subjugation, it had been quietly rallying its forces, and now made the attack when its victim was least expecting it.

No wonder the temptation was stronger than half intoxicated reason. Why, it was stronger than *love*, and Cainsford was borne away as if upon the bosom of a vast, impetuous, irrestible flood.

True, the game which immediately followed, with the party of five, was altogether genteel, and at the time seemed next to harmless, as they played merely for pastime, and only a fifty cent limit. Of its far-reaching effects, not one of the animated players dreamed for a moment. Alas, in the case of the one with whom we are most interested, the train of events which that seemingly innocent game of draw poker set in motion was as far reaching as eternity.

The little game played in the beautiful room of that palatial home was to Chris Cainsford like a spoonful of cool water given to a man dying of thirst. It only produced a mad ungovernable longing for more Nothing would satisfy the greed of his ravenous disease . but play—play—play.

During the days which followed, before starting on the proposed trip, if opportunities were not forthcoming at the Allen home, Cainsford sought them elsewhere, regardless of the run of luck his passion to gamble remained paramount. He almost forgot his beautiful wife and lovely child in his useless efforts to satiate the horrible craving of the glutenous monster.

All other pleasures palled upon him. Even when on board the Gladys, Mr. Allen's large beautiful yacht, bound for the St. Lawrence and surrounded by cheerful faces and happy hearts, his sly fiendish enemy held first place in his thought, and a new pack of cards held first place in his pocket.

Mrs. Allen and her husband had discovered sometime previously that Cainsford never after the first time he yielded hesitated to indulge in wine or any other stimulant offered him. They also discovered with a degree of regretful wonder that he was passionately fond of gambling, and had frequently excused themselves from joining the games he proposed, at the same time telling him good-naturedly that he was too fond of draw bluff.

Not so the wealthy widow, Mrs. Clair. She was always willing, but played with such greedy careful-ness that Cainsford was often disgusted. However, this same greed and care on her part had made a big hole in his funds. More than once had he been obliged to ask his generous host to become his banker and cash a check.

On the day in question, they started early from Charlotte, and when about half way across the blue water of Lake Ontario, heading for the gap near Kingston, the bell rang for dinner, and they sat down to a meal fit for a prince. They tarried, and talked long over the wine; but Cainsford ws the only one who indulged freely.

Mrs. Allen rose suddenly, as she said: "Now for some music," and entering a cabin, it was not long till she returned, and with lady-like grace, handed Cainsford her husband's famous violin, as she said sweetly:

"You see, Mr. Cainsford, I did not forget to bring it. Now please favor us. The music of the splashing water will add to the effect," and her beautiful eyes rested on Cainsford's flushed face, who looked at the violin with a fown, then while laying it on the table, said almost churlishly:

"Please excuse me. I'd much prefer playing draw poker with a new deck, than playing a pokey fiddle with an old bow."

Then smiling at what he evidently considered his own wit, coolly asked if they would not like a game. For a moment Mrs. Allen's eyes flamed on him with a glance of contemptuous reproach, then beckoning to Miss Howard, without another word went up on deck. No wonder she felt hurt, no wonder she never repeated the request.

During the afternoon, before entering the gap, Cainsford induced Mrs. Clair to play. The fleshy widow did not hesitate to comply when she noticed that the young man was partly intoxicated; and she got up from that game a well satisfied winner.

That night the Gladys remained at Kingston Harbor. Mr. Allen desired the pleasure of the run down through the islands in daylight, and did not continue the cruise till the next forenoon. Cainsford fretted at the delay. His burning wish was to meet congenial spirits, with whom he could gamble, and if possible retrieve his losses. He felt sure that dame fortune would smile on him if he could only run across players as bold as himself, who played for the love of the game, and believed Alexandria Bay would be a likely place to find such. This desire filled him, even to the exclusion of the power to appreciate the ever-varying beauty of the scene as they ploughed along, out and in, among the islands so famous for their picturesque loveliness. On the evening of the same day our party reached their destination and put up at the popular Crossman House.

The next morning Cainsford could not refuse to accompany Mr. Allen on a fishing excursion. The latter was a very enthusiastic fisherman and prided himself on his skill as such. He had made arrangements on the previous evening, having secured a boat and the services of a guide. The party started early in the morning, and upon reaching the spot, said to be the best on the St. Lawrence for Black Bass fishing, imagine Mr. Allen's chagrin and annoyance to find that the guide who rowed them had by a stupid blunder failed to put in their pail of minnows. The

fact that they were six miles from the Bay added to
his anger and disgust.   If ever mortal man received
a blowing-up for unpardonable thickheadedness, his
guide got it that morning.

The angry words were still rolling o'er the waves
when another row boat hove in sight. As soon as
within hearing distance, the penitent guide hailed it,
and the boats were soon alongside, and Mr. Allen
explained the situation to the occupants. These
gentlemen were also after bass, and very soon our
party had plenty of bait.   The off-hand generous style
of the two strangers, as they willingly divided their
minnows, impressed Cainsford strongly in their favor.

Then followed a day of rare sport, and both boats
returned to the Bay with a fine catch.   Mr. Allen was
jubilant.   His skill or good luck had not deserted him,
for he landed the two largest bass caught that day.
He might well be proud of the pair of beauties.   One
weighed five and a half pounds, the other turned the
scale at six.   Of course, they were packed in ice and
sent to Rochester.

The gentlemen from whom the minnows had been
secured informed Cainsford that their home was in
New York, and were just out for a holiday having arrived at the Crossman House two days before. When he
saw them again that evening, they were faultlessly
dressed in the style of the day. Their appearance
would indicate that they were cultured gentlemen
with plenty of means. It did not take our young
lawyer long to discover that they drank freely, played
recklessly, and spent money lavishly.   They appeared
as favorably impressed with Cainsford as he was with

them, and during the days and nights which followed played many games of draw poker, from which Cainsford frequently rose a winner. At such times they would praise his skill and luck, and laugh at their own loss.

Our young Canadian became so infatuated with their company that he sometimes neglected the Allen party altogether, and when the day arrived on which they were to continue their trip, he excused himself from accompanying them, stating that as he only had a few more days to spend away from business, he thought it wise not to go further. He was profuse in his studied phrases of thanks for their great kindness to him, and as he bade them good-bye, knew they were disappointed, very much disappointed indeed; and although there was no spoken word of reproach, knew also that he had lost their respect forever, and was as fully aware that he deserved to lose it; but does a gambler ever think of the feelings of others when his mad passion for play beckons him on? Very seldom, if ever. The immortal Charles Dickens furnishes an example in the character of "Little Nell's Grandfather."

We are sorry to state what followed in the Cainsford case, and will endeavour to be brief. Before the Allens departure he had drawn every dollar that stood to his credit in the bank at L——. Their presence at the Crossman House had been a partial restraint upon the impetuous Chris. Now that they were gone, the coast was clear and he cast himself loose.

Then followed days and nights of draw poker and debauch. Regardless of the run of luck, Cainsford's desperate passion kept its hold, till he wakened one morning to discover that he was a financial ruin and well nigh a physical wreck. Had he been cheated? Hard for him to say. He could only remember that during the games of the previous night the stakes were heavy, brandy plenty, the room hot, and his opponents keen and cool.

A sober sharp-sighted onlooker might have noticed as the last game progressed, that the New Yorkers managed to increase the stakes with consummate skill, and as Cainsford's recklessness increased, they grew cooler and more wary. Their eyes no longer beamed good-naturedly upon their victim, but began to emit eager cruel gleams, as they rested upon the huge pile of money which now constituted the pot.

When the hands at last were shown, Cainsford lost.

When he discovered this, he suddenly became dazed and scarcely noticed who raked in the money.

As he sat seemingly stupified, his opponents looked at him a moment as he rummaged through his empty pockets, then smiling grimly at each other, stretched themselves with a great sigh of relief, and one said with a cold laugh: "Never mind Cainey, old chap, better luck next time, you old Canuck. Ta-ta ta-ta."

Thus they left him, and he remained sitting half unconscious, while his noble head dropped lower, and lower, it caught rays from the dimly burning light, and as it gradually sank, the silvery locks at the temples seemed to whiten and whiten, and the lines on the broad brow seemed to deepen and deepen; then a heavy, weary, long drawn sigh told that Chris Cainsford, the GAMBLER, slept.

CHAPTER XXXIII.

A Telegram and What Followed.

The next morning Cainsford's New York friends did not meet him in the bar as usual. He was, therefore, obliged to drink alone, and needed it badly. He had carelessly been breaking physical as well as moral law. The fierce excitement of play and heavy drinking had already left their stamp upon his handsome face and manly form. Even after repeated glasses of his favorite brandy and soda, he still felt weak and shaky, and was not entirely free from the benumbing effects caused by the occurrences of the previous night, nor did he yet fully realize his position.

After waiting some time, he left the bar for the dining room, but did not succeed in eating his usual hearty meal. Then, with aching limbs and unsteady steps was on his way to the hotel verandah, when a messenger accosted him.

"Are you Mr. Chris Cainsford, sir?"

After receiving an answer in the affirmative, the boy continued:

"I have been looking for you, sir. Here's a telegram from Canada."

Then he looked on wonderingly, as he saw this big strong man tremble as he wrote his acceptance signature.

Cainsford waited till the lad was gone before opening the message, then read with burning eyes and throbing brain:

"At home.   Helen   slightly   ill.   Please come, if you can."   Signed,
Nora.

For some time he stood rooted to the spot, gazing at the words which danced before his reeling vision, then he groaned:

"Sunbeam—sick—and Nora—wants me.   Nora—wants—me? My—God!" and he staggered through to the bar, still mumbling to himself:

"Nora—wants—wants—me, and I'm a—drunken—pauper. Good Heavens—to think—its come—to this."

"Brandy, quick," he gasped to the surprised bartender, who at once set down the brandy decanter and stood watching Cainsford as he gulped down a huge drink, place the glass on the counter, then shook his head, as he watched him make his way towards the office.

As he stepped up to the waiting clerk Cainsford said:

"I'm called away suddenly," and showing him the telegram, continued: "The bank is not open yet, and am short of funds. My trunk is upstairs. Will leave it until I send money to pay my bill."

The clerk shook his head in evident annoyance, and Cainsford's face flamed angrily, as he almost shouted: "If you are afraid to trust me, I'll get the money in five minutes."

Then he rushed away to the double room occupied

by his New York friends. Rapped, then tried the
door, but found it locked. Returning to the office,
he asked hastily: "Have you seen Mr. Port or
Mr. Blackley this morning?"

"No," was the short answer. "They left by the
five o'clock boat, bag and baggage."

Cainsford looked at the speaker in utter bewilderment, put his hand to his aching head, leaned against
the counter, and murmured to himself:

"Oh, oh, what a poor weak deluded fool I've been,
and I thought, yes—I thought they were gentlemen."

Without saying another word he hastened down to
the dock and found the man from whom he had the
day before hired a steam launch to give his New York
friends the pleasure of a run through the islands.
Having nodded a good morning, he told him briefly
that he had met with a misfortune, was obliged to go
home, and requested the loan of ten dollars and a
passage on board his yacht across to Gananoque.

The man looked at Cainsford's flushed perspiring
face dubiously, and shook his head.

"Hold on," blurted the latter. "Here, take this
as security," and handed him a solid gold watch and
chain. (The chain was a birthday gift from Nora).

While both were being carefully examined, a greedy
glint shone in the man's small eyes, and he said:

"Durned if I like this sort of a job, but if you'll git
ready quick, durned if it isn't a go."

When the watch and chain had disappeared into his
capacious pocket, he drew out a fat purse, removed
two five dollar bills and reluctantly handed them to
Cainsford.

:   :   :   :   :   :   :   :   :

On the evening of that same day, when the nine-forty east-bound express thundered into the station at L——, a large man, with hat pulled well over his face, stepped off a second class car.. He carried neither grip, umbrella, nor raincoat, and when accosted by a cabman, said harshly: "No, I'll walk."

He then proceeded to the nearest hotel, with nervous haste, slipped into a private apartment, and ordered brandy neat. When it came, his strong hand shook as he raised the glass and drank greedily.

A few moments later he repeated his order, drank it; then left the place with firmer step, without showing the nervousness which had been noticeable at the time of his arrival.

As he walked along in the direction of Main Street he saw that the sky was full of racing clouds, and that the wind was rising rapidly. He stopped before a brilliantly lighted shop, and while peering in through the window, murmured:

"It's the new drug store. They'll scarcely know me here, and I must have a bracer before I can face Nora."

He looked carefully to see that no other customers were present, then entered the store, wrote a short prescription and handing to the clerk, requested him to put it up as quickly as possible.

The latter seemed a little surprised as he read the prescription, but soon had it ready. Before delivering the mixture, to his customer, which was in a four ounce bottle, he stuck a label on it, upon which was printed in red the picture of a skull and cross bones, also the word "Poison," then he said:

"I suppose you are aware, sir, that an overdose of

this is dangerous, even one-twentieth of a grain of strychnine is a stiff dose, and should not be taken more frequently than every two hours."

"Oh, yes," was the reply, "I fully understand. Have taken it before. Used to generally keep it on hand, but at present am out."

This was quite true. Once during examinations at Osgoode Hall Cainsford happened to drink more than was good for him, and feeling very rocky (as the saying is) the next morning applied to a young medical friend, who gave him a prescription which seemed just what he needed. It contained a romatic spirits of ammonia and strychinne. When again he required a bracer, he used the same prescription, and learned to write it himself.

This was the first time since his marriage, however, that he required to have it filled. During the day Cainsford had kept partially stupified with brandy. He had not allowed himself to dwell upon the awfulness of his fall and ruinous loss, but dimly realized that he must return to his waiting wife and child, as sober as his shattered nerves would permit. He was aware from past experience that as soon as the effect of the brandy wore off, if he had nothing to take as a substitute he would probably collapse, hence his care in securing the bracer, as he called it.

Choosing the darkest side of the street, he slouched along guiltily through the gusty wind towards his cosy home. Having reached it, he crept to the rear, and there in the darkness uncorked his bottle and took a small swallow. He recognized the unpleasant flavor, which following his recent potations of brandy, caused him to gasp, but soon he felt better. The depression was gone, and his heart beat stronger.

As he held the bottle in his hand he remembered the label, and if the light had been sufficiently strong, one could have seen a crafty expression appear on his haggard face.   He drew out his knife, and proceeded to scrape it off, and while he scraped, he whispered:

"If Nora happens to see it she will not likely ask questions when the bottle bears no grinning skull to frighten her.   I wish to heaven the meeting was over. I've acted the senseless brute, but this stuff is a treasure; and I feel this very minute that I could, if necessary, face the devil, and Nora is only a forgiving wife, so here's a go."

He walked quickly to the front and finding the door locked, tapped on the glass.   He thought to ring the bell might disturb little Helen.   In answer to his rap, Nora's voice inquired: "Whose there?"

"Only Chris," he replied, and in response to his voice he heard a joyous bark, and as the door opened, a huge hairy form was upon him, and a cool moist tongue licked his hand.   Then Pilot galloped round and round them, sounding short yelps of glad welcome, as Nora with a joyous cry and passionate sob, rushed into her husband's outstretched arms.   She gave him a lingering kiss; and a smile of sweet content rested on her lovely face as she laid her golden-head upon his broad bosom.   Then, with a dreamy radiance in her violet eyes, she looked into his face and murmured:

"Welcome, welcome home, dear Chris.   I've been so lonely, oh, so very, very lonely.   Just think, you have been away three weeks, and did not answer my last letter.   You naughty boy."

Here Chris interrupted hurriedly: "Oh, how is Sunbeam? Is she better?"

"Yes, nearly well," was the answer. "But longing for you. There she is now, Pilot has wakened her."

And a sweet childish voice could be heard calling: "Papa! Papa! tome up taies, to see lil dirlie."

"We will have to go," said Nora, and she led the way.

As Cainsford entered Helen's room, it seemed to him the very air suggested that innocence and purity lodged there, and his coming defiled it. As he bent over the snow-white bed, two soft little arms encircled his neck. Two sweet little lips were pressed to his, and a soft little voice cooed lovingly.

"Oh, Papa, I's dlad — oo tomed home to dirlie, and Pilo. We ause bofe so oney for zoo. Don't eave us any moea, will zoo not, Papa?"

"No, no, my darling," was the father's answer, as tears stole down his strong flushed face, and as he hurriedly brushed them away he noticed that Nora was gazing at him with startled anxious eyes.

"Oh, Chris," said she earnestly, "Have vou been ill? Your face seems strange to me. Has anything happened?"

He forced a laugh and said: "I did not sleep well last night, and I'm somewhat weather beaten, having been on the water so much. I tell you Nora holidays are not always what they're cracked up to be. I wish to God I'd never gone."

There was a tone of suppressed anguish in his voice which added to Nora's evident anxiety. Again she looked into his face, as she whispered:

"Oh, my husband, what is it? Do not fear to tell

your Nora.   You know she loves you with all her heart. Please do, dear Chris."

If he only had what grief and suffering the confession would have saved them both. He felt like telling the whole wretched story, but was so ashamed that he resisted the good impulse.

Suddenly his expressive face hardened and with a forced laugh, he said:

"Oh, its nothing, Nora.   Your telegram made me anxious."

"I hope you are not sorry I sent it, Chris," and tears glistened in Nora's eyes as she continued with a quiver in her voice: "I had not heard from you for so long, and was so very lonely, besides Helen's illness made me anxious."   Here a soft sigh told the parents that during their earnest conversation Helen had again fallen asleep.

"How long has the little darling been ill. She seems alright now," said Chris, as his eyes lingered on the child sleeping so peacefully.

"It developed the night we returned from the country.   Dr. Frank said it was a mild type of scarlet fever, and the most important thing was to look after her kidneys.   He mixed some medicine just before he left this evening and put it in that little four ounce bottle you see there on the table."

As his eye rested on the bottle, Chris noticed that it was very like the one in his pocket, and said:

"There is no directions on it."

"Oh, no," was Nora's reply, "Doctor had no label with him, and I guess thought an old ex-nurse like me might be trusted."

She smiled wanly, then continued:

"The dose is a tablespoonful every three hours.
Helen had some at nine-thirty, and will need it again
at half past twelve. You seem tired Chris, so you had
better go to bed and I will look after her. You look
so strangely haggard I think you must be ill."

"Not a bit of it, Nora. I assure you I could not
sleep if I did lie down. You have been working and
watching while I have been playing and idling, and
I know you are tired and weary, so please, dear, go to
bed, and let me watch this once. I promise to give
the medicine at twelve-thirty, and you know Sunbeam
will take anything for me without even a protest."

"I know she will, Chris, and the fact is I was so
depressed last night I could not sleep, although
Maggie's mother was here, kind soul, she forced me to
bed, but I felt that some terrible calamity was coming
upon us, and the night before my rest was broken by
such vivid, horrible dreams that the remembrance
of them makes me shudder."

Now she came closer, laid her hand on her husband's
broad shoulder, and looked with tired eyes into his,
as she whispered softly:

"Now that you have come, dear Chris, I'm sure if
I have dreams they will be pleasant ones, and indeed
I am so very, very tired, that if you will make yourself comfortable, and be sure and remember the
medicine, I'll go and lie down. Should you need me,
call. By the way, here is the evening paper."

"That is right, my poor tired wifie," said Chris, as
he pressed his burning lips to her cool brow, and gently
pushed her toward the door; then turning seated
himself in the big arm chair. He felt a light touch on
his shoulder, and as he looked up from the paper,

was a little surprised to see Nora standing at his side.
There was a dreamy gladness in her lovely eyes as
again, and yet again, she pressed her ripe lips to his
and murmured:

"Good-night, my love, remember a tablespoonful
at half past twelve."

Then gliding to the hall, Nora turned quickly, and
Cainsford never forgot the picture she made standing
there framed in the door way, as she smiled with
bewitching langour, and threw him an airy kiss.

CHAPTER XXXIV.

Little Helen Dies of Poison.

For some time after Nora had gone her husband sat
still, listening. When he thought sufficient time had
elapsed for her to be undressed and in bed, he looked
around stealthily, drew the four-ounce bottle from his
pocket, gave it a shake and whispered: "I feel that
horrible depression and those wretched cramps
stealing over me again and must have another
bracer."

Then uncorking the bottle, he placed it to his
trembling lips and took a small swallow. Having
carefully returned it to the inside breast pocket of his
coat he tried to read, but his eyes burned so that he
could scarcely distinguish the words. He threw the
paper down impatiently, as he said:" By Jove, this

heat is stifling," then noiselessly took off his coat and placed it across the foot of Helen's bedstead.

Seating himself he drifted into a partial stupor, and his mind was filled with wild, half-defined, ever-varying thoughts, while great beads of perspiration gleamed all over his brow.

Thus he sat for a long time, then suddenly glancing toward the bed he felt for his watch. At first his face wore a surprised expression, but changed to disgust, as he said hoarsely:

"My God—now—I—remember—its gone. A poor drunken—gambling—dupe—called Cainsford—had to pawn—his—wife's—present—in order to—bring—his —besotted—carcass — back — to — her — pure — presence. A very—pleasant—recollection—indeed," and he laughed a low reckless laugh.

While removing his boots he continued whispering to himself: "I'll have to go downstairs and look at the clock. It must be nearly time for Helen's medicine." He hastily put on his coat, and tip-toed through the door. In doing so he nearly stepped on Pilot, who was lying on the mat, wide awake and quietly watchful. The latter whined a low glad note and followed his master as he, softly descended the stairs, and felt his way to the kitchen. Having struck a light and found the tap, he drank greedily, then passing to the dining-room he said, as he looked at the clock, "By Jove, I'm five minutes late." Then quickly returned to his charge.

*   *   *   *   *   *

Not more than a minute after Cainsford had gone downstairs, a rosy girlish face peered in at the half-open door of Helen's room, then a little white-robed figure stole softly to the bedside of the sleeping child. It was the housemaid, Maggie, who had worked hard that day, and been induced by her thoughtful mistress to retire early.   She was in a sound sleep when Pilot's joyous barks of welcome suddenly wakened her, and she knew at once that the dog's master had returned. For a long time she tried to go to sleep but could not succeed.

A large tree which stood near her window creaked and groaned with the strong night wind, and the house appeared so very silent that she became apprehensive, and determined to see if the child she loved was all right. It did not take her long to slip out of bed, open her own door, and as we have said, enter the other, glad to find her treasure sleeping peacefully. For a moment her gaze rested on the sweet face, then hastily looking about her she noticed the newspaper lying where it had been carelessly thrown. Her instinct for tidiness caused her to mechanically pick it up, fold and make room for it on the table; then turning to take one more look at little Sunbeam, her keen eye noticed a small vial lying on the spread near the foot of Helen's bed. She wondered why it had been left there, but saw that it was securely corked, and placed it also on the table. She was bending over listening to the child's quiet breathing when she caught the sound of approaching footsteps and hastened to her room, just in time to miss Cainsford, who, with nervous haste, crossed to the bed, placed his hand gently on the child's brow and softly called her name.

Helen opened her large beautiful eyes, and yawned

sleepily: "Will you take the medicine Dodo left for Sunbeam?" said her father coaxingly, as he tenderly patted her peach-like cheek.

"I ont like medis, papa," said she, with a shake of her curly head, "but I des me'll tate it for zoo."

Lifting the four-ounce bottle from the table Cainsord carefully filled the tablespoon. As he held it to the pretty parted lips his hand trembled in spite of himself. "Please hurry, my pet, before papa spills it! That is a good girlie."

Helen heroically swallowed the large dose, which seemed to strangle her. She gasped for breath, and tears came into her eyes, but she merely said brokenly: "It vely bad medis, Papa, but Dodo say it make lil Sunbeam bette."

"So it will, my darling. Now go to sleep, and Pilot will come to see you in the morning."

Helen cuddled down, and remained very still for a few minutes. Then her eyes suddenly opened, and her father noticed a sort of wondering expression in their innocent depths, and that they were exceedingly bright and prominent. She commenced murmuring some words of the song entitled the "Gipsy Boy," then turning her pretty head, asked sorrowfully:

"Did poor lil Dipsy Boy have to tate bad medis too, Papa?"

"No pet. He did not have any kind Dodo to give it to him."

"Did poor lil Dipsy Boy die all lonie, Papa?"

"Yes," was the answer. And as the father looked at the lovely sympathetic face, tears came into his eyes.

"Is oo solley for lil Dipsy Boy, Papa?"

"Yes," brokenly.

"Dirlie is too, and she die some day, en ool be solley for lil dirlie, too, won't zoo, Papa?"

"Yes, yes, but please go to sleep. You are going to be well in the morning."

But Helen seemed very wide awake, and continued:

"Mama—and—Pilo—and—Dodo—and Madda—all be solley for Papa's dirlie—when she die too. What is to die, Papa?"

Again Cainsford entreated Helen to go to sleep.

"Dirlie not sleepy now," she replied, sweetly. "Please tell torey bout fishmans lil dirlie. Zen I do seep ser zoo, Papa."

Cainsford's voice was very husky as he repeated the story of the fisherman's child, who guided her father through the fog to home and safety by calling from the shore: "Papa come this way!" While telling it Helen's bright eyes never left her father's face. Then she whispered:

"Ta-ta, Papa Triss, oor lil dirlie will tall—to—zoo —some day."

Having closed her bright eyes, Helen kept quite still for some time till Cainsford thought she was dropping off to sleep. Suddenly she threw back her head, and her little form became almost rigid, while the muscles of her hands and face twitched convulsively. As she gazed at her father he noticed that the pupils of her eyes were greatly dilated. Although the paroxysm only lasted a moment, to the startled father it seemed an hour. He tried to cry to Nora, but his trembling lips refused to utter her name.

At last he managed to gasp: "Oh, my darling, what—what is the matter?"

At first the little jaws seemed unable to move, then the set lines gradually relaxed, and she smiled faintly, and murmured, "Papa, tiss poor lil dirlie."

He did so and was about to awaken Nora, when Helen called his name again, and as he bent over the little form, her eyes gazed into his as she whispered: "Dirlie—oves—oo, Papa."

Then she appeared to drift into semi-unconsciousness, and sang just above a whisper, but very sweetly: "A—lil—voice—talls—from—at shoca—Papa—tome—iss—way."

The low refrain died away tremblingly, as Cainsford said:

"My God in Heaven, I can't stand this." He felt the awful depression coming upon him again and thrust his hand into the pocket of his coat, thinking to take another bracer to steady his nerves before calling Nora. The bottle was not there, and for a moment his face showed a great bewildered surprise, then filled with horror, as his anxious eyes caught sight of the bottle from which he had given Helen the medicine. He seized it, held it near the light, and at once saw where the label had been scraped off with a knife, leaving some shreds of red colored paper still clinging to the glass. A horrible fear flashed in his pale face as he uncorked the bottle and smelled its contents. Then a hoarse cry rose and died away again, like the wail of a lost soul, and an agonized voice shouted in despairing tones:

"Great—God—of—Heaven! I've—poisoned my child. Nora!—Nora!—come—Oh, come!—your darling is dying—and I'm the cause—."

Looking toward the bed he saw that Helen was in

another paroxysm,and for a second he stood with glaring eyes and chattering teeth ; then rushed through the door and met Nora staggering along in white-faced terror. He could not speak, but pointing to the bed, gasped: "The doctor," then tore down the stairs, through the hall, and away up the street.

He reached Dr. Allgood's office, bareheaded, without boots, and frantically rang the night bell. While he stood there waiting and panting, a cold muzzle shoved into his hand, and he dimly realized that Pilot was with him. The door opened and Dr. Frank's tall form stood under the rays of the low burning hall light. There was startled wonder in his kindly face, as he said anxiously:

"Is it you, Chris, what is the matter man, your looks frighten me?"

"Oh, Frank, quick!—for Heavens sake hasten. I've poisoned your Sunbeam. Come or she'll die."

Then followed a bitter wail that appeared to rend the heart of the powerful man as he stood there shivering in the dark. The doctor quickly joined him, and without a word together they sped along the wind-swept streets to the Cainsford cottage. Panting for breath, the stairs were climbed to find Nora and Maggie, with streaming faces and trembling forms bending over little Helen's white twitching face.

"Oh—doctor!—my—child!—my child!—wailed the mother. What has happened my darling child? Tell me, is she dying? Oh, tell me quick."

As the doctor tenderly raised the delicate wrist, Helen's eyes opened wide and dwelt lovingly upon each face. She tried to speak, but seemed unable to articulate. Turning to her father, she raised her

dimpled hands, extended her snow-white arms, and a
heavenly radiance seemed to illumine her lovely face
as she managed to whisper, oh, so sweetly: "Papa,
tome—iss—way."

Then the glorious eyes rested on her mother, and
with the glimmer of a tender, loving smile radiating
from the parted lips, *little Helen died.*

CHAPTER XXXV.

On, On, On Through Smudge and Blackness.

Yes, beautiful, bright, loving little Helen was dead.
The gentle sweet-voiced singer had gone to join an
angel choir.

We will not attempt to depict Nora Cainsford's
heart-breaking sorrow; Dr. Allgood's lonely sadness;
nor Maggie Murphy's demonstrative grief; but ask the
reader to accompany a tall, bare-headed, wild-eyed
man as he rushes through the windy darkness, closely
followed by a large, long-haired dog. If it were not
so terribly dark, one could see that the dog limps as
he lopes along close to the flying footsteps of his
master's unbooted feet.

Chris Cainsford had fled from the room where lay
that still, little white-faced form, with the wild light of
delirium in his glaring eyes. As his shaking hand
turned the front door knob he felt that he was
being followed, and fiercely ordered Pilot back,

and shutting the door with a clang, bounded away
through the night.

For a moment after the door closed Pilot stood
with bowed head and drooping tail; suddenly he
turned, and with noiseless springs ascended the stairs.
It was then that Dr. Allgood noticed the sad face
peering into Helen's room, and two wistful eyes for
a moment dwelt on the form of a beautiful grief-
bowed woman, moaning out the agony of a breaking
heart. As they lingered, pain and sorrow were
stamped deeper in a melancholy piteous to see. Then
with a long drawn sound like a sob, the grave face
disappeared up the hall, and Pilot entered the sewing
room at the front of the house, the door of which was
open and window up. He sprang on the sill, sniffed
the night air; then with an anxious whimper the great
dog gathered himself and leaped his long length out
into the dark. The slither and scrape of strong claws
could be heard, as he went over the verandah roof;
then a loud thud told that the body had struck the
ground below. A vigorous shake followed, a mighty
spring cleared the front gate, and Pilot with nose to
scent of sock-covered feet, was in swift pursuit of his
mad master, who, when overtaken, was running in the
direction of the river and breathing heavily.

Soon they reached the dock, and as they fly along
the fierce wind of the approaching thunder storm
shrieks, wails, and lashes the black-rolling water into
flashes of foam. Amid the tumult and gloom, the
bootless, bareheaded man, thinks he hears familiar
voices of long ago angrily whisper: "Crazy Chris!—
Crazy Chris! you have poisoned Sunbeam. You
killed your child. Dear little Helen is dead. You

are guilty, guilty! Drown yourself! you drunken, gambling, miserable wretch."

He stops at the end of the dock, and with rolling eyes and burning eyeballs gazes into the dark depths of surging water, and leans out—out, out, as if fascinated.   The voices seem nearer, and continue to whisper and hiss: "Crazy Chris! Crazy Chris! you're guilty, guilty, and not fit to live."

Suddenly a blinding flash of lightning breaks the spell.   It is closely followed by crash and boom, and as the thunder rolls and re-echoes o'er the wind-swept waves, he hears in sweetest tones, a childish voice in thrilling accent call without the blackness behind him: "Papa!—dear—Papa!—tome—iss—way."

As he turns he thinks he sees a bright, angelic face smiling at him entreatingly.   For a moment he stands trembling and irresolute, then drops his head, and while a groan bursts from him, a cool damp nose touches his hot feverish hand, and he hears a low tremulous whine, while two glowing eyes are raised to his with a steadfast light.

"Oh, my God, what will I do?   What will I do?"

As the cry is borne away on the wings of the wind his long arms are raised in an unspoken, helpless appeal to heaven; then, with lowered head, the man flies back toward the shore as if pursued by a thousand furies.   Again his ears catch the awful medley of accusing voices.   Horrid forms and hideous phantoms seem to surround and pursue him; then as a fierce blast nearly takes him off his feet, a chorus of curses from unseen fiends resound through his ringing ears, adding one more touch of madness to his delirious brain.

"I'm going crazy," he gasps, and rushes to the edge

of the dock to hurl himself from it.   As he draws in his breath for the wild leap, he is again arrested by the sound of that childish voice, calling: "Papa, dear —dear—Papa, I—oves—oo—so.   Papa—tome—iss —way."

As he gazes into space, Helen's sweet smiling face again appears to his imaginary vision, and her brilliant eyes look into his with an irresistible supplication in their humid depths.

The mad father, now filled with a strange awesome fear, flies from the dock and turns up the shore, still followed by the persistent Pilot.   They stop beside a large boat-house, gloomily outlined in the darkness. The man feels for the door, and the rattle of a heavy padlock follows.   After a pause, a stooping figure can be discerned searching among the rocks along the shore, suddenly it rises bearing something in its hands, then from in front the boathouse can be heard rapid blows of stone against iron, which continue till a crash mingles with creaking hinges.   The opening door leaves a void of densest darkness, through which man and dog disappear.   Then comes the noise of groping and stumbling.   Finally the door next the water rolls back with a groan, followed by the sound of heaves and heavy breathing. and a long dim shape slides out, and strikes the water with a dull splash.

It is evidently a large boat, and is soon swept to leeward of the shadowy building.   The head line is made fast to something invisible, and a moment later a tall form is more distinctly seen standing on the dim plunging deck.   He seems in nervous haste, for very soon a high mast is hoisted and the stay ropes made fast.   The man must possess prodigious strength to accomplish this unaided. His dusky four-footed friend is patiently watching, and now he too clambers on board.

The rattle of pulley blocks and flapping of canvas accompanies the appearance of a large white sail rapidly ascending the dimly outlined spar. It shows out huge and ghostly against the inky blackness of hurrying storm clouds, and as the long boom swings too and fro, the increasing breeze, now almost a gale, hurtles by with a howl.

The man who has been in frenzied haste, for a moment pauses, and turning a wild despairing face up to the lowering sky, the lips part, and a cry as if from a soul in torment, bursts from them; then an agonized voice can be heard above whistling wind and rushing water: "Mercy! Mercy!" it cries. "Great—God— have—mercy. I'm—mad—I'm crazy. My—brain —is—on—fire."

The cry is strangled by an extra fierce gust as the angry gale seizes and shakes the towering canvas with cruel delight.

Again the bowed head is raised. Again the white quivering face and gleaming eyes look skyward with haunting agony in every line, and now a despairing wail gurgles from a throbbing remorse-charged heart. "No! No! No—mercy for—me. No—mercy—for— Crazy—Chris—the drunken gambler, who—poisoned —an—angel—child, and broke a—loving—wife's— heart."

As the sound of the despairing voice dies away, the man springs to the bow of the plunging boat, and leaning far over, with hasty slashes of a large knife severs the straining head line. As soon as released,

the restless vessel pays off, and as helm is seized, and
sheet rope fastened, she is caught by the resistless east
wind, and thrown clear down; then slowly righting,
flies away through the darkness like a doom-frighted
ghost.

For a brief moment the solemn moon unveils her
face and two phantom-like forms can be seen on board
the fleeing craft.   The one with uncovered head and
long waving hair stands at the helm; while the other,
with sad face upraised, and paw uplifted, sits be-
seechingly near.

As the dim white craft mounts a mighty billow, her
name "Nora" can for a second be seen in golden
letters across her stern. Then while bouyantly bearing her burden of *haunting, hopeless remorse* and
staunch, steadfast love, the spectre-like barque plunges
into the night, and amid flying foam and wailing wind,
ploughs on! on! on! through *smudge* and *blackness*.

PART IV.

DEFEAT AND VICTORY.

CHAPTER XXXVI.

Helen's Tomb—A Mother's Prayer.

On gently rising ground close to the majestic
St. Lawrence, and overlooking its blue waters, can
be found a quiet grave-yard which is both hallowed
and historic. It lies quite close to the highway,
and not far from the busy town of P——.

One summer afternoon a funeral procession
could be seen slowly driving through the rustic
entrance gate to this peaceful spot, and here close
to the graves of her grandparents, (Nora's mother
and father), little Helen Cainsford was buried, a
more appropriate place for the long silent sleep could
not be found.

A lovely spot indeed, over which venerable
pine trees whisper and keep guard, and to which
the rolling water of old St. Lawrence sings a solemn
lullaby.

Till after Helen's funeral Mrs. Cainsford had borne her crushing weight of sorrow with christian fortitude, but her husband's continued absence gradually increased her load of grief and despair, until it seemed greater than she could bear, and culminated in a serious attack of brain fever. Had it not been for Dr. Allgood's skilful treatment, and Mrs. Mike Murphy's assiduous care, Nora would have gone to join her darling child. However, the critical stage was past, but it was weeks before she was strong enough to be conveyed to the Littlejohn homestead, where for a long time she remained in a sort of melancholy stupor from which it seemed impossible to rouse her. Dr. Allgood did all in his power to awaken hope and renew her courage, telling her that although there had been no reply to oft repeated advertisements for tidings of her hsuband's whereabouts, still the fact that Pilot had not returned was a strong proof in favor of his belief that the dog's master was still alive.

The Dr. was aware that Cainsford's sailing yacht "Nora" was gone, and surmised (rightly too) that in his wild delirium and remorse, believing that Nora could never forgive him, his poor friend had employed the yacht as a means of escape from the horrible consequences of his awful mistake. The Doctor's opinion that he was still alive was proven to be correct by a short, somewhat mysterious communication which Nora received, stating that the report that her husband was probably drowned was untrue, as the writer knew for a fact that he had been rescued by his faithful dog. He stated further that having given a solemn promise, he could not reveal where or when the rescue had taken place. Neither could he give any information with regard to Mr. Cainsford's whereabouts.

The letter closed with an earnest appeal to the bereaved wife to put her trust in God, and not lose hope, as the writer felt convinced that the missing one would return safe and well in the course of time. He merely signed himself, "AN OLD FRIEND OF THE FAMILY."

Although this news was very unsatisfactory it had a tendency to awaken Nora from her condition of hopeless despondency, and following this came the imperative duty of nursing her aunt through a serious illness, which caused her to partly forget her own trouble in attending to the wants and troubles of another.

Dr. Allgood at once noticed hat employment was the very best thing to prevent Nora from dwelling upon the loss and misery of the dark past. He therefore determined to keep her busy, if possible. He secured the co-operation of her Uncle George, and eventually Nora's consent, to take up her former profession of nurse. This was a wise decision, for now that she had an object in life her courage and faith gradually revived, and from this time she never ceased to hope, watch and pray for the return of her erring husband. She became the friend of every dog she saw, and was ever on the look out for a tall, honest, white-faced Setter.

One day Dr. Allgood called at the house of a wealthy invalid lady, where Nora at the time was engaged, and requested the latter to accompany him for an afternoon's drive, telling her that he had a little surprise in store which he hoped would meet with her approbation.

Nora had gone out very little since her bereavement, and at first hesitated to comply, but when told they would probably visit little Sunbeam's grave, she seemed greatly pleased.

Having arrived at the peaceful spot, imagine her surprise to find flowers in bloom on the little grave, and at its head a white marble slab bearing on its top the form of a dove in the position of flight, and beneath it the following inscription, exquisitely wrought:

IN MEMORY OF

HELEN CAINSFORD,

OUR PRECIOUS, PASSING SUNBEAM.

Born——18——Died——18——
and underneath this again the following lines:

> "A little childish voice is stilled
> Two little lily white hands are crossed;
> Two little eyes forever closed;
> The sound of pattering feet is lost.
>
> A little form from out our home,
> Was borne by loving hands away;
> But still I seem to hear a voice,
> Within my heart, it says each day:
> "Pa-pa come this way. Pa-pa come this way."
>
> A little voice calls from that shore,
> "Papa come this way."

Nora read and re-read the inscription; then turning her beautiful tear-dimmed eyes to the Doctor, grasped both his hands, and said, oh so earnestly:

"Doctor Allgood, my more than brother, may God reward you for all your great kindness. I cannot express the debt of gratitude I owe. Your friendship for me has been as a glowing beacon in densest darkness; ever sending forth rays of hope to a sorrowing grief-striken woman, lost in the gloom of despair."

Then she knelt close to the white marble, raised her arms to heaven, and with streaming face upturned to the azure sky, poured out the longing, earnest pleading of a desolate heart:

"Oh, Thou Almighty Merciful Being, who didst restore to the sorrowing widow of Nian her only son, wilt Thou in Thine infinite compassion hear my prayer and restore to me my lost husband. May his life be spared to visit this peaceful spot, hallowed by the sweet memories which surround his darling child's tomb. Oh, God, grant that her pure spirit may become his guardian angel, and may her sweet voice ever continue calling to him, till he returns to me, to his home, and at last to Heaven. Amen."

CHAPTER XXXVII.

Pilot Saves His Master.

"Well, Jake, what do you make her out to be?" shouted Captain Sherman to his first mate, big Jake Simmons, who was clamoring down the rigging of the *Tranchemontagne*, a large schooner, as she was humming along merrily under a great cloud of canvas, headed across Lake Ontario for Oswego.

"It's purty hard to tell exactly," was Jake's answer, "but she's a small yacht, carryin' about a seventy-five yard main sail, and no jib, for it's blowed to bits. I think she's in a purty bad shape; acts as though she might be half full of water, and her peak's dropped, preventin' her havin' steerage way."

"Could you make out how many were aboard, Jake?" enquired the Captain.

"Oney two, as I could see. Seemingly a man and a boy, and the man's asleep, dead or drunk, I couldn't make out which."

While the captain and mate were talking, the schooner was rapidly lessening the distance between herself and the boat in question, which appeared off her port bow, but if she did not change her course, would pass half a mile or more east of the small vessel, which had by her erratic movements awakened the interest of the schooner's crew.

The *Tranchemontagne* was owned and sailed by
Captain Sherman, whose home was at the town of
Darkton.   On this trip she was carrying a full cargo
of lumber, having secured her load at Mill Point,
opposite Bridgeville, on the Bay of Quinte. Not
only was her hold full, but the deck load was built
up so high that there was just sufficient space to
allow clear passage of her great booms. It was because of this prodigious deck load that the practical
Captain remained at anchor inside the Gap, to allow
the fierce east wind which had been blowing almost
a gale for two nights and a day, to blow itself out or
change to another quarter. On this occasion it had
been obliging, having gone down about midnight, and
sprung up again from the North-west about two
in the morning, giving Captain Sherman just the
chance he wished for—to up anchor, and make a
splendid offing through the Gap, which already lay
five miles astern.

Captain Sherman was a man respected by all
who knew him, was also honoured and admired by
his crew. Some people thought him eccentric,
because he would not allow swearing on board his
vessel, neither would he sail on Sunday, even if
coaxed to do so by shipping companies or by a
fair wind.

In the schooner's forecastle were two framed
mottoes, one of which read: "Keep Holy the Sabbath
Day," the other: "Thou shalt not take the name of
the Lord thy God in vain." It can easily be understood that a man who carried such mottoes, would
be willing to lend a hand to the unfortunate, no matter what their condition, and if necessary make a
sacrifice for their benefit.

When the captain heard the report of his first mate, he climbed the rigging himself, glass in hand, and very soon the man at the wheel received a command to alter the schooner's course two points, causing the small sail to be overhauled very rapidly.

Having returned to a spot on the forepart of his vessel which furnished a good look out, the Captain again focused his glass, then beckoned to Jake, and said:

"She certainly is in a bad way. Here take a look. It seems to me there is just a man and dog on board, and judging by his actions, one would think the dog saw danger, and was doing his best to rouse the sleeping or unconscious man."

"That's so, Captain; but mercy save us, she is nigh full of water. Her boom is dragging so that she can't come into the wind, and she's gettin' fuller with every sea that breaks. My opinion is that if she carries sandbag ballast, she'll sink inside of ten minutes."

Again the Captain took a hasty look through the glass, then sung out to the man at the wheel:

"When you are near enough, Pete, run the Old Girl into the wind, and keep her hove to as near yon yacht as possible."

As the vessel responded to the helm, Jake Simmons sent a loud hail across the wind-swept water, and an answering bark could be indistinctly heard coming from the deck of the laboring vessel. Now Jake shouted in tones of alarm:

"By gracious, Captain, she's founderin', sure as a gun. What will we do?"

"Man and lower the yawl, quick, quick," was the sharp command.

Then amid the flapping of great sails, and excited
shouts of the crew, the schooner was run into the wind
and hove too. As she lost way the ropes ran through
the davits with rattle and creak, followed by a dull
splash as the yawl struck the water manned by three
sailors. Big Jake stood in the stern, and with rapid
sweeps of his powerful arms skulled, while his companions bent their backs and rowed with frantic haste
toward the water-logged yacht. Before the yawl
had gone a dozen lengths, however, the former
rolled heavily, then, as she recovered an even keel,
she plunged forward, the stern elevated, and while
her sharp bows made way for herself, Nora's name-
sake dove down, down, down into the depths,
never to be seen again by mortal eye, leaving in the
midst of angry bubbles and hissing spray, a large
bare-headed, bootless, unconscious man, and a gaunt,
long-haired, pale-faced, struggling dog.

"Quick, quick, Jake, quick, roared the captain, or
you'll be too late." Then he said to himself. "Oh,
how I wish we had changed our course sooner. I
fear the poor chap is a goner; yes, oh, oh, there he
goes, what a pity. Ah! no, the dog has grabbed
him. Well done, well done. If he can keep his head
above the water for twenty seconds, he has a chance.
Ah, ah, God have mercy! they are both under."

The Captain turned away for a second; but looked
again to see the dog frantically struggling and
trying to support the helpless burden he had again
brought to the surface.

"Hurry! lads, hurry!" was the Captain's loud
command to the men in the yawl who had been
straining every nerve, and now backed water furious-

ly, as Jake leaped to the bow, and leaning far out, seized the man's long hair just as he was going down. The noble dog had become completely exhausted from his great exertions, although he still hung on. Jake was not a second too soon, for while he was exerting all his gigantic strength to haul the helpless pair out of the water, a huge sea broke about them with swish and roar. He succeeded, however, and now they lay on the floor of the yawl, entirely unconscious of their rescue.

"I guess the man's a goner," said Jake, feelingly. "And it was a mighty close shave for the dog. Blamed if I don't feel sorr'rier fer him than fer tother, and if he lives, I'd like to adopt him."

He again seized the skulling oar and headed for the fast drifting schooner. She was soon overtaken, and the yawl and its burden hauled up to her stern. By this time the great gaunt dog had recovered sufficiently to watch every move of the men as they placed his master's dripping form upon a spare sail.

The work of resuscitation immediately commenced, and as the *Tranchemontagne* was got under way the rubbing, rolling and chafing began and was continued on the part of Captain and mate, until they were both tired out. Then the man's jaws were opened and brandy forced down his throat, after which the large sunken eyes opened for a moment, then closed again wearily; but the Captain seemed overjoyed, as he straightened himself and said:

"Boys, here is another proof that the Great God watches over His creatures. He certainly has a purpose in snatching this poor fellow from a watery grave, but they both look half starved and I think we had better take the man to my cabin, where we can remove his wet clothes and have cook get him some hot broth. I don't believe he has eaten for days. Wonder who he is, and where he and his dog came from? I am sure these two have a history."

"Nora was the name of his boat," said Jake. "I see it plain just before she took her last dive, and I have seen somebody that looks like this chap what sailed her; but I can't make out for the life of me who it is."

As Jake and the Captain were gazing on the prostrate form, the large eyes again opened and languidly rolled about. He tried to raise his hands but seemed too weak. The dog had remained crouched at his side, and noticing the movement, whimpered gladly and licked the hand and face, then with a long drawn, weary sigh, assumed his former position, and laid his white striped face along his paws.

When his master was raised and borne down the steps to Captain Sherman's cabin, the dog followed, uttering occasional low growls of warning. The form was heavy, but the kind hearted men succeeded, and while removing the clothing from the poor helpless chap could not but admire his magnificent proportions. The Captain had some difficulty in getting off the socks, for they were worn to shreds, and the feet were all bruised, swollen, and bleeding.

When all was done the cook brought hot broth for the man, which was swallowed with difficulty. He seemed almost starved, however, and managed to consume quite a quantity. Then, with a weary sigh, dropped off into a sleep of complete exhaustion, which continued the whole day through, while the faithful dog, having devoured some food, stationed himself beside the low bed and with closed eyes that never slept, kept watch.

The *Tranchemontagne* made splendid time across the Lake, and before sundown signalled for a tug, which met her and she was towed safely to Oswego harbor, where her sails were furled, fenders arranged, and her lines run out and made fast. But amid all the energy, noise and turmoil overhead no one but his dog knew that the once brilliant lawyer, Chris Cainsford, was below in the Captain's cabin, being slowly restored to life and remorse by nature's great healer, restful slumber.

CHAPTER XXXVIII.

ASLEEP IN THE CAPTAIN'S CABIN.

After arranging for the unloading of his vessel and attending to various other duties, Captain Sherman visited his rescued passenger. The first thing he noticed upon entering the cabin was a pair of glowing orbs shining in the gloom close to the bedside. He spoke kindly to the silent watcher, then listening to the heavy breathing of the man, whispered to himself:

"The poor chap must have been greatly exhausted, but if that sleep continues during the night, it will do him great good." Then with another kindly word for the dog, the good Captain went to the fore part of the schooner, arranged his bed, and retired for the night.

About daylight the following morning, he again entered the cabin to find unchanged conditions. The man was in the same profound slumber, the dog quietly watchful. This continued during the day. Amid all the rattle and hubbub occasioned by the removal of the schooner's great load the man slept; the dog watched. Twice the cook brought food, but the sleeper was not aroused. The dog, however, seemed grateful for his, and having eaten, resumed his silent vigil and thus he was found by the Captain after the day's work was done.

The latter lit his lamp, and seating himself, heard unintelligible sounds coming from the prostrate form on the bed. By leaning over, his keen ear distinguished these whispered words: "Nora! Oh, Nora! Frank! Frank! Quick! Quick."

Then louder, in a horrified tone: "My God! My darling is dead. I've poisoned my child," and with a startled cry the man wakened, trembling like a leaf.

He turned his face toward the Captain, and as they gazed at each other for several seconds, the two men recognized each other; and while one face filled with shame and despair, the other expressed astonished compassion, then their hands met in an eager, trembling clasp.

A long, broken, oft - interrupted conversation followed, which lasted till the mate, Jake Simmons, while on his last round before turning in for the night, noticed a light still burning in the Captain's cabin. Jake had been much interested in the rescued man, and drew near to see if anything peculiar was amiss. As he listened he could distinctly hear his Captain's voice in earnest pleading prayer, which coming as it did from out the gloom, was very solemn and impressive, and Jake never entirely forgot the words.

"Oh, Thou Great all-loving Father. Thou Ruler of the Universe. Thou helper of the helpless, we place this sad case in Thine Omnipotent hands. Here is a poor weak sinner, who has been saved from a watery grave by Thy tender care. Now he thinks himself beyond hope of pardon or redemption. He acknowledges his guilt. Sorrow and remorse are breaking his heart. He is weary and heavy laden, and Thou hast bidden such to come to Thee for rest. Thou Helper of the helpless, wilt Thou in Thine infinite mercy raise him, who was intended for one of Thy noblemen, from the slough of despond. Help him in his great weakness to put on the armour of faith, renounce the evil, cling to the good, and endeavor by Thy grace to redeem the dark past, and Oh! for the sake of Him who came seeking the lost, receive his precious soul at last. Amen."

As the prayer ended Jake heard a muffled heartbroken moan. Then the Captain's voice, in tones of encouragement:

"Do not despair, my friend, never lose hope. I think you are certainly mistaken with regard to the feelings of your noble, true-hearted wife. You say that under the circumstances she must necessarily despise and hate you. How very sad it would be if you were wrong, and only increasing her misery by remaining away. I think that probably at this very moment she is longing for your return."

Here Jake caught the sound of low, despairing words in reply: "No, No, Captain, I wish with all my heart it might be possible, but—it—cannot—be, No!—No!—it cannot be! Great—God!—to—think that—Nora—hates—me."

The words ended in a stifled groan and the Captain's voice again was heard:

"Well, if you have decided that you cannot go back with me, I am sorry, but I will leave a little money here in your pocket, just to show that I still have confidence in you." (Here Jake heard a protest, but the Captain continued.) "And for the sake of your noble father, mother, and sister, and because of what you have told me, I will keep your sad secret, and ask the crew to do the same, here is my hand on it. Now good-night, and God be with you till we meet in the morning."

They did not meet the next morning, for when it came the passenger and his dog were gone, and they never met again in this world. Possibly they may in the next. If so, it will be on the morning of the great resurrection.

We are sorry to inform the reader that the *Tranchemontagne* was afterwards wrecked in the very port where Captain Sherman prayed so earnestly in behalf of the despairing man, who was so filled with remorse he could not be comforted.

The loss of his schooner was a great blow to the worthy captain, who not long afterwards was called to a haven of rest, where shipwreck, sin and sorrow are unknown.

CHAPTER XXXIX.

A Tangle-Haired Tramp.

Were the prayers of a forsaken wife and her husband's faithful friend ever answered? If we could have seen what Mrs. Frederick Allen saw on a bright summer's evening, nearly three years after the fervent supplications were offered, we would have said, "No, and they never can be now, for the subject of those prayers is sunken too low, has become too degraded, ever to be reclaimed."

What did Mrs. Allen see? Oh, only a big, bloated, besotted, ragged, red-faced, tangle-haired tramp, sitting on a log by the roadside, binding up the paw of a large, long, silky-eared, white-breasted Setter dog.

How did she happen upon such a sight? Oh, simply enough. She was visiting some relatives residing in the town of A——, situated about one hundred miles east of Oswego, and on the afternoon in question was returning from a drive through the country, accompanied by her nephew, when suddenly their spirited team shied, and the handsome lady turning her head at once saw the cause of their momentary fright, namely, the tramp and dog already mentioned. It was certainly anything but a pleasing picture, but there was something in the position of the two wayfarers at the time, which touched a chord of sympathy in Mrs. Allen's breast, causing her to have the carriage stopped. The ragged man had been too intent upon what he was doing to notice the approaching team. When they halted in front of him he raised his large uncovered head, (for his hat and a worn blue bag were lying on the log at his side), and fixed on Mrs. Allen a pair of dark, bleary, melancholy eyes. As they took in the details of her lovely face, a vivid flush appeared on the man's broad, furrowed brow. He hastily placed the weather-worn hat on his head, then lowering it, mumbled something to himself, or probably to his dog, for the latter turned on him a look of such worshipful devotion that Mrs. Allen's generous heart was touched. She opened her purse and flung a silver dollar in the man's direction, which the dog immediately recovered and carried to him.

When Mrs. Allen's nephew saw the dog's prompt action he shouted at the tramp: "I say, where the mischief did you get that dog?"

At the question the man who had been dejectedly looking at the coin he held, raised his head, and with an ugly glance in his blood-shot eyes, said shortly:

"None of your business, but I did not steal him,

and by the way, here's the lady's money." Saying which he came over and dropped the silver dollar into Mrs. Allen's lap; then as he saw the manifest surprise in the faces of the occupants of the carriage, he continued: "We thank you, kind lady, but although pretty low my dog and myself are not quite beggars yet."

Here the young man haw-hawed, and broke in with:

"Say, Mr. High and Mighty, although your personal appearance is not a recommend for the character of your dog, I'd like to buy him anyway. What is your price?"

"Not for sale," was the gruff answer.

"Oh, come now, you may as well drop your airs, they do not fit your apparel. I'll give you enough to buy a new suit of clothes. Here," and he held out a ten dollar bill.

There was a momentary flash in the tramp's dark eyes, as he said:

"No, young man, ten times ten dollars would not buy him. Why, he's the only friend I have in all the world. Perhaps I do not deserve this one, but money will never take him from me."

Then with a sweeping bow, he picked up his blue bag, a heavy cudgel, chirped to his dog, and without ever turning to look back, slouched away in the direction the carriage had come.

"My eyes! Isn't it a terror how cheeky some of these tramps are, Auntie?" said the young man, as they sat watching the receding pair. The lady did not answer, but seemed greatly perplexed. She had noticed something in the manner of the tramp, or in the tone of his voice, which reminded her vaguely of someone else, or was it possible that she had met this very man in different circumstances, if so, where in the world could it have been?

"Oh, shaw," she murmured to herself, as they drove on. "The idea is preposterous, but it does seem so strange." And do what she would, Mrs. Allen could not forget that bloated face nor its despairing expression as he called to his dog.

The haunting memory still clung to her. Even that night after she had retired it caused her sleepless hours, and she was disgusted to find that the very first thing she thought of in the morning was the big, ragged tramp, and his long-haired dog.

Had she been told that her own fair hand had been the one to start this wreck of humanity on his downward course she would have laughed the thought to scorn.

The next afternoon she and her brother, while taking a walk through one of the parks belonging to A——, noticed a small crowd of men, women and children collected under the branches of a wide spreading elm tree. Near the tree and from out the centre of the crowd came the notes of a violin, mingled with an occasional abrupt command, in a hoarse voice. At first curiosity, then interest was awakened. In order to satisfy both they climbed a rustic bench, and what Mrs. Allen and her brother heard and saw that afternoon lived in their memory for many a day. They had a fairly good view, and as she looked Mrs. Allen said: "My goodness, Jack, it's that ragged tramp."

Before she could say more a husky voice addressed the crowd and again that vague remembrance came to Mrs. Allen as she listened.

"Ladies and Gentlemen, now that we have secured your attention by the preliminaries, we will proceed with our open-air performance. Allow me first to introduce to your notice the wonderful performing dog, Pilot, who is half-brother to the world-renowned trotting dog, "Dock." I assure you, ladies and gentlemen, that Pilot is in many ways superior to his illustrious brother, and feel convinced that you will acknowledge the statement correct, after seeing him perform. It may possibly add to the interest when I inform you that this noble dog has more than once saved my worthless life at the risk of his own."

"Now! all ready, Pilot? Bow to your audience." The handsome dog seemed delighted to comply. As he rose on his hind feet, there was a proud light in his eye; then elevating his ears, he made a profound courtesy, at which everyone was pleased and clapped their hands while he remained sitting erect on his haunches waiting for his master to announce the first act.

"Now, ladies and gentlemen, Pilot will give you his laughable imitation of a dancing bear."

There was a motion of the violin bow, and the dog raised his honest face, elevated himself on his hind legs, and with lolling tongue and drooping paws, revolved about his master, while the latter, in imitation of the Italian bear tamer, croaned the guttural "Ra—doo—ang donge, Ra—donge—donge," so familiar to all.

The imitation was so comically perfect on the part of both man and dog that every person roared with laughter.

The "Ra—donge—donge Ra—donge" continued, as round went the dog; then was heard the quick command:

"Bar, climb telle pole. Ra—donge—donge Ra—doo—ang," and in perfect imitation of an erect bear, Pilot waddled over to the elm tree and made as if to climb it. Then as his master produced a long drawn minor chord on his violin, he dropped on all fours, rolled over like a flash, and with a bound was at his master's side, seemingly joining in the applause he so richly deserved.

"The next act we will introduce, ladies and gentlemen, is entitled, 'Dog, leap frog,' but Pilot requires five or six lads to assist in this simple performance."

The lads were quite willing, and were soon arranged in a row, with bent backs, bowed heads, and hands on knees in the old-fashioned style; then while accompanied by wild shrieks of the violin, and loud shouts of the crowd, Pilot charged the row more swiftly than any hurdle racer, and with mad leaps cleared one lad after another, then back again, adding shrill barks to the noisy din coming from that wonderful fiddle.

The "Ra—donge—donge" chant again sounded, and Pilot with hind legs in air, swaying tail, and head down, marched on his forelegs, and turning a complete somersault, was again sitting erect on his haunches by his master's side, evidently expecting the thunders of applause which followed.

"You will now see Pilot in his own inimitable waltz. Kindly notice with what perfect grace he carries himself."

Having listened to a charming prelude, Pilot raised himself majestically and started to move his hairy hind feet in perfect time to the sweet strains of waltz music which came so mysteriously from the dingy old violin. He moved with as much nimble grace as he had shown laughable awkwardness while performing the bear dance; and as the music became faster he appeared like a rapidly revolving mass of tawn colored hair. Finally with a great flourish of his silver tipped tail he made his elaborate bow, and sat listening to the plaudits of praise, but panting and blinking from his great exertion.

Then came numerous interesting tricks, never surpassed by any travelling dog show. Pilot doing the difficult parts with such glad willingness that the crowd were captivated.

"Now, ladies and gentlemen," said the tramp solemnly, "the offering will be taken. You know the importance of it, and I think you will certainly say that the poor dog has earned his bone and his master a bed." Saying which, the tramp removed his weather worn hat, tossed it to the dog, who caught it adroitly, then holding it by the rim, started on his rounds, stopping before each person with a silent request for a contribution in his deep honest eyes that never told a lie.

CHAPTER XL.

"Oh, Jack! 'Tis He! 'Tis He!"

During the dog's performance, Mrs. Allen and her brother had been interested spectators, and were about to step from their elevated position when the tramp made the following announcement:

"Ladies and Gentlemen, while Pilot is securing the needful, I will endeavor to entertain you for a few moments by playing this dusty fiddle, which was given me by a dear friend. You need not laugh, he was a much better man than I, and taught me what little I know about violin music. The kind gentleman set great store by this instrument, and used it for many years. I am not capable of playing as he played, but will do my best to give you an idea of his style."

The music which followed held the listeners still and almost breathless. Never had such weird strains been heard in Lincoln Park as upon that quiet summer afternoon. It was produced without apparent effort, by a ragged, dissipated tramp, whose very appearance caused the music to seem the more mysterious. At times it was so exquisitely sweet and pathetic that it brought tears to the eyes of many. This was followed by a mystic melody, suggestive of singing birds, balmy breezes, sunshine

and flowers. Then, in strong contrast, came wild
strains of awesome music, never before heard, and
minor chords which seemed to whisper of dark deeds,
breaking hearts, and human suffering. It ended in
a climax of bewildering sounds, as of hopeless despair,
and a final muffled groan seemed to come from the
very heart of the old worn fiddle, and as the slowly
moving bow stopped, the listeners shivered in wondering sympathy, then remained silent, while the
player in a dazed sort of way mopped his broad,
perspiring brow.

Perhaps the most interested person in that appreciative crowd was Mrs. Frederick Allen. She had
been so absorbed by the dog's performance that she
paid little or no attention to his master till the latter
removed his hat. Then came the same puzzling
haunting memory she had experienced before, and
as the wondrous music rolled from the fiddle, her
eyes were riveted on the player's bloated face and
uncovered head. As she gazed, the man straightened
himself and seemed carried away from a consciousness of his surroundings. Then for the first time
she noticed white locks mingled with the black hair
which covered his large head, and her mind travelled
back three years, recalling distinctly another well remembered scene in which an old violin figured.
She started to tremble, and turning horrified eyes
to her brother, gasped:

"Oh, heavens, Jack, 'Tis he;' 'Tis he; can it be
possible that the handsome clever lawyer has come
to this?"

She wrung her hands, and tears came into her
startled eyes. "Why, Gladys," said her brother,

"what in the name of wonder is the matter? Has the tramp's music set you crazy? Why you are as pale as a ghost."

"Oh, Jack, Jack, I see a ghost in that ragged violinist. A ghost of the past. He stands revealed to me as the embodiment of a prematurely wasted life."

"For goodness sake tell me what you mean?" said the brother earnestly.

"You will laugh at me, and I am almost ashamed to tell you, Jack; but three years ago I was more interested in the man who appears to-day as a degraded tramp, than anyone I have ever met. At that time he was not only a brilliant and refined gentleman, but the handsomest man in New York state."

"Why, Gladys, you do surprise me; but what in the name of goodness has brought him to this?"

"It's a dreadful mystery, and you had better ask him," was the reply. "But here is his wonderful dog taking up a collection."

"Well", said the brother, "his performance and that music is worth more than I have with me; but there is a dollar, old chap." Saying which the gentleman dropped a bill into the hat. Pilot looked his thanks, and was moving off, when Mrs. Allen extended her hand and let fall a shining gold piece among the dimes and nickles which the hat contained.

As she and her brother occupied a position on the outskirts of the crowd they were the last persons to whom Pilot came. Now he sedately carried the hat to his master, who, having emptied the collection into his hand, was about to transfer it to his pocket, when suddenly he paused, selected one coin from the others, and held it up between finger and thumb, as he said:

"Ladies and gentlemen, there has been a mistake. Someone has dropped this ten dollar gold piece into the hat, probably thinking it was a nickle. If the party will come forward, it will only give me pleasure to return the coin to its rightful owner."

"I put it in on purpose, Jack," whispered Mrs. Allen, "do go quick and tell him. Say it came from an old friend of other days. I'll keep in the shadow of the tree, and he will not recognize me."

As her brother left, Mrs. Allen murmured:

"Oh, how sad. What a pity to see him thus. It makes my heart bleed. What in the world has happened? I wonder if we can do anything to help him."

Again she heard the tramp's voice:

"Ladies and gentlemen, I have just received a very great surprise. I am informed that this coin is a freewill offering from a friend of better days. Why I tell you, citizens, I did not think I had a living friend on earth, except my dog, but he is a valuable one. See all he has earned for us to-day," and he held out his hand, containing cents, nickles, dimes, and a one dollar bill. Then dropping the money into his pocket, he continued:

"This gentleman asks my name. Ha, ha, I have no particular reason to withhold it, but I tell you it is not very illustrious, and it is not likely you will re-member, but such as it is you're welcome to know. It's John C. Tomkins, D.G. Ha, ha, I thought you'd laugh."

"What do the last letters stand for?" asked a spruce young man in the crowd. The tramp laughed again, as he replied: "Why my appearance should almost lead you to guess. D.G., why, Drunken Gambler, of course. Ha, ha. I see you think it appropriate, and so it is. John C. Tomkins, Drunken Gambler, that is me," and his face wore a cold bitter smile as he touched his bosom with a trembling forefinger.

"I'm no relation, though, to honest John Tomkins, the hedger and ditcher, who, although he was poor, did not want to be richer. By the way, that quotation reminds me of a poem I once recited at a school examination in the happy long ago, and for which I received a prize. Say boys, little I thought the story told in that poem would ever fit my case; but it does, and you'll say so too, if you listen to the lines. I am sure its author, John Townsend Trowbridge, if alive, will forgive me for repeating some of the verses, with just sufficient change to tell fully the brief sad story of John Tomkins, the drunken, gambling fiddler, and his faithful, performing dog."

"Here, Pilot, lad! You're one of the audience, so show your manners." There was a motion of the violin bow, and Pilot sat erect on his haunches, quietly attentive while his master continued: "The poem I will endeavor to recite is very appropriately entitled, *"The Vagabonds."*

A quiet titter followed this announcement, and there was a momentary flash in the speaker's eyes but he said sadly:

"No, I do not blame you for laughing. I told you the poem suited the case to a 'T'; but I hope the story may be a warning to all."

Then straightening his powerful frame, the tramp
in a deep distinct voice, which had not entirely lost
its mellow tone, repeated the following lines with
rare impressiveness:

"We are two travellers, Pilot and I.
  Pilot's a lad;—sit up you scamp;
Wink at the girls,—with just one eye;
  Hold up your paws,—don't look like a tramp;—
The rogue is growing a little old;
  Three years we've tramped through wind and weather,
And slept out-doors when nights were cold,
  And ate and drank—and starved together.

The truth is, now I reflect,
  I've been so sadly given to grog,
I wonder I've not lost the respect
  Of all things on earth, even of my dog,
But he sticks by through thick and thin;
  And these old clothes, with their empty pockets,
And rags that smell of tobacco and gin,
  He'll follow while he has eyes in his sockets.

There isn't another creature living
  Would do it, and prove, through every disaster,
So fond, so faithful, and so forgiving,
  To such a miserable, thankless master;
No, lads,—see him wag his tail and grin;
  By George! it makes my tired eyes water!
To know he still loves, after all my sin,
  And fairly chokes a fellow. But no matter!

Why not reform? That's easily said;
  But I've gone through such wretched treatment,
Sometimes forgetting the taste of bread,
  And scarcely remembering what meat meant,
That my poor stomach's past reform;
  And there are times, when mad with thinking,
I'd sell out heaven for something warm
  To prop a horrible inward sinking.

Is there a way to forget to think?
  Once I had home, fortune, friends,
A pure wife's love—but I took to cards and drink—
  The same sad story; you know how it ends.
If you could have seen these classic features—
  You need not laugh; they were not then
Such a burning libel on God's creatures;
  I was one of your handsome men.

If you could have seen our child so young,
  Whose head was so happy on this breast,
If you could have heard the songs she sung,
  While I played low chords, you wouldn't have guessed
That even I, a tramp, should be straying
  From door to door with fiddle and dog,
Ragged and penniless, and playing
  To you to-day for the price of grog.

Cards and drink drove me from my wife.
  'Twas better for her that we should part—
Better the saddest, loneliest life
  Than be near the one who had broken her heart.
It makes me wild to think of the change;
  But what care you for poor Tomkin's story
'Tis not amusing, and is far from strange;
  May it stand as a warning, and guide some to glory.

I'll go seek a strong glass, to deaden
  This pain; then Pilot and I will start.
I wonder has he such a lumpish, leaden,
  Aching thing in place of a heart?
He is sad sometimes, and would weep, if he could,
  No doubt remembering things that were,—
A well-bedded kennel, with plenty of food,
  And himself a sober, respectable cur.

Now Tomkins paused, seemingly overcome by emotion. He had rendered the above lines with such intensity of feeling that his little audience seemed almost magnetized. Not only were there tears to be seen, but stifled sobs could be heard, and when he concluded Pilot looked into his face as if to ask, "What next?" A motion of the violin bow caused him to range himself alongside, and in conjunction with his master, they made an elaborate bow, as the latter said brokenly. "We thank you for all your kind attention, and generous offering."

Then turning in the direction of Mrs. Allen and her brother who still occupied the rustic bench; the tramp with weather-worn hat in hand, again bowed, with

a grace which proclaimed him a gentleman, irrespec-
tive of rags, tatters, bloated face, and tangled hair,
and as he straightened himself he said, in tense tones:

"Allow me to thank the kind lady for the gold coin,
and give her the assurance that it at least shall not
be used for gambling, neither will it be squandered
in drink; and now my friends (if you will allow a poor
tramp to call you such) the last words I address
to you will be the closing lines of Trowbridge's
immortal poem:

"I feel better now; your sympathy is warming—
   Pilot, lad, limber your hairy feet,
We must be fiddling and performing
   For supper and bed, or starve in the street.
Not a very gay life to lead, you think?
   But soon we shall go where lodgings are free,
And the sleepers need neither victuals nor drink—
   The sooner the better for Pilot and me.

CHAPTER XLI.

Back to Canadian Soil

"Haw! haw! haw! Hello, Patsey! Where did you get the jag? Where did you find the man? Who owns the dog? By jove, but he's a beauty. You certainly must be smuggling Patsey Farrol."

"Troth, your mishtaken, intoirly, Mr. Fitz. Onless ye do be callin' it smugglin' to be carryin' a dhrop too much yankee whuskey, which same hes tangled up both me and me frind a wee bit, jist what ye'd notice."

The hearty laugh came from a fine-looking, grey haired customs officer in uniform. The abrupt questions were addressed to a thick-set, red-faced jolly-looking man, wearing a check tweed suit. He and a tramp, with whom we are familiar, were the last passengers to leave the ferry steamer which plied between Prescott and Ogdensburg. After she had been made fast to her dock on the Canadian side of the St. Lawrence, and the other passengers had gone, they staggered off the gangway, arm in arm, followed by Pilot. As the man who was called Patsey had said, they were badly tangled with something, for they swayed from side to side while making their way along the dock toward the shore, and when accosted by Mr. Fitz, who was, perhaps, the most popular customs officer along the river, they came to an unsteady halt and the above dialogue took place, after which Mr. Fitz addressed Patsey's companion:

"Well, my good man," said he, "what is your name? and what do you carry in the blue bag?　Ha! ha!　Not smuggling, I hope."

"My name, is—hic—John C. Tomkins—D.—hic—G," was the labored answer, in a thick voice, while its owner looked vacantly at his questioner. Then unslinging from his shoulder a worn blue bag, he continued:

"This, my dear—hic—sir, is an old fiddle, which—like its—hic—owner, has seen better days."

"Where did you find the dog?" was the next question.

"Didn't find him.　He's mine—hic—.　Are you not, lad?"　And the tramp's large meaningless eyes tried to fix their drunken gaze on the dog, who, when addressed, elevated his ears and blinked back a look of anxious, undying love, while he whimpered softly in reply.

"You can see he knows me, Mr.—Mr.—Officer."

"Yes, he knows you alright, and I guess he knows more good about you than I do; but I guess you do not abuse him, even if you do get drunk."

"No,—sir,—Oh, No.　Abuse—hic—Pilot, well no. Why sir,—I tell—you—he's the only friend—hic—friend—I've got."

"Well, I guess he's a pretty good one, but you had better brace up before entering the town, or you might be run in."

"Divil the fare ave that," said Patsey, who had been quietly listening to the conversation.　"Bedad it's mesilf that'll look afther that saim.　Why, bless ye'er koind heart, Mr. Fitz, it's the gran' fiddler he is ahl-out, and his dog, the craythur, fairly bates the worruld, for perfarmin'.　Och, it would warrum

yere heart to sae him walutz, so it waud.   Be gorra,
it was the foin thricks the lad went through wid,
over ferninst at the Burg, that led me to take up
wid his masther, and it's the happy man Oi am thish
day becase we mit, fer he's the bist company, and
the foinest lad fer a little game wid the carrds, ye
iver kim acrost; but bad cess to me bad loock, he
clained me out intoirely.   Then wint to worruk
and spint narly ivery blissed cint ta fill us up wid
tangle leg.   Whin I axed him where he lived, and he
told me nowhere's in particular, well thin, says I,
yiz'll jist be afther comin' roight acrast the ferry wid
me, and be me owan welcome guest, thish very day."

"No, no, says he at firsht, but we drank some more
an thin Oi coaxed some more, and bedad, here wees
are; but parthon me fergitfulness, Mr. Fitz, fer not
axing about wee Bessie.   Bliss the swate face av
her.   Is she bether, sor?"

"Oh, very much better, indeed, thank you, Patsey.
She has greatly improved since we secured the
services of a trained nurse."

"I'm glad to hear ye say ut, Mr. Fitz.   Indade Oi
am, fer it's an angel she is ahl-out; but Oi sae ye'er
onaisy to be goin' and O'ive blathered a good-ale,
but ye nade hive no fares fur me frind here, and if
ye'll jist cum round ta the St. Lawrence House thish
avenin', ye'll hare and sae somethin' that'll warrum
the cockles of ye'er koind heart, sor.   Arrah, but
it's the truth Oi'm tillin ye.   Will ye plase come,
Mr. Fitz?"

"Yes, Patsey, if I have time, but now I must be off.
Be very careful not to get in trouble.   So long, be
kind to that lovely dog," and Mr. Fitz hurried from
the dock.

CHAPTER XLII.

FARROL CASTLE AND WHAT IT CONTAINED.

The morning Lawyer Cainsford left the cabin of the schooner *Tranchemontagne*, three years previous to the day Patsy Farrol heard a tramp fiddler play, and saw his dog perform, he decided to adopt the name of Tomkins.

During the long conversation which had taken place between Captain Sherman and himself, after their mutual recognition, he informed the latter, among other things, that he had not the slightest idea of how he came to be five miles south of the Gap in a sinking sail boat on the morning of his rescue. All he could remember was the fact that he had, by a horrible mistake, poisoned his child, and then fled in despair. Pilot alone was aware of what the yacht "Nora," his mad master, and himself passed through up to the time the sinking boat was sighted off the schooner's port bow, by Jake Simmons, the first mate.

Cainsford set out with the resolve to discontinue both gambling and drink, and was not long in securing employment. The work was distasteful, and he only held the position a short time, when overcome by temptation, he endeavored to drown loneliness and despair by a protracted spree, the result of which was a peremptory dismissal on the part of his employers. It was during his wandering in search of another place, that chance led him to a meeting with the German professor, who years before had given him lessons on the violin. This old gentleman knew at once that his former pupil was in great trouble, and did his best to cheer him up, and finally presented him with the old violin already referred to in this simple tale.

Not long after receiving the gift, Tomkins left Oswego in disgust and almost penniless, to seek employment elsewhere. He met with oft-repeated disappointments, till driven to desperation, as a last resort he made use of Pilot's ability to perform, his own knowledge of the violin, and gave an out-door entertainment. The hardest part of which was the humiliation of taking up a collection, but it had to be done, steal, or go hungry, and the amount received at this his first attempt was far beyond his expectation.

Then came to him what he termed an inspiration. He therefore set to work assiduously to teach Pilot an important part of the performance, namely to pass around the hat. We are already aware how proficient Pilot became.

Even at this occupation Tomkins' natural cleverness was so great, and his dog's ability so pronounced, that had the former kept sober and strangled his passion for play, he could have soon established a bank account with a substantial amount to his credit. He did not do either, however, but gradually sank lower and lower, till he became what Mrs. Frederick Allen found sitting on a log by the dusty roadside.

It chanced that Patsey Farrol while on one of his periodical sprees, crossed over to Ogdensburg, happened to see Pilot perform, fell in love with him at once, and became his master's friend on the spot. We know something of what followed.

Patsey Farrol was a jolly, generous, kind-hearted Irishman, who owned a small farm a few miles from Prescott. He did not depend entirely upon farming for a living, however, for he was a typical egg buyer, and made considerable money during the summer months at this business. He had recently purchased an old tumbled down building on the outskirts of the town, which he used as a sort of storehouse for egg cases, etc., and had been known to sleep there occasionally, as he had a shake-down in one of the two rooms in the upper story. Since the death of his wife, which occurred about a year previous to our introduction, Patsey's sprees became more frequent, and the day before he met John Tomkin's, in a fit of lonely melancholy he had come to town, put his horse in the stable adjoining his old house, and before dark was three sheets in the wind. That night he remained in the old house, and the next morning crossed on the ferry to O—, returning as we have seen, arm in arm with the drunken fiddler he called his friend.

Having made this brief explanatory digression, we will take up the thread of our narrative.

After Mr. Fitz had left them, the friends made their way to a restaurant, familiar to Patsey, where they secured a much-needed meal, then Patsey thought of his horse, and induced his companion to accompany him while he went to look after its needs.

This rollicking Irishman never let anything depending upon him go hungry. He remembered Pilot at the restaurant, and now his sleek-looking horse received a bountiful feed; after which Patsey introduced his visitor to the mysteries of "Farrol Castle," as he called the place; showed him where the huge, old-fashioned key of the front door was kept concealed; at the same time informing him that "if iver he wuz harr'd up fer a noight's lodgin' he was as welcome to the castle as the flowers av May."

He then led him through a passage, between barrels, boxes, etc., up a narrow stair, to a garret room, lighted by a dingy, uncurtained, broken-paned window. The only furniture the room contained was a small table and a backless cane-bottomed chair, which Patsey set out for his guest, while he rummaged about in the adjoining room. He soon emerged, carrying a pair of well worn boots, and throwing them down, he said:

"There yiz are, put them on ta yer fate. Oi'd loik if they wus betther, but it's not ivery gorsoon Oi'd lit stan' in me shoes, and bedad, they'er a good dale more loik a gintleman's togs, than thim pair ave howly terrors, wid out any hales, which saims a disgrace to the illigant walk ave yiz. And now ye'er luckin' foin. Arrah, but it's a good male, wid lots ave timattie pickles, or the loik, to pit the whuskey to floit. Bad scran ta ut. I wisht Mr. Fitz could jist pape at ye now. Be-gorra, yer as sober as a jidge, and can walk as straight as awny wan on the policest force; and now we'll take a wee droph of the craythur in honnor of thish blessed

day, whin I found ye widout a frind.   Here yiz
are."

Saying which Patsey opened a drawer in the little
table and produced a flask which was about half
full of Canadian whiskey, then continued:

"This'll pit us in great fettle for the avenin's
performance, but there is wan thing Oi'd loik ye
ta do fer me thish noight—it's ta sing a rail Orish
song, fer me an the bys. Will ye do that saime
fer yer frind av ye plase?"

Here Tomkins, who had been busy changing his
boots, raised his head, and willingly accepted a
drink from the bottle. Patsy did likewise, and after
returning the flask to the drawer, brought out a
worn leather case, which contained a revolver. As
he opened it, he remarked:

"Luck at that. Be-dad, O'ive carried that saim
on ivery thrip Oi've made buyin' hin eggs since the
poor ould Jew peddler was robbed and noigh killed
wan noight lasht fall. I've niver bane obleeged ta
foire it aff yit; but Oi kape it loaded all the saim,
but there, faix it's a wicked lookin' craythur an'
Oi'll pit it back where it belangs. The question is
will ye sing that Oirish song?"

"I'll do my best to remember one, Mr. Farrol."

"Na, na, don't Mishter me, jist Patsey plase,"
interrupted that gentleman. "An' lit's have jist
another wee sup."

"Alright Patsey. I thank you for your boots,
and all your kindness, but I must not drink too often
or I will not be able to sing or play either. I cannot
stand as much as I once could."

"Me nathur," said Patsy, as he emptied the bottle.
Then they descended the narrow stair.

Three hours later the sound of a violin, hilarious laughter, and loud hand claps, came from a crowd which had been attracted to a large room adjoining the bar of the St. Lawrence Hotel. When the enthusiasm was at its height, Patsy Farrol's voice could be heard above the din of applause:

"Now, me frind, plase kape ye'er promise, and give us a rale Oirish song."

The player tried his best to excuse himself, but in vain, for Patsey insisted. Then the notes of a rollicking Irish air came from the old fiddle, and the song entitled "Pat Malone Forgot That He Was Dead," was sung in a voice that at one time had most certainly been both rich and musical. It was a little thick upon this occasion. The brogue, however, was almost equal to Patsey's and helped conceal the roughness in the tone.

The crowd was more than delighted, and continued their uproarious applause till the hotel proprietor came to demand a cessation of both noise and performance. Then every man present insisted upon treating the singer and his friend Farrol. As they were both willing, it was not long until they were in a very mellow mood. Then Patsey recalled the fact that he had promised to return to his home in the country, and after considerable persuasion Tomkins consented to accompany him.

Of course, before leaving, they each secured a bottle, and half an hour later were on their way, and had not gone a mile before one botrle was emptied and the other attacked vigorously, with the result that they were soon almost helplessly drunk. Poor Patsey lolled in the seat, and his passenger, having mechanically seen that his violin was beside him, spread himself out on the hay which covered the bottom of the long box of the low spring waggon, and a moment later was fast asleep.

When Patsey's steady-going horse was two-thirds of the way up a steep hill, he suddenly felt his load become lighter. He did not stop, however, but diligently toiled to the top and disappeared, before a sprawling heap staggered up, dimly wondering what had happened.

It was a huge mystery to the bewildered Tomkins, but very easily explained. While lying in the bottom of the wagon one of his heavy boots was thrust with considerable force against the end board, which chanced to be on hinges with spring hooks to secure it at the top. The blow from the boot caused the hooks to let go, and down went the board. Then as the hill was steep and somewhat rough, the jolts of the wagon gradually shook Tomkins and his hay bed, till they quietly slid out behind.

When this occurred, Pilot who had been solemnly marching along abreast of the wagon, turned back and sniffed wonderingly at his master, who, although only partially roused by the severe jar, managed to scramble to his feet. While he stood swaying in the darkness, the watchful Pilot drew his attention to the fact that his much-valued violin, incased in its blue bag, was lying on the road. At the third attempt Tomkins picked it up and hung it on his shoulder, then slowly staggered his way to the top of the hill. He continued his course for a short time, but as he could not hear or see anything of the wagon, and fairly overcome with weariness and whiskey, determined to rest. He was still too much muddled to reason clearly, but realized that a secluded spot would be best.

While glancing about him he noticed a group of tall pine trees outlined in the gloom quite close to the roadside, also a gate. With some difficulty he managed to undo the fastenings of the latter and passed through. It seemed a quiet, inviting spot, with deep soft grass, which would make a good bed.

Having drank what remained in Patsey's flask, Tramp Tomkins, and his Performing Dog, disappeared in the shadow of a pine tree, with thick foliage, which stood there grim and *silent*, in the *darkness of night*.

CHAPTER XLIII.

A Madman's Wild Laugh.

Never more blue was the water, never more pure was the sky, never more gay were the wavelets and careless in innocent glee, than the next morning when God's sunshine peeped over the distant purple hills and sent its glancing light across the majestic St. Lawrence, leaving in its path myriads of dancing sparkling ripples, like diamonds indued with life.

As it reached the Canadian shore it touched the trees with its magic wand and they burst into brilliant golden green, which wakened their feathery lodgers to gladness and song. The flowers too seemed to rouse and nod a sweet welcome, and the grass was certainly pleased, for thousands of its blades shed joyous dew drops, straightened themselves, and with a soft whisper embraced the merry shimmering brilliance of a new day.

The coming of the morning light wakened more than birds, grass and flowers, for until it came heavy snoring could be heard, coming it seemed from the foot of a venerable pine tree. But as its thick boughs were touched into gorgeous green, the noise ceased, and as the golden rays penetrated the shady spot, they first illumined into shining splendor a pure marble slab, then gently rested on the bloated unshaven face of a sprawling tramp, whose large head had pillowed itself upon a little flower-bedecked grave, and in its heedless heavy rolling had crushed the hearts out of dozens of sweet innocent flowers.

For hours its owner had been noisily sleeping off his last debauch, while a glossy-haired, pale-faced companion silently kept watch; and now as the golden sunbeams lighten up the drink-disfigured face, the ragged man moves uneasily, as if ashamed of his appearance even in his sleep. As he moves, the watcher raises his head, and as his deep mysterious eyes blink steadfast unending love, he tenderly licks the dirty sun-browned hand carelessly thrown out from the mighty shoulder belonging to this huddled heap of degraded humanity.

With a throat gurgle the man's mouth closes, the blood-streaked eyes open, and a drunken gambler glares about and mutters hoarsely: "Where— the —devil—am—I?" Then he pulls himself together, and sitting upon his heels his eyes slowly become accustomed to the light.

Finally they rest on the pure white marble tombstone which stands there calm and silent, almost within reach. At first his eyes follow the letters of the inscription without apparent comprehension. Then they open wide in startled wonder, and seem to telegraph a familiar name to the benumbed intellect, and the man's whole being quivers as he reads:

IN MEMORY OF

HELEN CAINSFORD.

OUR PRECIOUS, PASSING SUNBEAM.

Born——18—. Died——18—.

As he repeatedly reads the heading his powerful frame sways from side to side, and perspiration pours from the twitching face and dims the sight of his burning eyes. He quickly wipes them out, and by a mighty effort steadies himself to read the verse so beautifully cut in the white marble, ending in the familiar words which had for three terrible years been re-echoeing through his tortured brain:" Papa, come this way."

Having finished he got upon his feet shivering as with cold, and a great cry was partly suffocated in his breast by the panting of his heart as he gasped:

"Dread God! how did I get here? Oh, to think that I the besotted one should have desecrated my angel child's grave." And a hellish groan of misery bursts from his heaving breast, and there in the golden glory of a summer's sunrise, beside a quiet solemn tomb, underneath the boughs of a mysteriously whispering pine which guarded this hallowed spot, came the climax of a gnawing agonizing remorse, which would drive a desperate husband and father to hell, or coax a repentant sinner to heaven.

In a dazed mechanically way he picked up his hat and fiddle, and trembling like a leaf tip-toed a short distance, paused, stopped, tip-toed back again, and for a brief moment his parched trembling lips were pressed to the cold marble where the name "Helen" was cut. As they lingered a sweet voice seemed to whisper: "Poor, dear Papa, tome ---iss—way."

Now filled with a vague familiar awesome fear, the man flies away and away, clearing the fence with astonishing agility and swiftness, down the road he ran as if for life, closely followed by swift flying, soft padded feet.

* * * * * *

An hour later a huge old-fashioned key was turned in the lock of the weather-beaten door which gave entrance to the house called Farrol Castle, and a panting, trembling, wild-eyed man, and a melancholy, white-faced dog passed through and the door was closed. As they climbed the narrow stair, Tomkins felt as though he might be a million miles from any living soul except his dog. There was such utter desolation in his heart, such horrid throbbing in his head, and such unutterable despair in his whole being, that he groaned aloud in hopeless anguish.

As he took his seat on the only chair the barren room contained, he noticed the staff lying where he left it the day before while changing his boots. It called to mind his lonely wanderings, his useless life, and present degraded condition. He dimly recalled the events of the previous night and the awful awakening, to find that he had defiled his child's last resting place by sleeping off an overdose of whiskey on her grave. The thought was maddening. He was seized with such terrible loathing that he cursed himself and the day he was born. Then sat in a sort of stupefication, while delirious dreams possessed his brain, and like a maniac he raved incoherently.

This seemed to startle the attentive Pilot. His ears elevated, and his rich luminous eyes gazed at his master in a mute appeal, as if anxious to learn the meaning of those queer unfamiliar sounds.

Suddenly Tomkins left his seat, entered the adjoining room, and returned with a whiskey flask. When he discovered it was empty he flung it down with a curse, mopped his streaming face, and took off his ragged coat, revealing the fact that he wore neither vest nor braces, and that his shirt which was open at the neck was torn, faded, and almost buttonless. A russet leather belt supported his trousers, which, like the rest of his scanty apparel betokened poverty and want.

For a moment he stands irresolute; then his wandering eyes rest on his threadbare coat lying on the floor. The sight appears to anger him for with vicious kicks he sends it flying into the next room. As he turns a new thought appears to enter the delirious brain, for he quickly opened the table drawer, removed Patsey's revolver, and took it from its case.

As he fingers the weapon he looks gloatingly upon it, and his eyes fill with a mad light.

"Ah-ha," he whispers, "I guess I've found a friend at last. The devil is after his own."

He placed the revolver upon the little table; then, while taking off his boots, muttered to himself: "I do not think I was intended to die in another man's shoes. Oh, no," and he chuckled harshly.

While removing his worn out sock, he peered at Pilot long and stealthily. The peculiar gaze seemed to effect the dog, for he heaved a loud sigh and started pacing up and down uneasily.

Now his master removed the violin from its blue bag; produced a soiled pack of cards from his pocket, and laughing a low reckless laugh, said to himself:

"A clever lawyer like me should arrange all his earthly possessions and make a will before going on the dark journey. My heirs will not have much to quarrel over, however. Oh, no. Ha—ha—ha—."

Laying the fiddle on the table, he shuffled the cards, and as he did so, nodded his head and talked to them:

"Yes—you—and that (pointing to the bottle) and the devil, have made me what I am; and the three of you are welcome to your victim. You have been after me for long, but I'll not keep you waiting at the finish. Ha—ha—ha—ha—ha—ha." And the moist, dead, comfortless room re-echoed a mad man's wild laugh.

Picking up the violin, while tuning it, he talked to it in the same cold creepy voice: "Just a chord or two from you, my old friend, before I say farewell forever."

Then wails and shrieks seemed to fill the stagnant air of the low garret room, and as he continued to draw the bow, Pilot sat scanning his master's face; his own filled with wondering anxiety.

Suddenly the turmoil of sound ceased and was for a time replaced by a delicious intoxicating melody. Then a familiar air gradually developed, till the violin strings seemed to whisper, softly and tenderly, "Pa-pa, come this way, Pa-pa, come this way." As the player's strong arm ceased to move he looks about him with an indescribable fear in his shining eyes and unshaven face. He placed the bow gently on the table, and rising with noiseless feet crossed the floor and hung the violin on a rusty nail driven into the door casing; then turning to the narrow stair he peered down and listened intently, and while doing so a cold muzzle was thrust into his hand, from which he recoils as if stung. As he turned his head he saw Pilot staring and blinking at him in dumb white-faced wonder, and the crazy gleam in his master's eyes softens as they rest upon that steadfast faithful friend, and he whispers words which seem to fairly drip with tears:

"I am very sorry, lad, yes very, very sorry to leave you, Pilot. But you will be much better off when I am gone, and really I cannot bear the burden of my hellish existence any longer. If the torments of the damned are as great as mine have been since I wakened at daylight on Helen's grave Satan himself must be sorry. Oh,—Oh,—the misery—to think of what might have been; and it is always with me —yes, always with me. I can—not—No,—I cannot bear it longer. I envy you, Pilot, lad. If

there is a heaven for dogs you'll sit on the throne,
and I'd willingly lie at your feet—but come on lad,
I will not give you the pain of seeing me die; come
on!" and the dog followed his master down the
creaking stair.

Before the front door was opened a trembling brown
hand stroked and patted Pilot's broad brow, gently,
tenderly; then a quivering voice said: "Now off
with you, lad. Go seek a new home and worthy
master."

As Pilot reluctantly passed out and the door
slowly swung to, a rending groan could be heard,
and a forlorn voice quavered: "Good-bye, Pilot,
lad, Good-bye."

CHAPTER XLIV.

A Prayer to Heaven for Aid.

"See here, Mrs. Cainsford, I do think you stay in
too closely. Why, you have scarcely been out of
the house since you came, and now that Bessie is
so much better you might just as well take a walk
every day. Please, go now, the early morning
air will do you all sorts of good. It is so delightfully
fresh and balmy. It would be a shame to miss it."

These words of advice were addressed to a golden-
haired nurse in uniform by Custom Officer Fitz.
As she listened, the lady smiled somewhat sadly,

and although a glance at her expressive face would have informed one that she had had some great sorrow, Mrs. Chris Cainsford was still a very beautiful woman. There was a subdued melancholy about her expression seldom seen. It would suggest that although sad and lonely she was not without hope.

As she gazed through the drawing-room window, she replied in a low musical voice:

"You are very thoughtful and kind, Mr. Fitz. The morning is truly inviting, and I think I will take your advice and stroll out on the lawn. I agree with you fully that a sun bath is conducive to health, and in order to secure a full benefit one is better without wraps." Saying which Mrs. Cainsford passed out, and made a very attractive picture as she crossed the lawn, clad in her pale blue and white uniform. The little cap only partially concealed her gleaming, golden hair, and seemed an appropriate crown for goodness and purity.

As her graceful, beautifully-rounded form disappeared behind the heavy boughs of a dark green spruce tree, Mr. Fitz heaved a sigh, and murmured to himself:

"If ever an angel woman lived upon earth there she goes. How any living man could desert such a wife knocks me cold. I understand she has not heard from her husband for three years. He must be a brute, and should certainly die and give a decent man a chance."

For some time after Nora reached the front gate she was completely absorbed by the beauty of the scene and while still looking across the sparkling waters of Old St. Lawrence she heard the bark of

a dog. Suddenly her ear caught a tone of anxiety
in the sound, which appeared to come from the **front**
of a forsaken looking tumbled down house, standing
by itself a short distance away on somewhat **lower**
ground, and slightly in the rear of Mr. Fitz's brick
dwelling.

As she looked across a tall dog raised himself and
began clawing frantically at the front door, as if
determined to gain admittance.

"That seems strange," thought Nora. "I do not
believe the house is occupied."

As she watched, a mournful howl was borne to her
on the balmy breeze, and again the dog stood erect
with paws well up on the dark weather-beaten door.
It formed a background which even at the distance
caused the dog to stand out in bold relief.

As Nora gazed a startled expression could be seen
on her lovely face; and at the sound of another
loud pleading bark she opened the gate and rushed
away. There was a ring of hope in her voice as she
said excitedly: "Oh, Heavenly Father, can it be
possible that my prayers are answered, and he has
come at last?'

The thought appeared to lend wings to her feet.
She turned off the road, and fairly flew up the weedy,
uncared-for path. "It's Pilot! It's Pilot!" she
gasped. "But where, oh, where is his master?"

As she drew near the dog turned, looked at her
inquiringly, dropped on all fours, sniffed her skirt,
licked her hand, and then with a great joyous yelp.
reared himself and almost embraced her; then galloped round and round, mouthing gladness at every
leap; after which rushing to the door he whined
piteously and clawed at the knob.

Nora placed her arms about Pilot's hairy form, laid her golden, cap-crowned head upon his tawny coat, and as tears rolled down her flushed face, whispered brokenly: "Oh, Pilot, your master. Where is your master?" In response the dog licked her face, whimpered and again fiercely clawed the knob.

Now, all of a tremble, Nora opened the door and passed through into gloom and disorder, Pilot leading the way. As his mistress followed, she was filled with an uneasy unexplainable dread which increased as they reached the narrow stair. When about to leap forward Pilot was prevented by Nora, who buried her hand in the depths of his soft hair, seized a tuft and said pleadingly: "Oh, Pilot, lad, wait, please wait just a minute. I am so terribly frightened."

As they stood thus, every sense on the alert, suddenly Nora's heart almost stopped beating, for she heard a low mumbling voice, and as she waited, trembling,and scarcely breathing, she could indistinctly hear these words:

"Good-Bye— Pilot—lad—Good—Good-Bye, old— boy. You have been a faithful friend. Good-Bye —Good-Bye my lovely—much-wronged—wife. Oh, —I—did—love you so—Nora. Oh—God—to think —that I made her hate—me, but I did—not mean to —poison—our—child. I thought I could—hear Helen calling just now—but I can not go to—her, No,—No, I'm too wicked and accursed. It's too— late—too—late—there is no—mercy for me.—"

Then followed the sound of a groan, mingled with a sharp click, click, and Nora with a shudder released Pilot and sprang after him as he sped up the stairs.

Arriving at the top she was for a moment spellbound at the sight she beheld. Could it be possible that this cowering, gibbering, wild-eyed wretch, with cocked revolver pointed at his head, was her once handsome husband?

"No, oh, no, it cannot be," she whispered.

But as she gazed, she perceived that white hair mingled with the black tangled, uncombed locks covering his massive head.

With a suppressed cry she sprang to his side, seized his wrist, and raising her arm aloft breathed a fervent prayer to heaven for aid.

As he felt the firm cool touch of the hand, and the pressure of those delicate fingers the man shrank away, while his large glassy eyes remained fixed in a hopeless, helpless demoniac stare. He seemed to think that the white-robed figure was an apparition, and shivering as with cold, clutched at his heart, as a muffled scream came from his parted lips.

While the trembling nurse grasped the wrist of the hand which held the weapon, Pilot placed his hairy paw on the other and whined anxiously, thus telling his despairing master that help had come.

As the would-be suicide heard Nora's cry of terror he seemed to harken! harken! and hold his breath as his trembling form sank lower and lower still on the backless chair. It seemed as though a new thought as last found lodgment in his bewildered brain. Did he recognize the loved tones of long ago? It must have been the case for he was evidently thrilled by some great emotion as these words fell on the heavy air:

"Oh, God of Heaven, Thou Mighty One, who hath promised to be the helper of the weak and helpless, come to my aid this moment and save a human life from self-destruction."

Then bending over her husband's ill-clad form, she cried: "Chris! Chris! Oh, Chris! do not despair. Your wife Nora has come to help you. She does not hate you as you think—far, far from it. Why, she still loves you with all her heart. Oh, Chris, listen! listen! and for my sake, for Helen's sake, for Heaven's sake, drop that Awful Weapon. I know God in answer to my many prayers has guided me to this spot in order to save you from yourself. Have courage. He will help and forgive you, for have not I? Oh, my husband, hear me! Drop the weapon, for I Love you still."

As the last words were uttered the crouching form on the chair quivered from head to foot. The trembling hand released its hold, and the heavy revolver fell to the floor and exploded with a flash. As the echoes of the report were dying away; regardless of rags, tatters, tangled hair, bloated face and shrinking form, Nora fell on her husband's neck and sobbed forth the joy and grief of a desolate, sore-tried heart.

Thus they met after three years of courageous waiting, watching, hoping and praying on the part of one; and three years of cowardly, purposeless wandering and sinning on the part of the other. Nora felt that God in his goodness had answered her prayers, and used the faithful Pilot to guide her to her husband's side. She was rejoiced to accept the prodigal without reproach or protest, no matter how low and vile his condition.

The loving, faithful devotion of a noble forgiving wife, and the staunch steadfast friendship of a true-hearted dog, guided by a merciful Providence, had prevented a man who was intended for one of God's noblemen from dying the awful death of a cowardly suicide, and rescued the homeless, despairing, degraded wreck of the man they loved from the very gates of hell; and to what purpose? Would the brand thus plucked from the burning reform and redeem the dark past?

As Nora knelt at his side and prayed that this might be so, he was suddenly seized with violent trembling, and as he gasped, "Oh, God of Heaven help me," sank to the floor in helpless unconsciousness.

As Nora was bending over the prostrate form her alarm was increased by the sound of a heavy tread ascending the creaking stair. Very soon a thick-set man, dressed in a check tweed suit, appeared, and as Nora got upon her feet, and with tear-dimmed startled eyes looked his way, he stopped and gazed at her in wild-eyed astonishment, and for a moment stood as if spell-bound; then in an awed tone said, hesitatingly: "Howly—Saints—it's a—shoinin'—angel — from— glory—or—the — blissed — vargin — hersilf—what's—kim—ta visit—me ould—castle."

CHAPTER XLV.

OLD FRIENDS.

About the same time Tomkins was wakened by the golden sunbeam, Patsey Farrol was roused by the soft whinney of his brown horse which stood waiting patiently at the stable door out at the farm. Patsey yawned, stretched himself, and while looking about with blinking, bleary eyes, muttered: "Bedad, Prince, but ye'er a koind, cliver lad, so yiz are, to have brung ye'er ould toired masther safe home be ye'er lone and niver disthurbed me paceful slape, at all, at all. Arrah, but it's the proud man Oi am to be the owner ave sich a sinseible craythur as yersilf; but where in the name ave Saint Patrick is our frind, the fiddler? Oi well moind ave startin' out wid him besoide me, and ave joinin' him in a wee sup ave ould John Sagrim. But divil the thing else do Oi remimber. Bad scran to the sthrong stuff that slips down wan's throat loik new made milk and stales up to wan's brains loik ould Satan himself."

Here Patsey was interrupted by another whinney from Prince, and now managed to clamber from his wagon, unhitch and feed his hungry horse, then go to the house to rouse the sleeping inmates. While eating a hastily prepared breakfast, he wondered why Tomkins had not come all the way. The more he thought about it the more mysterious it seemed, till he became anxious and determined to go back in search of his missing gues'.

As Prince was slowly descending a steep hill his master noticed some hay lying on the road, and upon examination decided that it had been in his wagon box the night before, and that its present location had something to do with the disappearance of the man he was looking for. He could find no signs of the latter, however, and continued on his way till he reached the old house, and was not much surprised to find the key in the door, but was fairly astounded to behold a beautiful woman bending over the sprawling form of his ragged friend Tomkins.

Explanations followed, and Patsy's astonishment increased when he learned that this lovely golden-haired nurse was Mrs. Chris Cainsford, and that the drunken fiddler was her husband and the once brilliant lawyer of whom Patsy had so often heard.

When he recovered sufficiently from his surprise to speak, he offered to go for assistance, and if possible bring Mr. Fitz. Of course Nora gratefully accepted the kindness, and remained to watch.

*   *   *   *   *   *   *

We will now ask the reader to accompany us while we again make a brief early visit to the picturesque town of L——. As we turn up a certain street we are pleased to stop and admire a vine-covered house, still called Cainsford cottage. As we stand in the shade of a thrifty maple tree, we notice that the front window is up, but upon this occasion there are no joyous barks to be heard, no clapping of soft chubby hands, no dancing dog, no music, no laughter. All is very still.

While waiting we notice a brass plate on the door which informs the visitor that Dr. Frank Allgood's office hours are from 8.30 a.m. till 12, and from 1.30 p.m. till 3 p.m.   Now the door opens and a short, rosey-cheeked, fleshy woman appears, and while she looks down the street, a comfortable-looking carriage turns the corner and is driven up to the curb.   As a tall, fine-looking youth springs out, the comely hazel-eyed woman addressed him thus:

"Docthur has jist about finished his kaffey, and will be riddey in no time.   Arrah, ishent this a luvily mornin' fer a droive.   I'd well loike to be goin' mesilf and it's the luckey lad yiz are entiorly, Toney Tomkins, to be sarvin' the foin maun yiz heve fer a boss, who is always and feriver doin' somewan a good turn.   It's rale proud Oi am to be his housekaper, and since we've kim to live here, Moik, me good maun, niver titches a draph. Praise be to the Saints, and we'er ahl so happy that sometoimes I heve to wape fer jie, and thin when Oi think ave ye'er other boss's louvily sad woif, me heart does be nigh broke wid sorrow, but Oi belave this mornin' that some swate day her prayers and moy prayers will be anshwered fer sure, and Mr. Cainsford, God save him, will kim back and make her happy."

"I do hope so," said our old friend Toney.   "And I am very luckey indeed to have Dr. Allgood for a friend; and you couldn't guess what he told me yesterday, Mrs. Murphy."

"Oi'll bit it was somethin' rale foine," said she.

"It was for sure.   Why, he told me if I studied hard for six months he would send me to college.

Is'nt that grand? And just think of what he has done for your Maggie."

As she listened to the last words, Mrs. Murphy gave Toney a keen glance which caused the latter to hold down his head and blush vividly, and Maggie, the elder, knew for sure that Maggie, the younger, had a sweetheart, but she only smiled and said softly:

"Yis, yis, God bless him fer all his goodness. Why Misther Mitchel tould me himsilf that oor Maggie wus the cliverist toypewroiter he evir kim acrast, but whist, whist Toney, here is the Docthur."

: : : : : : :

It does seem good to look upon the tall Doctor's long face once more. Although the lines are a little deeper and the crows feet more pronounced, it still beams with goodness, sympathy and loving kindness. Many of his patients claim that Dr. Allgood's cheery words and bright smiles are more effective in producing a cure than his carefully prescribed medicine. Be that as it may he has been very successful, and is honored by all who know him.

While stepping into his carriage he nods a pleasant good-morning to Toney; then turning to Mrs. Murphy, says: "I am going to Prescott to see how my old friend's little girl is doing. It is not probable that I will be back for luncheon, but if Bessie Fitz is well enough I will return early in the afternoon and try and bring Mrs. Cainsford with me. I am sure you would be glad to see her, Mrs. Murphy."

"Indade an' I would, and ye may be sure Oi'll heve iverything riddy. Good-bye, sor, and may good luck go wid yiz."

*   *   *   *   *   *

As Dr. Allgood arrived in front of the Fitz home, he saw its owner hurrying down the walk accompanied by a thickset man dressed in a tweed suit. They both seemed excited, and as Mr. Fitz held out his hand, he said earnestly: "By George, doctor, you have come in the very nick of time. My friend Patsey, here, has given me some strange news that I can scarcely believe, but please come along and we will see. There must be someone in trouble, or Mrs. Cainsford would certainly have returned.

Without further loss of time the three men hurried across to Farroll Castle. We will not attempt to describe Dr. Allgood's surprise and astonishment, nor the complete bewilderment of Mr. Fitz, as they reached the top of the stairs and found Mrs. Cainsford sitting on the floor of the dingey garret room, anxiously gazing upon the face of a coatless, sprawling, ragged man, whose large uncombed head was pillowed on her snow-white lap. She uttered a fervent "Thank God" as the Doctor appeared, then tears streamed from her lovely eyes, as she said brokenly:

"Oh, Doctor, he has at last come back. Your old friend and my poor homeless husband is here. Truly God is good. Oh, Doctor, please feel his pulse, quick, I think he has just fainted from weakness and emotion. You are always so skilful I am sure you will soon restore him. Do you not think you can, Doctor?"

"Heaven helping me I will do my best, Mrs. Cainsford, but he is greatly changed, and seems entirely unconscious. Oh, what a pity."

As he examined his dear old friend of other days, the Doctor was filled with varied emotions—gladness, sorrow, regret, dismay, hope, were all inter-mingled. As he continued doing his best to restore him; he only met with partial success, for his patient remained in a semi-unconscious condition for hours after he had been placed in the cleanest, sweetest bed John Tomkins, D.G., had known for years.

Mr. Fitz, in his big-hearted kindness, had insisted on placing Mrs. Cainsford's husband in the large airy front room which contained the best bed in his house.

It was only by skilful treatment and careful attention on the part of the Doctor, and self-sacrificing devotion and tender care on the part of his loving nurse, that Tomkins escaped a serious attack of the awful disease known as delirium tremens. His iron constitution was in his favor, however, but it had been greatly shaken and impaired by exposure, careless living, and over-indulgence. At last after ten days of anxiety on the part of his friends Chris Cainsford was able to sit up, clothed and in his right mind. We may perhaps be able to judge somewhat of his condition if we listen to a conversation which took place one day after Patsy Farrol had called to see him.

"Where did you meet that generous Irishman first, Chris?" asked Nora, as she sat by the table working the initial "C" in the corner of a silk handkerchief.

For some time Cainsford's face wore a puzzled expression, then turning to his wife his large eyes glistened with tears as he said brokenly:

"Oh, Nora, Nora, my much wronged wife, when I endeavor to recall the events of the past three years they seem to me like the indistinct remembrance of a prolonged dream of hideous horror, peopled by demoniac demons and spirits of evil who have ever been on the alert to drag me down, down, lower and lower, to an awful abyss of despair and death, from which I could not possibly escape, but through all my wanderings, degradation, drunkenness and vice, it seems as though a good spirit has also continually watched over and protected me. The more I tried to drown sorrow and remorse by gambling and drink, the oftener would I hear little Helen's sweet voice calling to me, oh, so tenderly, in the words she loved to sing: "Papa, come this way."

"Many, many times after partially recovering from a drunken debauch, my remorse and misery were so great that I would decide to end all my trouble by suicide,—full as many times have the hissing demons who appeared to surround and urge me on, been put to flight by that sweet voice and angel presence, and I would gradually return to a conscious realization that I did not possess the power to end my own miserable life, while so carefully guarded by my ever watchful friend Pilot, and darling Sunbeam's spirit. Again would come the haunting thought of what might have been, followed at once by the awful remembrance that I had poisoned our child, broken your heart, and made you hate me. This last was the hardest of all to bear. Oh, Nora, Nora, how I have *suffered*, and made you *suffer*. If I only had known that you did not hate me. Oh, if I only had known." And a quavering groan heaved from Cainsford's breast as he sat there pale and wan in the mellow light. While his hand drooped over the arm of the easy chair, a cool muzzle shoved into it, Pilot's tender way of telling his poor, weak, trembling master that the sympathising, staunch, courageous friend whose name he had mentioned was near——."

CHAPTER XLVI.

THE BLACK NIGHT IS PAST.

Before entering the room Pilot had looked through the hall window and noticed a dapple grey horse and phaeton carriage approaching, driven by a sturdy-looking old gentleman. We do not know what the dog's thoughts were, but he immediately pushed through the door, which stood slightly ajar, and in doing so left it invitingly open, then took up his station at his master's side. Pilot's expression, like that of his mistress, seemed to have undergone some mysterious change. There was a joyous light in the rich depths of his honest luminous eyes, and as his master stroked and patted his broad brow, and softly whispered his name, he wagged his silver tipped tail, then sitting erect on his haunches, looked from master to mistress with eyes filled with admiring love and devotion.

Nora had been greatly moved by her husband's recital of his terrible experiences, and as he uttered the last words, so burdened with sorrow and regret she too softly stole to his side, and placing her cool firm hand on his bowed head, murmured:

"Courage, Chris, Courage. It's all past and gone.
The dark night is ended; the morning is here. Oh,
Chris, my husband, you know now that 'God is
good.' How thankful we should be when we remember your miraculous preservation from the awful
death of the suicide. Just think of the means He
employed to save you. Truly His ways are mysterious and past finding out; and I know He is wil-
ilng and able to keep, for I have proven it over
and over again during the past three sad years.

"Yes, yes, Nora, I do believe it, and am truly
thankful, but although I love you with all my heart
and would willingly lay down my life for your sake
I am afraid of myself. I have not forgotten, nor can
I ever forget my former good resolutions, and the
many, many promises I gave you; but when temptation really came I broke them all and went down
before it with scarce a struggle. Thus proving conclusively that I am just a poor weak vacilating coward, not able to stand alone; and when I think of the
degradation through which I have come, I fairly
loathe myself, and wonder you do not do the same.
How you can for a moment regard me with feelings
of anything but hatred and scorn is a profound
mystery to me this very moment.

"Why, I tell you, Nora, when you came upon me
so unexpectedly in that garret room, I thought it
was to denounce and curse me before I had time to
die. Imagine my surprise, when, instead of curses,
I heard prayers, instead of reproach, loving words
of forgiveness and hope. No wonder I became unconscious."

For a moment Chris sat silent, then continued in a
loud eager tone:

"Oh, Nora, Nora, my darling wife, would to God that I could in some small measure atone for the misery I have caused you, but I am so weak and unworthy; so weak and unworthy," and Chris Cainsford sat with bowed head and trembling form. while he sobbed like a child.

"Believe on the Lord Jesus Christ and Thou Shalt be Saved." As these words sounded through the quiet room, spoken in a rich mellow voice, husband and wife looked up in startled surprise to see George Littlejohn standing near by, with trumpet adjusted, head to one side, and while his grey eyes glistened with grateful thanksgiving and joy, he said earnestly: "I know you will forgive an old deaf man for entering without rapping, but Mr. Fitz, the kind gentleman, sent me right up, and when I found the door open, the joy of seeing you again united, fairly made me speechless, till I heard the groans and sobs of a truly repentant sinner, then I had to speak the words of the precious promise."

Here George Littlejohn seized both of Cainsford's hands and gazing into his face long and earnestly, said in sympathetic tones:

"I see you have suffered. Truly the way of the transgressor is hard, but you have not an idea how glad I am to be able to hold your hand once more, and thank God for bringing you back. I would have come sooner but was away from home when Nora's letter came bearing the good news I had prayed for and expected so long, and now : *"This my son was dead and is alive again, he was lost and is found."* I heard you say that you were so weak and unworthy, Chris. Why bless me! listen to the words of the prophet after whom your noble father was named: *"Oh Lord God, Thou hast made the Heavens and the earth by Thy great power and stretched-out arm, and there is nothing too hard for Thee."* Now, Chris, my man, do you believe what Jeremiah says of God's power, and that nothing is too hard for Him?

"Yes, yes," was the trembling answer.

"Then, do you not also believe that if He promised to keep a poor weak chap from gambling and drink He'd do it?"

"I cannot help but believe when I think of what He has already saved me from. Oh, Mr. Littlejohn, my noble generous friend, your life and character, my father's and mother's holy example, my loving wife's devotion, forgiveness and care, and my recent rescue from an awful death, all proclaim the fact of God's power to keep, protect, and save."

"Of course they do, Chris, and listen to His words: *"Come now and let us reason together, saith the Lord. Though your sins be as scarlet, they shall be as white as snow. Though they be red like crimson they shall be as wool."* Why, bless me! bless me! what more do you want? Those are God's own promises, and you know His *great power*. Will you believe what He says, and ask for His help?"

"Yes, I will, I will," cried Chris. "How simple you have made it all. Oh, at last I have hope, and I believe the all-powerful God *will* give me strength to keep this solemn vow which I make this day before you, dear Nora, my sweet loving wife; before you, uncle George, my generous kind friend, and before you, staunch Pilot, my noble dog, and also before the

great God who knoweth my heart. I do vow and
promise that from this time forth I will never drink
intoxicating liquor, I will never indulge in gambling,
and never take part in any game of chance. I further promise that so long as I live and have sufficient
strength I will pray to God each day to save me
from all evil and help me keep this sacred vow."

"I thank Thee, O Lord, for sparing my life to hear
these words," whispered George Littlejohn, then
turning to Chris he said joyously:

·"Never fear, my son, only trust and pray, and
He will forgive all thine iniquities'; '*He will heal
all thy diseases*'; *He hath redeemed thy life from
destruction*'; *and now* '*He will satisfy thy soul.*'
Why, bless me! bless me! the joy of it all makes
me cry," and while tears stole down George Littlejohn's ruddy face, and gleamed in his grey side
whiskers, Nora with a glad cry flung herself into her
husband's outstretched arms, pillowed her golden
head for a moment on his broad breast, then raising
it, she pressed her lovely trembling lips to his, and
with quivering musical voice, whispered softly:
"Oh, Chris, my love, you have made me so very,
very happy."

Then there was silence, only broken by sighs
and Pilot's soft whimper, as he sat there looking
on with elevated ears and gently wagging tail, while
his honest eyes blinked forth a brilliant sparkling
light, which could only come from a Great,—Glad—
Generous-Hearted—HERO.

*   *   *   *   *   *

The Bible tells us that joy shall be in heaven over one sinner that repenteth. Chris Cainsford proved conclusively that in his case, at least, there was also joy upon earth.

Uncle George and Dr. Allgood had everything their own way in arranging the program to be immediately followed by Chris and Nora.   The first move suggested was that they should return to their former home, which was occupied, as we know, by Dr. Allgood. Chris was somewhat reluctant to comply, but finally consented, and met with a very great surprise indeed the evening he and Nora arrived at the familiar cottage, to find it filled to overflowing with old friends, who were delighted to welccme them back. How the kind words, spoken by these steadfast friends, warmed Cainsford's heart and filled Nora with delight. How their hearty hand clasps thrilled them through and through.

But perhaps the most joyous among the many persons present at this memorable reception was Mrs. Mike Murphy. Although she was very busy, and kept somewhat in the background, one could see by her beaming face and shining eyes, that her honest Irish heart was filled to overflowing with happiness and joy; and sturdy Mike, her husband, was not a whit behind and showed his pleasure to the full.

Their pretty daughter Maggie, and our old friend Toney were also glad and happy. All the more so because of the fact that they were given the opportunity to be near each other, and praise their former master and mistress in soft whispers.

Of course, Mr. and Mrs. George Littlejohn were there with smiling faces and light hearts, and you

may be sure Pilot was by no means the least important of the many guests. Oh, how glad he seemed
when his master tuned the old violin and asked him
to dance.   He had been applauded many, many times
before, but never by such a happy, warm hearted
audience.

Chris Cainsford retired that night filled with gratitude for all the kindness he had received, and the
next morning, while dressing, was surprised to find his
old bank book lying on the bedroom table, and more
than astonished while looking through it, to discover
that $450.00 stood to his credit in the Bank of Mont-
real. Who in the world put it there was his mental
question, and his eyes filled with tears as he thought
of this another proof of love and regard, and the very
delicate manner in which it was manifest. Again he
thanked God for giving him such noble, generous
friends.

This same day, in reply to a long letter written by
Chris to his mother and sister, which had brightened a
gloomy home, and gladdened a widow's heart, he received an urgent invitation to bring Nora and come to
see them at the town of Darkton.

The invitation was accepted, but we will not attempt to describe the pleasures attending this long
deferred visit. However a trip to the Bluff by way of
Big Light on board the old Widewave, with Dummy
Deacon at the helm, was not among the least; neither
was it a small pleasure to again shake Jock Quiggley's
brown hand, and hear his "Well—Well—Well! if it
ain't my own true fren Chris Cainsford at last come
back to Darkton. I'm gladder an a 'Gleamin' Goldfish' to see yer face, shake ye by the hand, and hear
ye call me jist plain Jock."

The manifest pleasure of all the old acquaintances he met,convinced Chris that there were far more kind, good, people in the world than he had ever dreamed of. However, during all the days of recreation he was filled with an ever increasing longing to get to work.

After consulting his relatives and intimate friends Chris decided that under the circumstances, a young, thriving western city would be the most suitable place in which to establish himself in order to quickly develop a successful practice as a lawyer, besides now that he was reclaimed himself he was very anxious to lend a helping hand to other unfortunates,and believed that the West would be a suitable field in which to labor.

Having returned to L—— Chris and Nora went to see Patsey Farroll, who seemed greatly pleased, and tendered them true Irish hospitality. Before saying good-bye Chris induced the worthy Patsey to sign the pledge, and three months from the day a tramp fiddler and his dancing dog gave their last open-air performance at Ogdensburg, Chris Cainsford and Nora his wife, bade their many friends a fond farewell, and accompanied by the faithful Pilot boarded a West bound passenger train.

While shaking hands good-bye, George Littlejohn gave Nora a sealed package, charging her not to open it till she and Chris reached their destination. Imagine their feelings of gratitude to find that it contained fifteen one hundred dollar bills, and the following note written in Mr. Littlejohn's own bold hand:

My Dears,

Please accept the enclosed amount as a
token of esteem from Aunt Nellie and Uncle George.
We trust that it may add in a measure to the comfort
and happiness which is sure to be yours in your new
home. And say, Chris, my man, never forget the
words of the Psalmist, *"Thou hast delivered my soul
from death. Wilt not Thou deliver my feet from falling."* Why, bless me, of course he will Chris, if you
only trust him.

Yours always and ever the same,

GEORGE LITTLEJOHN.

CHAPTER XLVII.

The Whitest Man in the West.

Exactly four years and six months from the
memorable day upon which Chris Cainsford gave his
promise and sealed his vow, Lightning Billy Bonter,
who was now one of the trusted drivers on the great
C. P. Railway, having brought his passenger train,
called the Cannon Ball, safely through his portion of
the run from the East, to a Western city near the
coast, and having thirty minutes to wait, left his
engine in charge of the fireman and sauntered down
the platform. He seemed a little surprised when

he noticed a very tall man wearing a silk hat, a medium sized woman wearing a white veil, and a huge fat man wearing a blue cap, and as he drew near he heard these words spoken in a big voice: "Cab, sir, and lady? Cab, sir, and lady? Cab? Two dandy hosses, and the best outfit in town." Billy evidently recognized the tall man and listened for his reply, which was this:

"I would like the use of your cab if you know where Mr. Cainsford, the lawyer, lives."

"Do I know where HE lives? Well, if anybody on this green earth had otter know where Chris Cainsford hangs out it's me. Why everybody in this young city knows the smart lawyer; but he's mostly called 'Silver Locks,' and is more popular than the Mayor. Why dog-gone-it the wildest cowboys that come to town would fight for him till the last drop of their blood, and be glad of the chance, for they all think he's the whitest man that ever struck the West, and I can take you to his house in a jiff. Do you want to go, sir, and lady?"

"Yes, Mr. Barlow, but we would like to give him and his wife a little surprise, and arrive when they are both sure to be at home."

"Well, naouw, Dr. Frank Allgood! ye took me all unbeknownst!" fairly roared the big man; "I know ye all right now though, but that there high hat and them there side-whiskers, and you bein' with a lady, puzzled me all to bits at first. Say, Frank, pon my socks, I'm gladder to see you than a gold mine, and this here large world aint so all-fired big after all, is it?" Ned Barlow seized the other's hand and gave it a mighty shake, and before he released it Lightning Billy stepped up to do the same.

When the Doctor introduced the graceful looking, dark-eyed woman as his wife, Ned grinned broadly and said: "By gum, Frank, I never thought you'd come to it, and I'm more'n glad ye heve. You deserve a good one, and if I'm any jedge, by graceous sakes, you've got her," and he made a prodigious bow to the lady, who first blushed scarlet, then joined the hearty laugh which followed.

For some time these four people who had met so unexpectedly, chatted merrily; then Billy Bonter saying, "I will see you again, Doc," strode back to his engine.

Having placed his lady in the back seat of a handsome cab, the Doctor excused himself and mounted the driver's seat beside Big Ned. As the horses started the latter said: "The best way will be to drive for an hour seein' the sights, then Chris will sure to be home from his office. He is purty nigh as regular as a clock; besides I'd like to tell ye some things your old chum 'Silver Locks' has done."

"Why do you call him Silver Locks?" inquired the Doctor.

"Mostly because his wavey hair has turned like snow, besides the white things he's always been doin' helped to give him the name. He looks purty nigh as young as ever, barrin' his hair, but it's so white you can often spot him by its *gleam* as he goes along through the dark leadin' some staggerin' drunk home, or when he's trying to comfort some poor cowboy who has like enough lost his wad playin' poker. Pon my word, Frank, I believe old Chris has done more good in this here wicked city than half the churches in town.

Now, jist look at me; at them hosses; at that harness; at this dandy cab! Who do you suppose got me braced up, and helped me to get 'em together, and by doin' so made my little wife happy? Why, 'SILVER LOCKS'. Who do you suppose saved big Larry O'Ryan, the shoe maker, from hangin', fer killin' a man in a drunken row? Why, 'SILVER LOCKS'—the clever lawyer. He used to know big Larry before he moved out here from Merry-vale; he had to work awful hard to save him, but he did though, and he's helped more gamblin' toughs to brace up and be men than you heve fingers and toes."

"Oh, Ned, I am more than delighted to hear such news," said the Doctor joyously; "But say? would you mind telling me how he helped you. I am really anxious to hear, and you can let the horses walk."

"Oh, it makes me awful ashamed, Frank, but I'll tell ye jist the same, fer it's all over now. You know I always liked whiskey, but I steadied down after bein' arrested at Latchford fer knockin' out Gregg, which I never done.

"By the way, Ned," interrupted the Doctor. "Did you ever see or hear anything of Greggson, since you came back? You know he ran away soon after you left L———"

"Yes, I did, Frank. It was about a year ago when I run across an old miner who had bin workin a claim away out at Crasher's Diggins. He told me a queer story about one time he was called on to help the sheriff, and showed me the copy of the note he said he took from the pocket of a man who was found dead behind his own bar. It seems the feller had been runnin a sort of grog and gambelin den, and had made quite a pile. I remember what was in the note because of the name signed to it. And this is purty nigh what it said:

"Teary, you infernal sneak thief, I've found you at last. Your black glasses and big whiskers didn't fool me two minutes after I got a good squint at them long shaky fingers of yours; and by all that's great and good, I want you to shell out that $4,000 you stole from me that night long ago down in the Royal. I am hard up and desperate, and if you don't come down with the stuff right after you read this, say your prayers, for so help me God, your time has come "   GREGG.

After readin this note two or three times I told the old miner I thought I knowed both the fellers; then he went on to say as how the Sherriff had a big job chasin down the one they suspected, and never would have done it if they hadn't spotted him by his crooked nose and a gold tooth. They got him, though, and I guess Ance Greggson was the chap, and now he's seein how it goes to break stone in a jail yard."

"I certainly think you are right, Ned." said the Doctor. "Greggson was bad from a boy, and I guess deserves his punishment; but I am sorry I interrupted the story about yourself, and how Chris helped you to brace up."

"All right, Frank. As I was sayin, after my trip east I come back here, steadied down and married a sweet little girl, but soon went bad again, and got worse and worse, till I was so low down I didn't do nothin' much but hang round spongin' drinks, while my poor patient little woman took in sewin' and done the best she could to feed me, herself and the kid.

"One afternoon a gang of cow-punchers come to town and started to see who could blow in most money and swoller most grog, and I, glad of the chance, got fuller 'an a boiled owl. That night I managed to board a street car but clean forgot where I wanted to get off. After askin' me time and agin the fellers what run it stopped the car at a quiet corner, lugged me off, and did the best they could to brace me up agin a telegraph post not far from a street light. If I'd a stayed there long the police would have run me in sure,but before I could doze off to sleep along comes a man and commenced tryin' to git me on my feet. It was an everlastin' big job, fer I'm most allfired heavy, and I was too blamed drunk to tell who the man was, where I was at, where I wanted to go, nor tell me own name. I can jest remember, I got ugly as sin, mauled him round, dirtied his clothes, and was bound to fight; but he never gave me up, jest stuck to me like a leech, and finally helped me along to a drug store, sot me down on the sidewalk, and yelled in my ear: 'Ned, Ned, old man, be good, while I try to find out by the directory where you live.' I can jest remember that, and that when he come out, I was damnin' a policeman fer tellin' me to move on.

"How Chris saved me from the coop that night I can't tell even now; but he done it some how and took me home in a cab.

"What do ye suppose we found when we got there? I was still awful drunk, but when I see my little wife sobbin,' and heard my little boy cryin,' and looked at two low-down sneak bailiffs, sittin' on the only decent chairs we had, (which they'd seized) and both of 'em smokin', laughin' and givin' lip,

and I see where their big feet had plastered mud and
dirt all over the carpet my sweet little wife Gertie
had made, I got jist as mad as I was drunk; and you
know, Dr. Frank, that these here big shoulders of
mine, and these here big hands of mine, generally
does things when my dull brain is fired with whiskey,
and my soft heart's filled with hate.

"I made a lunge and got them two bailiffs by their
dirty necks, and if it hadn't been for Silver Locks
I'd a kept on grippin' till they died, then there would
heve been two low curs less livin' on earth, and Ned
Barlow's big carcass would have been dumped into
a murderer's shallow grave. I tell you, Frank, it
took Chris all his time to break my holt, and when
he did I turned on him, tore his shirt and collar to
bits, (he'd took off his coat) and hurt him pretty
blamed bad I know; but at last my wind give out,
and I had to quit.

"He took a sweet revenge, though. Yes, Chris
took a sweet revenge." Here Ned sobbed a mighty
sob, and continued huskily: "How do you think he
took it, Frank? It jist breaks me all up to tell you,
but my stars, think of it! just think of it! he paid my
rent, hustled the gaspin' bailiffs out, got me oysters
and pickles, made me eat, coaxed me to say I'd
stay in till he called with a bracer in the mornin.'
Made me promise I wouldn't drink any more grog
unless I got it from him; then kneeled down right
there and asked God to help me keep my promise,
coaxed me to ask Him—to—do—it—too. And
do you believe me Dr. Frank Allgood, Ned Barlow
hes—kept—that—promise, and Chris Cainsford, the
clever lawyer, has bin my sympathizin' friend an

'Guardian Angel' ever since. Do you wonder me and Gertie loves him? Do you wonder he is named 'SILVER LOCKS,' THE WHITEST—MAN—IN—THE—WEST?

"Just two things more, Dr. Frank, before ye climb down to open the door fer yer bride: Chris has a lovely wife called Nora. She is kind,—beautiful,—true as steel, and good as gold; and they have a little lad they call Fred Sunbeam. He looks like his mother and can sing like a lark. But here's their *house*, there's their DOG PILOT. Now—ye—are—alright. GOOD EVENIN.''

THE END

9 781442 651890